FELINE

"Little Mira... ...usch
A hardboiled ... ...vhen
the sole surv... ...murder is a
beautiful cat w... steals the detective's heart *and*
gives him the clue to the killer's identity.

"The Cyprian Cat" by Dorothy L. Sayers
In a signature story of psychological suspense,
Miss Sayers brings together a beautiful woman,
two men, and a phantom-like cat who may be real
or part of a terrifying madness.

**"The Cat and Fiddle Murders"
by Edward D. Hoch**
Sir Gideon Parrot, amateur sleuth, finds himself
stranded on a luxurious private island with twelve
other people—not counting the Czech violinist
who has been killed and left in the tiger pit of the
host's private zoo.

**And eleven more intriguing stories
of extraordinary cats and
uncommon crimes in**

More Mystery Cats

MORE MYSTERY CATS

Feline Felonies by
Lilian Jackson Braun
Ellis Peters
Dorothy L. Sayers
P. G. Wodehouse
and ten more masters
of mystery

Edited by Cynthia Manson

A SIGNET BOOK

SIGNET
Published by the Penguin Group
Penguin Books USA Inc., 375 Hudson Street,
New York, New York 10014, U.S.A.
Penguin Books Ltd, 27 Wrights Lane,
London W8 5TZ, England
Penguin Books Australia Ltd, Ringwood,
Victoria, Australia
Penguin Books Canada Ltd, 10 Alcorn Avenue,
Toronto, Ontario, Canada M4V 3B2
Penguin Books (N.Z.) Ltd, 182–190 Wairau Road,
Auckland 10, New Zealand

Penguin Books Ltd, Registered Offices:
Harmondsworth, Middlesex, England

Published by Signet, an imprint of New American Library,
a division of Penguin Books USA Inc.

First Signet Printing, September, 1993
10 9 8 7 6 5 4 3 2 1

Cover art by Robert Crawford

Grateful acknowledgment is made to the following for permission to reprint
their copyrighted material:

"Spectre in the Blue Doubleknit" by Bruce Bethke, copyright © 1988 by
Davis Publications, Inc., reprinted by permission of the author; "Cat Burglar" by Gene DeWeese, copyright © 1991 by Davis Publications, Inc., reprinted by permission of the Larry Sternig Literary Agency; "Little Miracles"
by Kristine Kathryn Rusch, copyright © 1992 by Davis Publications, Inc.,
reprinted by permission of the author; "Call to Witness" by Nancy Schach-
terle, copyright © 1972 by H.S.D. Publications, Inc., reprinted by permission
of Janet Schumer; all stories have previously appeared in *Alfred Hitchcock's
Mystery Magazine*, published by Bantam Doubleday Dell Direct, Inc.

(The following page constitutes an extension of this copyright page.)

Contents

Introduction

Here is the second book in the popular *Mystery Cats* series. Loyal mystery readers are continually entertained by these clever and amusing feline companions, and mystery writers are, too. From the pages of *Ellery Queen's Mystery Magazine* and *Alfred Hitchcock's Mystery Magazine* we bring you another wonderful lineup of authors and cats in starring or supporting roles.

For starters we have "The Sin of Madame Phloi" by Lilian Jackson Braun, whose popularity is worldwide; no mystery cat collection would be quite complete without a story by the Queen of Cats. In addition, we have stories by Ellis Peters, Dorothy L. Sayers, and P. G. Wodehouse. This collection includes a wide range of cat mysteries from upbeat tales like "A Case of Catnapping" by A.H.Z. Carr, to the darker side of humankind as reflected in "Animals" by Clark Howard, to the terrifying story "Little Miracles" by Kristine Kathryn Rusch, to a classic whodunit, "The Cat and Fiddle Murders" by Edward D. Hoch.

This collection for cat lovers and mystery fans should suit both *purrfectly*."

—Cynthia Manson

CATSPAW

by Sandra Woodruff

Died: Croft, Jane Gilberta. At her home, after a decline bravely borne. Survived by her great-nephew Alexander de Vries and her boys: Slyboots, Courtall, Crossbite, Ranger, Fainall, Vainlove, and Furpants. She will be missed. Orchids only, by request.

> Wisteria Cottage
> March 28
> Dear Boy,
> You will think me a morbid old woman, preoccupied with death. Do not. The thought is unworthy of you. I am alert and cheerful, as always. I write because Dr. McKillop informs me that after 83 years my heart is at last showing its age. "Tell me the worst, Doctor," I demanded. "I can take it." The man has no sense of cliche; he replied earnestly that I am failing. I deduce from his wafflings that I may linger and dwindle for a few more months or I may suddenly "pop off," as the saying goes. Accordingly, I am setting my affairs in order. My obituary is enclosed. Insert it in the quality papers, *The Globe and Mail* and *The Times*, I think, exactly as it stands. I have omitted my age because I have no wish to satisfy the appetite of the curious and because an unexpected feeling I can only describe as superstitious awe prevents me from anticipating the time of my own death.

I have also made my will. Since you are my only living relative, it is a simple one. As you know, I have a strong sense of family obligation and an aversion to dividing property unnecessarily. I have appointed you and my solicitor, Mr. Swaine, as my executors. His firm handled your trust fund from me and your inheritance from your parents. At Mr. Swaine's excellent suggestion I have added a codicil to my will giving full legal force to any letters describing specific bequests which are found in my possession at the time of my death. These I can alter as I choose without consulting anyone. When the time comes, you will find them in the top left-hand drawer of my desk.

Believe me, it is important to attend to these matters. However distasteful they seem to you young people, be reassured that they do not unduly distress

Your affectionate aunt,
Gilberta Croft

Aunt Gilberta's letter knocked me for a loop. Don't get me wrong. I'm used to getting letters from her. Though she lives only fifteen miles from me, she refuses to use the telephone. She claims it makes communication too ephemeral. I thought nothing she did could surprise me any more, but finding her obituary in my mail Monday morning was something else.

Aunt Gilberta took me over when my parents were killed in a car accident fourteen years ago. I was twelve. She had just been widowed, and there was no one else to have me, really. "I owe it to your poor dead mother," she said at the time. My parents always made a big thing of accepting people as they are. They had a poster that said *Dare To Be Different* over the kitchen stove. So Aunt Gilberta seemed ordinary by my standards, but my friends all thought she was a hoot.

Take the cats, for example. Every stray tomcat that wandered by got fed, neutered, and adopted as one of her boys, just like that. I'm not even sure they were all homeless to begin with. We named them together, one by one. I remember Aunt G. taking it very seriously.

"I've been doing research on the theory of cat naming," she announced. "Many people, it seems, name their cats after the nobility out of a misplaced wish for social status. Not I. My cat names must call well. The sound of the call is all important, never forget, dear boy." She had a point. "Here, Furpants" echoing on the night air is memorable. I ought to know—I had to do the calling.

In the evenings she read "the great comedies" aloud, to make me civilized—though she always regretted that she got me too late to do the job properly. We worked our way through Congreve, Sheridan, Feydeau, and her favorite Mr. Wilde and Mr. Coward. One Feydeau night she slammed the book shut in the middle of Act One and said, out of the blue, "Your Uncle Henry was always unfaithful to me. I can never forgive him for showing me that infidelity is not funny. It has quite spoiled my enjoyment of bedroom farce."

She really talks like that. Dear boy, she always calls me. I protested at that once. "But, dear boy," she answered, "I don't like your name. My niece called you Alexander against my wishes, to please my sister, so you shall be 'dear boy' or possibly 'dear' to me. You *are* a dear boy," she smiled, patting my hand.

She wanted me to be a lawyer, but took it pretty well when I dropped out of law school and went into the property-development business. I buy houses, fix them up, and sell them at a profit. Actually, Aunt G. gave me the money to buy the first houses I restored. "Seed money, dear boy," she breezed, "but from now on you must make your own way." The old girl has been good to me by her lights. After her epistolary bombshell, I decided a visit would be a good idea.

Aunt Gilberta lives in chintz-lined seclusion at the edge of Oakes' Corners, a village about eighty miles east of Toronto. Her house is an ordinary Ontario Victorian brick cottage, but you'd never know it. The little white gate, the hedges, the lane with the church at the bottom of the hill all look like Olde England. Aunt G. has preserved herself from the least taint of Canadianism since her family came out from England sixty years ago. She still carries on the lifestyle of her Edwardian country girlhood. Actually, I think she makes up her girlhood as she goes along.

I have to say that the visit was like all our visits. Aunt Gilberta was very much herself. As usual, I knocked and let myself in. She called from the living room, with Furpants (fat and striped) on her lap and Crossbite (lean and black) on the back of her wing chair.

"Hello, dear boy," she greeted me. "Does the house smell of cat?" This is Aunt Gilberta's usual greeting.

"No, Aunt G., it smells of lavender and hyacinths," I answered truthfully as she presented her cheek to be kissed. We have played this scene many times before.

"Good," she replied, right on cue. "In my child-hood, of course, the best houses smelled of dogs and damp. It was a mark of social distinction. Cat is merely common."

I quickly changed the subject. "Where is Mrs. Nelles today?" Mrs. Nelles, apart from the fact that her stout dignity prevents any such term, is a dogsbody. She cooks, cleans, and copes with the daily round. She also keeps her distance.

"She is out, dear boy." Aunt Gilberta sounded huffy. "She now requires two afternoons off a week instead of one whole day. It is most inconvenient, but she claims that I shouldn't be left alone for too long any more. In case," she added darkly in a faithful imitation of Mrs. Nelles' gloom. She brightened again. "We can talk after tea."

By talk, of course, she meant a discussion of her decline. We canvassed the subject thoroughly. Aunt G. was obviously hedging her bets. She was determined to prove her doctor wrong while at the same time obeying his instructions for babying her heart. Trips upstairs were rationed but walks to the post office permitted. As further justification for these daily trips, she trotted out one of her maxims: "Never put temptation in an inferior's way." I could imagine temptations, but not in Aunt G.'s mail.

She absolutely insisted on what she calls arranging her affairs herself.

"You will be glad I have planned carefully when the time comes," was all she would say. She had never shown the least interest in things financial before. I've certainly tried to talk about my business with her often enough. Whenever I've mentioned money she has cut me off with an Aunt Gilbertaism: "I am too well off to understand finances myself, I'm thankful to say. Concern for money becomes a man, I agree. On a woman, it is loud, like tartan trousers." There is no way to answer a thing like that.

I tried to rouse her a bit as I was leaving, partly because she had me worried, partly because it dawned on me that if Aunt G. got really sick she might become my full-time responsibility. I didn't know if I could handle it.

"You know, Aunt," I said, "you should try to meet more people. Otherwise, you'll begin to brood. Find yourself a nice young man to take your mind off your troubles." If she were the rib-elbowing kind I would have elbowed her in the ribs.

I was flabbergasted to receive another letter a week later.

Wisteria Cottage
April 3
Dear Boy,
You will be glad to know that I have taken your advice and have made a new friend, a young man named Alvin Ferrars. He is one of the Dundas Ferrars, I knew his grandfather. While I was arranging my affairs, it occurred to me that I might offer the art gallery one or two of those Sickerts that your Uncle Henry collected so devotedly. They are dreary things, but enjoying a vogue again, I believe. I wish to donate them now but not have them delivered until after my death. Mr. Ferrars sees to acquisitions for the gallery. He was thrilled to the marrow at my generous offer, he said. In many ways, Mr. Ferrars reminds me of your uncle when he was young. He so loves beautiful things, though he cannot see them without wanting to save them, hoard them, I might almost say. He was quite distressed at finding my small Turkoman rug by the front door in the path of dirty feet, and he actually became flustered about Courtall's blue dish. It seems that it is the best kind of carnival glass and very collectible. This seems extraordinary. Carnival glass is

not what I would call good, collectible or not. As you know, I have always been one for enjoying my things, not pussyfooting around them. Courtall is particularly fond of his dish. I am sure he wouldn't drink his tea out of anything else. It was a pleasure to talk to such a cultured and considerate young man. Vainlove quite took to him, too, and you know how particular he is. The time flew. Fortunately, he will need to come again to complete the arrangements—evaluations, gift forms, and so forth. I hope you will visit soon, dear boy. I don't see enough of you.

Your affectionate aunt,
Gilberta Croft

She may not see enough of me, but when I did stop by for a few minutes later in the week to say that I would be away for a while, she hardly spared me a thought. It was Mr. Ferrars said this and Mr. Ferrars did that and Mr. Ferrars made such a hit with all the cats, not only with Vainlove the particular but with Ranger, who never sits on laps but sat on Mr. Ferrars' lap, who didn't even mind when he shed white hairs all over his trousers. By the time I left, I was fairly fed up with Mr. Ferrars.

The next month was incredibly hectic. I was away on business more or less continuously. Actually, the business had hit a bad patch. In my line, cash flow is everything. You have to buy at a good time and sell at the right time or you're in trouble. A sale that I had been counting on fell through and I needed to raise money right away. A loan from Aunt Gilberta would tide me over, but I didn't have any real hope of one. The few times I've wanted to borrow money from her before, she has resisted pretty firmly—refused outright, to be frank.

"You cannot expect me to pay for what I cannot approve" or a version thereof is her standard response. She's getting her own back at me for quitting law school, I guess. It's maddening, actually. Anyway, I was tired and strung out when I got home. I put down my suitcase and stooped to pick up a month's worth of mail from the hall carpet (industrial-quality grey tweed, made to withstand dirty feet). Right on top of the pile was a letter from Aunt Gilberta on her usual thick creamy paper.

Wisteria Cottage
May 4
Dear Alexander,

I hope you have concluded your business satisfactorily. In my experience, most men, even your Uncle Henry I regret to say, choose to put their work before their families and friends. It is almost a mark of masculinity. My dear Alvin is such a refreshing change; he puts the proper value on home life, friendship, and pleasant surroundings. The dear boy has been kind enough to say that my house feels like home to him. I have come to rely on him so much during your absence, particularly as I have had one or two worrying turns.

Mrs. Nelles continues to insist on her two free afternoons each week. She is quite obdurate on the subject. I must confess to feeling a shade nervous that she might leave me altogether if I were to forbid her outings. When he can, Alvin arranges his afternoons off to coincide with hers and spends them with me. He works queer hours at the gallery and is often free during the day. He is such a comfort to me. I have made him some small gifts to show my gratitude—just a silver salt cellar, Georgian your uncle always claimed, and a small porcelain dish, Meissen I believe. He was so delighted and so modest. "Don't think of giving me anything," he protested. "Leave me some small memento if you like, but nothing more." "Don't worry, dear boy," I told him, "you will be remembered in my will." Of course, I have made some alteration in my will now that I know him. The letter with instructions is in my desk with the others. Come to see me if you can spare the time.

Your aunt,
Gilberta Croft

On top of everything else, this letter made me really angry. That putting-work-before-family crack was cheap. It was obvious that young Alvin Ferrars of the Dundas Ferrars—damn Aunt Gilberta's mania about good families—didn't put anything before himself. Don't think of giving me anything, my eye. He couldn't wait to get his hands on Aunt G.'s money—my money, as a matter of fact. I couldn't for the life of me think of what, but I knew I'd have to do something about him.

I didn't have to, however. Young Alvin overplayed his hand, the dear boy. I spent a restless few days after my trip clearing up the backlog of paperwork and trying to persuade the bank manager to give me a bridging loan. He wouldn't hear of it. He not only refused, he refused in the managerial way. "Your business is already overextended and your prospects, quite frankly, are very insecure," he said. "It wouldn't be prudent for us to lend you further monies at this time. Don't hesitate to approach us again if you can demonstrate some really solid prospects."

With one thing and another, I hadn't had a chance to visit Aunt Gilberta and I didn't much feel like it, either. I knew that I would have to go soon and at least ask her to lend me the money. I wasn't looking forward to it. Just as I finally psyched myself up to do it, I got another letter from her, in very shaky handwriting. I hardly recognized it.

> Wisteria Cottage
> May 9
> Dear Boy,
> Please come to see me very soon. That fool Dr. McKillop wanted to ring you when I was very low, but I refused. The idea of a quasi-deathbed scene offends me. However, I have important matters to discuss with you. I am afraid that I have been badly mistaken in Alvin Ferrars. He is not the innocent lover of beauty that I supposed. He is regrettably acquisitive, and I fear that mention of some small bequest—you know that I remembered him in my will—has made him greedy. Indeed, he looked at me quite fiercely the other day when he came to call. His eyes fairly glittered. I fear that he had designs on my life. I blame myself in part. I have broken my own rule and put temptation in his way. I have asked him not to come again. Do not desert
>
> Your affectionate aunt,
Gilberta Croft

Things were obviously getting serious. Either that creep Ferrars was dangerous or Aunt G. had really flipped out this time. It was Thursday, one of Mrs. Nelles' afternoons off, so I went over right after lunch to have it out with her privately. I was fuming. Spring was in its golden phase, the time of year I usually like best, so to calm down I drove over the back way, through open country, and down her lane from the top of the hill.

About halfway there, it hit me like a ton of bricks that the simplest solution to all my problems (hers, too, for that matter) was to kill Aunt Gilberta myself.

At first the thought made me so queasy I had to stop the car. I couldn't believe I could even consider such a thing. I mean, she had raised me, after a fashion, though she didn't hesitate to abandon me for Ferrars when it suited her. Finally, I got hold of myself well enough to drive on, but I still felt unreal when I arrived.

I went in at the side door. She must have heard the car because she was standing on the upstairs landing clutching a shabby housecoat around her. She looked really feeble.

We got off on the wrong footing right away. For one thing, she kept us standing in the upstairs hall. She looked ready to keel over, but she wouldn't lie down and she wouldn't sit. There were no greetings, no social niceties. All she wanted to talk about was the ingratitude of Alvin. That was fine—I didn't have a good word to say for him, either.

Warming to her theme, she went on to my own ingratitude: a) for not warning her of the evil in Alvin's heart: b) for not paying enough attention to her myself; and c) combining her grievances—for going away and leaving her in Alvin's clutches. She was completely unreasonable. I should have just left and come back later. I knew it was no time to ask for a loan, but I was desperate. I had only until Friday evening to raise the money and she was my only chance. Besides, other times I'd waited for the best moment to ask and it didn't make any difference. I just wanted to get it over with.

She didn't take it well. I would almost have welcomed one of her chilly little pronouncements. What I got was pure fishwife at top volume. I didn't know she had it in her. The gist was that she wouldn't lend

me money, now or ever. We were all the same, Uncle
Henry, Alvin, and I. We had all betrayed her and
used her.

At first, I tried to soothe her down, though I was
pretty upset myself. She was practically hysterical. I
even tried to joke with her that a lady always controls
her temper. That was a mistake. She called me shallow and utterly lacking in sensitivity. Finally I lost my
temper, too. I started to shout.

"You can't stand anyone getting the better of you,
can you, Aunt? You've always laid down the law and
doled out favors to other people. You don't know
anything about being dependent on another person's
whims. How do you think I feel asking for money I
need badly and being treated like something sub-
human? Do you think I enjoy it? Look at me! You've
only given me what you thought I should have, not
what I wanted. I'm not a person to you, I'm a puppet.
You're not interested in me for myself. Actually,
you're not interested in anyone—you just want to control people. You're selfish and tyrannical and bogus.
Without your eternal posing you're nothing!" By this
time I was beginning to feel better. I had done a lot
of holding in over the years.

I was just starting to calm down when she smiled.
She actually smiled. She was laughing at me. I felt a
surge of pure rage. I reached out and shook her. I
could have gone on and on doing it, just to see the
pretense ooze out of her, but she wrenched away from
me. She fell backward down the stairs and lay in a
little heap at the bottom. One hand was reaching out
to save herself, the other was still clutching her old
housecoat, as if I might try to take it from her.

The first thing I thought when I saw her lying there

was that she never was a good listener. The second was that she was dead and I had killed her.

I checked for a heartbeat just in case, but of course there wasn't any. My knees started to shake so much I had to sit on a step. The shouting must have disturbed Ranger, the big white cat, because he came out of the living room and, ignoring Aunt Gilberta, sat on my lap. I don't know what Aunt G. was on about—he'll sit on any lap going.

Suddenly I became cool and clearheaded, sitting there with a cat on my lap and Aunt Gilberta heaped below us in her housecoat. I looked at my watch. I had been in the house fifteen minutes.

I was about to call the doctor to say that I had found Aunt Gilberta dead, but I decided that would be asking for trouble. He would know right away that she had just died. There was no way I could explain to him what really happened—he wouldn't understand. So I decided to wait until Mrs. Nelles found Aunt G. that evening. Even if somebody saw me come to the house, by then she would have been dead long enough that a few minutes wouldn't matter one way or another. The obvious thing was to leave quickly. But I had to get rid of the letter to Alvin Ferrars first.

The letters were, as Aunt Gilberta had directed, in the top left-hand drawer of her desk. The Alvin letter was right at the back. It was short: "To Alvin, in gratitude for your attentions to an old woman, I leave you Courtall's blue dish, the one you have admired so often. I ask only that you substitute an ordinary blue glass dish for it. Courtall is fond of blue."

I could have laughed out loud—a dish, a piece of junk. Poor sod, all that effort wasted. For a moment

I didn't even begrudge him the Georgian silver. In a
burst of good will I put the letter back.

I left quietly a minute later. No one saw me. When
Mrs. Nelles phoned to tell me the news, I managed
to summon convincing surprise and grief. I made the
funeral arrangements with my usual efficiency and
placed the obituary in the quality papers, as instructed. Aunt Gilberta was to be buried on Monday.

The waiting time was terrible. It felt just like when
my parents died. I've heard Aunt G. say a million
times, "You are my only living relative, dear boy,"
and she was my only living relative, too. But I never
really thought about what it meant. Now I know. It
means that I am completely alone. I have friends,
sure, but nobody who goes back all that far or who
really cares about me. I told myself it was all for the
best. Aunt G. couldn't have lasted much longer, the
way she was looking. Even if she had really declined
for any length of time (obituary or no obituary), she
would have hated it.

I can't deny that I was relieved that my future was
looking better. I took the risk of phoning the bank
manager on Friday morning and arranging the bridging loan. I was a bit hasty, I know, but I had to be.
Word had evidently gotten out, because he spread his
oily charm all over me. Overnight, I had become a
valued client. He had the gall to offer his condolences
on the loss of my aunt and to congratulate me on my
now secure prospects in the same breath.

After the funeral, at which there was no sign of
Alvin Ferrars, I returned to Mr. Swaine's office with
him to discuss the will. Mr. Swaine was tall, thin, and

solemn. Whether he was always mournful or whether I was seeing his funeral manner I couldn't decide. He wasted no time in chat.

"Your aunt gave me to understand that you were familiar with the general tenor of her will," he began. "As you know, we are her executors. We shall discuss arrangements in due course, but for now Mrs. Croft left a letter for you, with instructions that you be left alone to read it." With that, he handed me a bulky cream envelope and beat a stately retreat.

I was surprised, but not worried. A letter from beyond the grave was a very Aunt Gilberta touch. It did give me a shock to see her handwriting firm again, though, as if she had been revitalized. The letter was dated six weeks earlier. It read:

Dear Boy,

By the time you read this, you will have killed me. You are surprised that I know when you may not even have formulated a plan for my removal. Indeed, I am not so callous as to expect malice aforethought from you, but in the end it will come to the same thing. Eliminating an ailing, possibly burdensome relative will begin to seem the expedient course, and you have always been fond of expediency.

I must confess prematurely, since I am unlikely to have a deathbed for confession, that I, too, have taken the line of least resistance. My death was not murder, but suicide at arm's length. I have been dreading the prospect of lingering death. I do not precisely relish the prospect of death at all, but given the choice I prefer quick to slow. Accordingly, I have been issuing little challenges to my heart, to no avail. An extra trip or two upstairs each day, the walk uphill from the post office, a laughable attempt to skip, even. I have survived all these.

I have, therefore, been obliged to enlist your help. You are my only living relative, and this is a familiar matter. I have decided to arrange an argument with you. You are slow to anger, but when it does erupt your temper is violent. I shall await a suitable occasion, then provoke you until you retaliate. With angry words? With an actual blow? A push downstairs? It is best that I do not know. I shall put temptation in your way and rely on you and my faint heart to do the rest. If my resolution does not falter, this scheme may even add some interest to days increasingly barren of it.

I have one other confession. To further my plan, I have practiced a small deception. I have implied strongly (though I did not lie outright—I never lie) that you would be my heir. This is not really the case. I am leaving you no money. Under the circumstances, it would not be good for your character to profit from my death. Moreover, I am a woman of strong family feeling. It has been my principle that my dear ones should be well looked after in my lifetime and not be obliged to wait until my death for financial benefit. The provisions I have already made for you and the inheritance you have from your parents should, with care, keep you comfortably. Your wildcat schemes are your own concern. You are so clever with money, dear boy. I have had the pleasure of seeing you established in life and of having discharged my responsibility to you as your only relative. I am leaving you my pink lustre teaset to remember our afternoon teas together. Do not neglect afternoon tea. It is a meal for children and the upper classes.

As my executor, you are entitled to a small fee. This fee is a convention merely; my will is an undemanding one. You know where my letters are. All of my property—the house and contents and my capital—I leave for the care of the cats. Mrs. Nelles will stay on in the house at her present salary, with increments at your discretion. Should she leave, you must find a suitable replacement at once. Spare no trouble or expense. The cats must stay in their own home until the last one dies. They are so very attached to the house. Fainall would pine anywhere else and Slyboots is not as robust as he might be.

Ultimately, the house and contents should be sold and the proceeds donated to the British Anti-Vivisection Society, a group I have long supported. They have an office in Harley Street. Look after my boys as I would, and as they grow old see that they have the best veterinary care. Under no circumstances are they to be put down. Their deaths will not benefit you and in general I am against killing. I sign myself this last time,

Your affectionate aunt,
Gilberta Croft

THE SIN OF MADAME PHLOI

by Lilian Jackson Braun

From the very beginning Madame Phloi felt an instinctive distaste for the man who moved into the apartment next door. He was fat, and his trouser cuffs had the unsavory odor of fire hydrant.

They met for the first time in the decrepit elevator as it lurched up to the tenth floor of the old building, once fashionable but now coming apart at the seams. Madame Phloi had been out for a stroll in the city park, chewing city grass and chasing faded butterflies, and as she and her companion stepped on the elevator for the slow ride upward, the car was already half filled with the new neighbor.

The fat man and the Madame presented a contrast that was not unusual in this apartment house, which had a brilliant past and no future. He was bulky, uncouth, sloppily attired. Madame Phloi was a long-legged, blue-eyed aristocrat whose creamy fawn coat shaded into brown at the extremities.

The Madame deplored fat men. They had no laps, and of what use is a lapless human? Nevertheless, she gave him the common courtesy of a sniff at his trouser cuffs and immediately backed away, twitching her nose and breathing through the mouth.

"*Get* that cat away from me," the fat man roared, stamping his feet thunderously at Madame Phloi. Her companion pulled on the leash, although there was no need—the Madame with one backward leap had retreated to a safe corner of the elevator, which shuddered and continued its groaning ascent.

"Don't you like animals?" asked the gentle voice at the other end of the leash.

"Filthy, sneaky beasts," the fat man said with a snarl. "Last place I lived, some lousy cat got in my room and et my parakeet."

"I'm sorry to hear that. Very sorry. But you don't need to worry about Madame Phloi and Thapthim. They never leave the apartment except on a leash."

"You got *two*? That's just fine, that is! Keep 'em away from me, or I'll break their rotten necks. I ain't wrung a cat's neck since I was fourteen, but I remember how."

And with the long black box he was carrying, the fat man lunged at the impeccable Madame Phloi, who sat in her corner, flat-eared and tense. Her fur bristled, and she tried to dart away. Even when her companion picked her up in protective arms, Madame Phloi's body was taut and trembling.

Not until she was safely home in her modest but well-cushioned apartment did she relax. She walked stiff-legged to the sunny spot on the carpet where Thapthim was sleeping and licked the top of his head. Then she had a complete bath herself—to rid her coat of the fat man's odor. Thapthim did not wake.

This drowsy, unambitious, amiable creature—her son—was a puzzle to Madame Phloi, who was sensitive and spirited herself. She didn't try to understand him; she merely loved him. She spent hours washing his paws and breast and other parts he could easily have reached with his own tongue. At dinnertime she chewed slowly so there would be something left on her plate for his dessert, and he always gobbled the extra portion hungrily. And when he slept, which was most of the time, she kept watch by his side, sitting with a tall, regal posture until she swayed with weariness. Then she made herself into a small bundle and dozed with one eye open.

Thapthim was lovable, to be sure. He appealed to other cats, large and small dogs, people, and even ailurophobes in a limited way. He had a face like a beautiful flower and large blue eyes, tender and trusting. Ever since he was a kitten, he had been willing to purr at the touch of a hand—any hand. Eventually he became so agreeable that he purred if anyone looked at him across the room. What's more, he came when called; he gratefully devoured whatever was served on his dinner plate; and when he was told to get down, he got down.

His wise parent disapproved this uncatly conduct; it indicated a certain lack of character, and no good would come of it. By her own example she tried to guide him. When dinner was served, she gave the plate a haughty sniff and walked away, no matter how tempting the dish. That was the way it was done by any self-respecting feline. In a minute or two she returned and condescended to dine, but never with open enthusiasm.

Furthermore, when human hands reached out, the catly thing was to bound away, lead them a chase, flirt a little before allowing oneself to be caught and cuddled. Thapthim, sorry to say, greeted any friendly overture by rolling over, purring, and looking soulful.

From an early age he had known the rules of the apartment:

> *No sleeping in a cupboard with the pots and pans.*
> *Sitting on the table with the inkwell is permissible.*
> *Sitting on the table with the coffeepot is never allowed.*

The sad truth was that Thapthim obeyed these rules. Madame Phloi, on the other hand, knew that a rule was a challenge, and it was a matter of integrity to violate it. To obey was to sacrifice one's dignity. . . . It seemed that her son would never learn the true values in life.

To be sure, Thapthim was adored for his good nature in the human world of inkwells and coffeepots. But Madame Phloi was equally adored—and for the correct reasons. She was respected for her independence, admired for her clever methods of getting her own way, and loved for the cowlick on her white breast, the kink in her tail, and the squint in her delphinium-blue eyes. She was more truly Siamese than her son. Her face was small and perky. By cocking her head and staring with heart-melting eyes, slightly crossed, she could charm a porterhouse steak out from under a knife and fork.

Until the fat man and his black box moved in next door, Madame Phloi had never known an unfriendly soul. She had two companions in her tenth-floor apartment—genial creatures without names who came and went a good deal. One was an easy mark for between-meal snacks; a tap on his ankle always produced a spoonful of cottage cheese. The other served as a hot-water bottle on cold nights and punctually obliged whenever the Madame wished to have her underside stroked or her cheekbones massaged. This second one also murmured compliments in a gentle voice that made one squeeze one's eyes in pleasure.

Life was not all love and cottage cheese, however. Madame Phloi had her regular work. She was official watcher and listener for the household.

There were six windows that needed watching, for a wide ledge ran around the building flush with the tenth-floor windowsills, and this was a promenade for pigeons. They strutted, searched their feathers, and ignored the Madame, who sat on the sill and watched them dispassionately but thoroughly through the window screen.

While watching was a daytime job, listening was done after dark and required greater concentration. Madame Phloi listened for noises in the walls. She heard termites chewing, pipes sweating, and some-times the ancient plaster cracking; but mostly she lis-tened to the ghosts of generations of deceased mice.

One evening, shortly after the incident in the eleva-tor, Madame Phloi was listening, Thapthim was asleep, and the other two were quietly turning pages of books, when a strange and horrendous sound came from the wall. The Madame's ears flicked to attention, then flattened against her head.

An interminable screech was coming out of that wall, like nothing the Madame had ever heard before. It chilled the blood and tortured the eardrums. So painful was the shrillness that Madame Phloi threw back her head and complained with a piercing howl of her own. The strident din even waked Thapthim.

He looked about in alarm, shook his head wildly, and clawed at his ears to get rid of the offending noise.

The others heard it, too.

"Listen to that!" said the one with the gentle voice.

"It must be that new man next door," said the other. "It's incredible."

"I can't imagine anyone so crude producing anything so exquisite. Is it Prokofiev he's playing?"

"No, I think it's Bartók."

"He was carrying his violin in the elevator today. He tried to hit Phloi with it."

"He's a nut. . . . Look at the cats—apparently they don't care for violin."

Madame Phloi and Thapthim, bounding from the room, collided with each other as they rushed to hide under the bed.

That was not the only kind of noise which emanated from the adjoining apartment in those upsetting days after the fat man moved in. The following evening, when Madame Phloi walked into the living room to commence her listening, she heard a fluttering sound dimly through the wall, accompanied by highly conversational chirping. This was agreeable music, and she settled down on the sofa to enjoy it, tucking her brown paws neatly under her creamy body.

Her contentment was soon disturbed, however, when the fat man's voice burst through the wall like thunder.

"Look what you done, you dirty skunk!" he bellowed. "Right in my fiddle! Get back in your cage before I brain you."

There was a frantic beating of wings.

"*Get* down off that window, or I'll bash your head in."

This threat brought only a torrent of chirping.

"Shut up, you stupid cluck! Shut up and get back in that cage, or I'll . . ."

There was a splintering crash, and after that all was quiet except for an occasional pitiful "Peep!"

Madame Phloi was fascinated. In fact, when she resumed her watching the next day, pigeons seemed rather insipid entertainment. She had waked the family that morning in her usual way—by staring intently at their foreheads as they slept. Then she and Thapthim had a game of hockey in the bathtub with a Ping-Pong ball, followed by a dish of mackerel, and after breakfast the Madame took up her post at the living-room window. Everyone had left for the day but not before opening the window and placing a small cushion on the chilly marble sill.

There she sat—Madame Phloi—a small but alert package of fur, sniffing the welcome summer air, seeing all, and knowing all. She knew, for example, that the person who was at that moment walking down the tenth-floor hallway, wearing old tennis shoes and limping slightly, would halt at the door of her apartment, set down his pail, and let himself in with a passkey.

Indeed, she hardly bothered to turn her head when the window washer entered. He was one of her regular court of admirers. His odor was friendly, although it suggested damp basements and floor mops, and he talked sensibly—indulging in none of that falsetto foolishness with which some people insulted the Madame's intelligence.

"Hop down, kitty," he said in a musical voice. "Charlie's gotta take out that screen. See, I brought you some cheese."

He held out a modest offering of rat cheese, and Madame Phloi investigated it. Unfortunately, it was the wrong variety, and she shook one fastidious paw at it.

"Mighty fussy cat," Charlie laughed. "Well, now, you set there and watch Charlie clean this here window. Don't you go jumpin' out on the ledge, because Charlie ain't runnin' after you. No sir! That old ledge, she's startin' to crumble. Some day them pigeons'll stamp their feet hard, and down she goes! . . . Hey, lookit the broken glass out here. Somebody busted a window."

Charlie sat on the marble sill and pulled the upper sash down in his lap, and while Madame Phloi followed his movements carefully, Thapthim sauntered into the room, yawning and stretching, and swallowed the cheese.

"Now Charlie puts the screen back in, and you two guys can watch them crazy pigeons some more. This screen, she's comin' apart, too. Whole buildin' seems to be crackin' up."

Remembering to replace the cushion on the cool, hard sill, he then went on to clean the next window, and the Madame resumed her post, sitting on the very edge of the cushion so that Thapthim could have most of it.

The pigeons were late that morning, probably frightened away by the window washer. It was while Madam Phloi patiently waited for the first visitor to skim in on a blue-gray wing that she noticed the tiny opening in the screen. Every aperture, no matter how small, was a temptation; she had to prove she could wriggle through any tight space, whether there was a good reason or not.

She waited until Charlie had limped out of the apartment before she began pushing at the screen with her nose, first gingerly and then stubbornly. Inch by inch the rusted mesh ripped away from the frame until the whole corner formed a loose flap, and Madame Phloi slithered through—nose and ears, slender shoulders, dainty Queen Anne forefeet, svelte torso, lean flanks, hind legs like steel springs, and finally proud brown tail. For the first time in her life she found herself on the pigeon promenade. She gave a delicious shudder.

Inside the screen the lethargic Thapthim, jolted by this strange turn of affairs, watched his daring parent with a quarter inch of his pink tongue hanging out. They touched noses briefly through the screen, and the Madame proceeded to explore. She advanced cautiously and with mincing step, for the pigeons had not been tidy in their habits.

The ledge was about two feet wide. To its edge Madame Phloi moved warily, nose down and tail high. Ten stories below there were moving objects but nothing of interest, she decided. Walking daintily along the extreme edge to avoid the broken glass, she ventured in the direction of the fat man's apartment, impelled by some half-forgotten curiosity.

His window stood open and unscreened, and Madame Phloi peered in politely. There sprawled on the floor, lay the fat man himself, snorting and heaving his immense paunch in a kind of rhythm. It always alarmed her to see a human on the floor, which she considered feline domain. She licked her nose apprehensively and stared at him with enormous eyes, one iris hypnotically off-center. In a dark corner of the room something fluttered and squawked, and the fat man waked.

"SHcrrff! *Get* out of here!" he shouted, struggling to his feet.

In three leaps Madame Phloi crossed the ledge back to her own window and pushed through the screen to safety. Looking back to see if the fat man might be chasing her and being reassured that he wasn't, she washed Thapthim's ears and her own paws and sat down to wait for pigeons.

Like any normal cat, Madame Phloi lived by the Rule of Three. She resisted every innovation three times before accepting it, tackled an obstacle three times before giving up, and tried each new activity three times before tiring of it. Consequently she made two more sallies to the pigeon promenade and eventually convinced Thapthim to join her.

Together they peered over the edge at the world below. The sense of freedom was intoxicating. Recklessly Thapthim made a leap at a low-flying pigeon and landed on his mother's back. She cuffed his ear in retaliation. He poked her nose. They grappled and rolled over and over on the ledge, oblivious of the long drop below them, taking playful nips of each other's hide and snarling guttural expressions of glee.

Suddenly and instinctively Madame Phloi scrambled to her feet and crouched in a defensive position. The fat man was leaning from his window.

"Here, kitty, kitty," he was saying in one of those despised falsetto voices, offering some tidbit in a saucer. The Madame froze, but Thapthim turned his beautiful trusting eyes on the stranger and advanced along the ledge. Purring and waving his tail cordially, he walked into the trap. It all happened in a matter of seconds: the saucer was withdrawn, and a long black box was swung at Thapthim like a ball bat, sweeping him off the ledge and into space. He was silent as he fell.

When the family came home, laughing and chattering, with their arms full of packages, they knew at once something was amiss. No one greeted them at the door. Madame Phloi hunched moodily on the windowsill staring at a hole in the screen, and Thapthim was not to be found.

"Look at the screen!" cried the gentle voice.

"I'll bet he got out on the ledge."

"Can you lean out and look? Be careful."

"You hold Phloi."

"Do you see him?"

"Not a sign of him! There's a lot of glass scattered around, and the window's broken next door."

"Do you suppose that man . . . ? I feel sick."

"Don't worry, dear. We'll find him. . . . There's the doorbell! Maybe someone's bringing him home."

It was Charlie standing at the door. He fidgeted uncomfortably. " 'Scuse me, folks," he said. "You missin' one of your kitties?"

"Yes! Have you found him?"

"Poor little guy," said Charlie. "Found him lyin' right under your windows—where the bushes is thick."

"He's dead!" the gentle one moaned.

"Yes, ma'am. That's a long way down."

"Where is he now?"

"I got him down in the basement, ma'am. I'll take care of him real nice. I don't think you'd want to see the poor guy."

Still Madame Phloi stared at the hole in the screen and waited for Thapthim. From time to time she checked the other windows, just to be sure. As time passed and he did not return, she looked behind the radiators and under the bed. She pried open the cupboard door where the pots and pans were stored. She tried to burrow her way into the closet. She sniffed all around the front door. Finally she stood in the middle of the living room and called loudly in a high-pitched, wailing voice.

Later that evening Charlie paid another visit to the apartment.

"Only wanted to tell you, ma'am, how nice I took care of him," he said. "I got a box that was just the right size. A white box, it was. And I wrapped him up in a piece of old blue curtain. The color looked real pretty with his fur. And I buried the little guy right under your window behind the bushes."

And still the Madame searched, returning again and again to watch the ledge from which Thapthim had disappeared. She scorned food. She rebuffed any attempts at consolation. And all night she sat wide-eyed and waiting in the dark.

The living-room window was now tightly closed, but the following day the Madame—after she was left by herself in the lonely apartment—went to work on the bedroom screens. One was new and hopeless, but the second screen was slightly corroded, and she was soon nosing through a slit that lengthened as she struggled out onto the ledge.

Picking her way through the broken glass, she approached the spot where Thapthim had vanished. And then it all happened again. There he was—the fat man—reaching forth with a saucer.

"Here, kitty, kitty."

Madame Phloi hunched down and backed away.

"Kitty want some milk?" It was that ugly falsetto,

but she didn't run home this time. She crouched there on the ledge, a few inches out of reach.

"Nice kitty. Nice kitty."

Madame Phloi crept with caution toward the saucer in the outstretched fist, and stealthily the fat man extended another hand, snapping his fingers as one would call a dog.

The Madame retreated diagonally—half toward home and half toward the dangerous brink.

"Here, kitty. Here, kitty," he cooed, leaning farther out. But muttering, he said, "You dirty sneak! I'll get you if it's the last thing I ever do. Comin' after my bird, weren't you?"

Madame Phloi recognized danger with all her senses. Her ears went back, her whiskers curled, and her white underside hugged the ledge.

A little closer she moved, and the fat man made a grab for her. She jerked back a step, with unblinking eyes fixed on his sweating face. He was furtively laying the saucer aside, she noticed, and edging his fat paunch farther out the window.

Once more she advanced almost into his grasp, and again he lunged at her with both powerful arms.

The Madame leaped lightly aside.

"This time I'll get you, you stinkin' cat," he cried, and raising one knee to the windowsill, he threw himself at Madame Phloi. As she slipped through his fingers, he landed on the ledge with all his weight.

A section of it crumbled beneath him. He bellowed, clutching at the air, and at the same time a streak of creamy brown flashed out of sight. The fat man was not silent as he fell.

As for Madame Phloi, she was found doubled in half in a patch of sunshine on her living-room carpet, innocently washing her fine brown tail.

CALL TO WITNESS

by Nancy Schachterle

The police captain himself came to see Allison. That pleased her immensely; but it's only right, she thought. The Ryder name still means something in this town, even if the last survivor is an old maid of eighty-three. Secretly she had been afraid that she had been in the backwater of age for so long that most people, if they thought about her at all, had decided that she must be long since dead.

Everett Barkley, he told her his name was. He was tall and well-built, filling his uniform to advantage, with little sign of the paunch that so many men his age allowed to develop.

Barkley helped himself to her father's big leather chair, slumping comfortably to accommodate his frame to its rump-sprung curves. Allison started toward a straight-backed chair suited to the erect posture of her generation, then yielded to the pleading of well-aged bones and lowered herself carefully into her familiar upholstered armchair.

The policeman surveyed the piecrust table at his elbow, laden with silver-framed photographs. Gingerly he reached out and picked up Dodie's picture.

"Mrs. Patrick. She must have been very young when this was taken."

"Nineteen. She sat for that four years ago." And she had watched, not an hour ago, Allison recalled, as they carried Dodie to the ambulance with a blanket entirely covering her.

"Did you know her well? As you probably know, I've been in town less than a year and I had never seen her before the . . . before this morning."

Allison shuddered slightly. Automatically her hand went to her lap to caress Snowball, to seek comfort in the warm, silky fur, and the pulsations of the gentle, almost silent, purr. With a start she remembered that she had let him out in the early hours of the morning, and he hadn't yet returned. Worry nagged at her.

What had Captain Barkley asked? Yes—about Dodie. *Did I know her well?*

"She came toddling up my front steps one day when she was about two, and we've been fast friends ever since. At that time she lived just up the hill, in the next block."

"And since they were married they've lived next door to you?"

"That's right."

"Miss Ryder . . ." The policeman shifted his position, slightly ill at ease. "Would you tell me something about Dodie? Anything you like. Just your mental picture of her."

Allison reached to take the photograph from him. "This shows her spirit well, those laughing, sparkling eyes. She was a happy girl. She used to come running up those steps—she never walked, always running— and she looked so full of life. Vital is the word that comes to my mind. Dancing, tennis, swimming, golf, singing—that was Dodie."

Allison looked down at the gray old hands that held the picture, with their knotted veins and their liver spots. Dodie had been the youth she herself had lost.

"I can see her right now, sitting on the porch railing, swinging those long, tanned legs. 'Frank finally asked me to the dance, Miss Ryder,' she told me. She was leaning so far out to look down the street that I was afraid she'd fall into my sweet william. 'Here he comes now. 'Bye. See you.' And she was gone, laughing and waving to him."

She had been pleased about Dodie and Frank, Allison remembered. All she knew of Frank Patrick was a dark, goodlooking boy with a quick grin and a cheery wave. She didn't know then that he was one of those helpless, hopeless creatures who feed on hurt. His charm swept up people like lilting dance music. Then, when they were dizzy from his gift of pleasure with themselves, he launched his barb and sucked at the wound. As his victims shriveled, Frank swelled with a grotesque satisfaction. Given the choice between kind and cruel, legal and illegal, moral and immoral, he'd rather go the lower path each time.

Allison handed the picture back to Captain Barkley. Carefully he placed it back among the dozen or so others that crowded the little table.

"Nieces and nephews, and their children," Allison remarked. "I even have one great-great," she told him, with visible pride. "But Dodie was closer to me than any of them."

The policeman shifted his cap between his fingers in a broken, shuffling motion as if he were saying the rosary on it.

"Miss Ryder," he said, lifting his eyes to meet hers, "it'll be out soon, so I might as well tell you, the doctor is virtually certain it was an overdose, probably of her sleeping pills. We'll know for sure after the autopsy. What I'm trying to do now is get a picture of her, of her husband, of her life. Now, the Patrick house and yours are very close, can't be much more than fifteen or twenty feet apart, and their bedroom is on this side. I noticed the window was open about eight inches at the bottom. Knowing how easily sound travels on these warm, summer nights, I wondered . . ." He paused, waiting for Allison to volunteer the ending to his sentence. She was wearing a look of polite attention, but said nothing.

"Well," he continued, "I just wondered whether you might have heard anything."

Absently Allison's hand reached again for Snowball's head. Where could he be? She had heard him yowling his love songs on the back fence about three this morning, so she knew he was near home. Then she shook herself mentally, and tried to remember what the officer had been saying. Oh, yes. *Did I hear anything?*

"My bedroom is on the far side of the house from the Patricks'. I'm afraid I can be of no help to you, Captain . . . Barkley, isn't it?"

Allison shrank into herself a little, half expecting a bolt of chastening lightning from above. But she hadn't lied, she decided. Her bedroom was indeed on the far side. She needn't tell him that most nights she didn't sleep well, and it was cooler out on the screened porch, practically outside Dodie's open window.

Barkley nodded, musing. "I understand Mrs. Patrick was a complete invalid for the past couple of years. Can you tell me anything about that?"

Allison sat a little more upright, legs crossed at the

ankles and hands quiet in her lap. Absurdly, a seventy-year-old picture flashed into her memory of the class at Miss Van Renssalaer's Academy for Young Ladies absorbing the principles of being prim and proper. What did any of it matter now, she wondered, after all these years? It was people, and what they did to each other, that mattered. Dodie, too, had gone to a private school, and see what happened to her.

She went out driving by herself one night," she told Barkley, "and . . . had an accident. Her spinal cord was crushed, and she was paralyzed from the waist down."

Allison remembered that night much too clearly. The stifling heat had been emphasized by the heartless cheerfulness of crickets. About eleven o'clock, Allison had prepared a glass of lemonade for herself, and moved to the old wicker lounge on the screened porch. It seemed cooler with the light off, so she sat in the dark, sipping the tart drink and resting. At first the voices had been muted, simply alto and baritone rhythms, then they had swelled and she caught phrases rising in passionate tones. Finally, there was no effort to hush their voices, and Dodie's anguish had cried across the night to Allison: "She's going to have a baby, and you expect me to be calm? How could you betray me so, and with a . . . a creature like that?"

Frank's voice had resounded with mocking laughter. "You can't be that much of an innocent! Do you honestly think your simple charms could be enough for a man like me? Susie wasn't the first, and you can be damned sure she won't be the last. Come on now, Dodie. You're a sweet kid, and your family's been real helpful in getting me where I want to go, but you just can't tie a man down."

Allison cringed, remembering Dodie's wounded cry. It had been followed by the slam of the screen door, then footsteps pounding across the porch and down the steps. The car door slammed and the engine roared to life. Gravel spurted as Dodie took off into the darkness.

Only Dodie knew whether the smashup truly was an accident. Perhaps she had simply tried to numb the pain with speed—but she had been twenty-one and she never walked again.

The policeman cleared his throat. "Miss Ryder?"

"Yes?"

"I hope you'll excuse me for asking you so much about your friends and neighbors, but you see . . . well, it's all going to come out eventually, and I'm sure you'll be discreet. There are only three possibilities to account for Mrs. Patrick's death. Crippled as she was, she had no access to the supply of sleeping pills. They were kept in the bathroom and her husband gave them to her whenever she needed them. It may be that she hoarded her pills, hiding them from her husband somehow, until she had enough for a lethal dose, and took them herself. Or it could be that Mr. Patrick was careless—criminally careless—and she received an accidental overdose. Or . . ." and he paused, while Allison's eyes searched his. "Well, you realize, we must consider the, uh, possibility that . . . perhaps the overdose wasn't accidental. Mr. Patrick wouldn't be the first man burdened by a crippled wife who took the wrong way out."

"Captain Barkley," Allison said. "There was no reason in the world for Dodie to kill herself. What does Frank say happened?"

"He insists she must have taken them herself. According to him she suffered a great deal of pain. He claims she must have saved up the sleeping pills, which rules out any chance of an accident. This is why I wanted to talk to you. You were very close to Mrs. Patrick. Was she in much pain?"

Allison's fingers unconsciously pleated the plum-colored fabric of the dress over her lap. Her head went a little higher, and an imperious generation spoke through her.

"I have already told you, there was no reason in the world for Dodie to kill herself. To my certain knowledge she was seldom, if ever, in pain. In fact, I can give you the names of three or four ladies who could confirm that fact, out of Dodie's own mouth. We'd often gather on the Patricks' front porch in the afternoon, so Dodie could be part of the group, and not a week ago we were discussing that case in the papers—you remember, the man who shot his wife because she was dying of cancer? Dodie was most upset. She was a dreadfully sympathetic child. She was torn between her distress at his immoral action and her sympathy with his concern for his wife's suffering. 'Perhaps I might judge differently,' she said, 'if I were in pain myself. I'm one of the fortunates, suffering only from the handicap. But even if I were in pain, I don't believe that anyone but God has a right to take a life.' The other ladies will bear me out on this, captain."

Yes, she said to herself, we were discussing the case. Maybe nobody else noticed, it was so skillfully done, but Dodie herself was the one who maneuvered the conversation around to mercy killing. *I didn't know then, Dodie, but I can see now what you were doing.*

"Mrs. Patrick said herself that she was in no pain? Ever?"

"At the time of the accident, and for several months afterward, yes, she did have pain. But not recently. I never once heard her complain."

There now, Allison, she realized, you did tell a lie; you can't wiggle out of that one. The same night as that get-together you told him about, remember?—and Sunday night—and last night . . .

The scene had been the same all three nights, and the script had followed the same lines. Allison had been in her comfortable corner on the porch, Snowball's faint purrs pulsing against her caressing hand, the creaking wicker of the lounge cool against her bare arms. That first night it had rained earlier, breaking the heat, and the lilac leaves had whispered wetly to each other in the dark. Gentle dripping from the eaves seemed to deepen the quiet, rather than break it. Dodie's blind had been pulled down only to the level of the raised window. The muted voices were carried across to her by the force of their intensity.

"Please, Frank! Please!" Never had Allison heard such pleading in Dodie's voice.

"I've told you, I just can't," he'd said. "If the pain's so bad, let me get a shot for you, or something. But you don't know what you're talking about, wanting to kill yourself."

"What good am I to anybody like this? And the pain—I just can't stand it any more." Her voice had risen with a startling anguish.

Allison, listening in spite of herself, had held herself tense, wondering. Just that afternoon Dodie had denied pain, yet now . . . Hot tears had welled in Allison's eyes as she listened to the tortured voice.

If she hadn't hated Frank so much for what he had done to Dodie, she might have been able to pity him as his voice broke with indecision. "Dodie, I can't do it! Don't ask me to. Even if you're ready to die, think of the position you'd put me in. They'd say I killed you. Think of me, Dodie! They'd give me the chair!"

The argument had gone on. Three different nights Dodie had hammered away. Then last night, while Allison, hypnotized, watched the shadows shifting on the drawn blind, Dodie had played out her drama. She had won. Frank gave her the pills.

Allison had no longer felt the heat of the night. Chilled with horror, she had fought her own battle. Her throat had throbbed with a scream to that silent window. She couldn't let Dodie do this! But a thin hand to her lips cut off that scream before it sounded. What right did she have to interfere? Dodie must hate with an unsuspected fury to die for her revenge. She wouldn't thank Allison for stopping her now.

Allison had sat quietly. Soon the Patricks' light went out. Only then did she rise stiffly and plod to her bedroom, where no one could hear her poorly stifled sobs.

The white cat had followed her to the bedroom. One soft, easy leap settled him beside the tired, sorrowing old lady. Allison remembered the day Dodie had brought him to her.

"Frank says he's allergic to cats, Miss Ryder. He won't have one in the house. But he's such a darling!" The vibrant face had gone quiet as she crooned over the kitten. "Snowball'd be a good name, don't you think? If you kept him, I could see him often. I could help groom him, and things. It wouldn't hurt so much if I knew you had him."

So Allison had kept Snowball, but Dodie had never visited him in his new home. The accident came only days later. That's what Allison resolutely called it, although she was very much afraid it was something else. Through those harrowing days the kitten grew, and comforted Allison. He was full-grown by the time Dodie left the hospital.

Please come home, Snowball, Allison begged in her heart, forgetful of the waiting policeman. I need you so. There's not much left for an old lady. I had Dodie and I had you. Now Dodie's gone. Snowball, don't you know how much I need you?

A tear that couldn't be restrained by a lifetime of self-discipline slipped down the wrinkled, gray cheek.

Captain Barkley, tactfully clearing his throat again, brought Allison back to the present. This policeman and his questions! Allison was weary. Please, no more decisions . . .

Barkley hoisted himself out of the deep leather chair. "Well, Miss Ryder, I think you've told us what we need to know. One thing—when you get the chance, could you just write down the names of those other ladies you mentioned, who heard Mrs. Patrick say she suffered no pain? I won't trouble you now. I'll send a man by later today for it."

Dodie wins, Allison thought, but she felt no elation. Yes, Frank had killed Dodie, killed her youth and killed her innocence, and pummeled her spirit until she wanted to die. Yet, did Dodie, or did Allison, have the right to sentence him? Heedless of the waiting policeman, Allison closed her eyes momentarily, yielding to the grief that closed around her like a gray fog. Dodie was gone—but Allison didn't have to decide. All she had to do was let things go ahead without her, and all those other people would have to decide.

Allison struggled out of her chair. Captain Barkley rushed to help her, but she waved him aside. "Thank you, young man, but I have to do things by myself nowadays."

Yes, Allison, she mused, you have to do things by yourself. Once you make this decision, don't fool yourself that somebody else sent Frank to the electric chair. They still execute murderers in this state, you know, and rightly speaking, Frank did not murder Dodie. For eighty-three years you've known right from wrong. You've faced up to the truths, whether you liked the result or not. Now . . .

"Captain . . ." she started. Then her taut nerves jerked her like a marionette as the doorbell shrilled.

"I'll get it," the policeman offered.

It was another policeman, a close-shaven young man too big for his uniform, who bobbed his head respectfully to her, then turned to the captain, "Morrison says to tell you they're all finished over there, any time you're ready to go back to the station."

Captain Barkley glanced in speculation at Allison. Her expression told him nothing.

"I'll be out to the car in a minute." He held the door open for the younger man.

"Oh, and I thought I'd mention that we don't have to worry none about that big white cat the neighbors said was yowling early this morning. We found it in the Patricks' trash can. Somebody'd wrung its neck."

The captain nodded and turned back toward Allison where she stood by her overstuffed armchair, one hand lightly touching the back for support. Dodie smiled at him from the piecrust table.

"You were about to say . . . ?"

Allison reached to pick a white cat hair off of the chair beside her. "Yes . . . I was going to say I'll start on that list you wanted right away. You can send someone over for it in about half an hour. Good morning, captain."

Head erect, shoulders straight, she shuffled resolutely across the room to close the door behind him.

A CASE OF CATNAPPING

by A.H.Z. Carr

The biggest fee I ever got was for finding a cat. That's the way it goes. I have solved murders and traced stolen jewels, but the only time anybody ever paid me 5,000 smackers, it was for a cat. I grant you, not an ordinary cat. This was the great Dizzy.

The funny part of it was that before there was even a case, the wife and I had been to the Orpheum just to see that act. *Dizzy—the World's First Performing Cat—With Dave Knight*—that's the way they billed it. My wife is a nut about cats—we have two of our own—and when she saw this publicity story in the newspaper, she read it to me.

It told how this Dave Knight had been a small-time entertainer, with a corny routine of comedy, tap-dancing, and ventriloquism—not very good at any of them, and pretty near down and out—when one night on the street this kitten rubs against his leg. It is just a handful of skin, bones, fleas, and miaows, and he does not care much about cats, but he says, "O.K., some milk," puts her in his pocket, and takes her to his little walk-up apartment in Greenwich Village. He feeds her and cleans her up, and the next thing you know, he has a cat, for he cannot bring himself to kick her out.

She turns out to be a kind of genius—as smart as any trained dog or chimpanzee—smarter, even. The article tells how Knight named her Dizzy when he noticed her doing somersaults while she played with a piece of string. Little by little he taught her tricks, until she would do them even on a stage and was not frightened by the lights and noise, as long as Knight was there.

Vaudeville was coming back just then, and when the booking agents looked over the act, they realized it was something new. Knight and Dizzy crashed the big time, touring all over the country. It says in the article there are supposed to be ten million house cats in the world, but Dizzy is unique—the only cat that ever got into the upper tax brackets. A thousand a week Knight was making, and he had Dizzy's life insured for $100,000.

The wife said she had to see it before she would believe it, and the next thing I knew we had our coats on and were headed for the Orpheum. We came in during an act called *The Three Graces—and the Disgrace* (a comedy dance team, and good too)—three girls, one a redhead, one a blonde, and the third a brunette, and a guy with a very funny dance routine. Next was *McIntyre, the Irish Magician,* who had a midget dressed as a leprechaun, and who did a lot of neat magic—mind-reading, card tricks, sword tricks, disappearances—the works. But it was Dizzy that wowed the audience.

Quite a cat. She had long silky gray fur, crossed with tigerish black stripes, a white bib and ruff, white boots, and a tail like a silver fox. Then there was her face. Most cats look pretty much alike, but this one had big golden eyes, long white whiskers, and an eager, innocent, gentle expression that made my wife coo.

She was the whole act. Knight is just a freckle-faced kid with a friendly grin—the college type, with a crew-cut and glasses—and smart enough not to compete with Dizzy. He started very easy, making her sit up, lie down, and play dead, like a dog. Anything a dog could do, he said, Dizzy could do better. She stood on her hind legs, with little boxing gloves on her front paws, and hit a little punching bag that he rigged up, in time to music. Then she did a series of somersaults and back flips, and jumped through three moving hoops. The orchestra played a rhumba, and they did a dance—very cute—with Knight tapping, and Dizzy moving around on her hind legs, with a little wiggle that made the audience roar.

The ventriloquist stunt was good, too. She sat on his knee, like a dummy, and he made her seem to speak in a high-pitched, miaowing voice, opening and shutting her mouth at the same time. At the end of the act he set up a contraption that looked like a little xylophone, with thin strips of metal hanging down loose. When she would hit one of these strips with her paw, it struck a note; and believe it or not, she jumps around, bangs the strips, and out comes *Home, Sweet Home*.

The audience loved it, and my wife couldn't talk about anything else for a week. So when my phone rang next Sunday morning and a fellow says, "Are you Jack Terry? This is Dave Knight," I knew who he was. He said the manager of the Orpheum—Eddie Thompson, who I went to school with—had suggested that he get in touch with me, and could he see me right away.

I told him sure, meet me at my office. When he showed up, there was a girl with him, and he introduced her as Miss Maribeth Lewis. I recognized her—one of The Three Graces—the dark-haired one. Very young, with one of these wide-mouthed, attractive faces, and a figure right out of a dream, as I knew from seeing her on the stage. Both of them were looking pale and worried, and Knight got right down to business.

"Dizzy is gone," he said. "I want you to find her."

"Look," I said. "I'm a detective, just an ordinary private eye, as they call them on TV. What you want is the SPCA or something. I'm sorry your cat is gone, but I wouldn't know how to begin to find a cat."

Knight was no dope. He did not argue. He just said, "I will pay you five thousand dollars if you find her. That's every cent I have saved so far, but you can have it."

"That's a lot of money," I said. "But suppose she has been hit by a truck or something."

Knight looked like *he* had been hit by the truck, and the girl, Maribeth, said, "Please don't say that, Mr. Terry!"

"Look," I said, "I don't want to scare you, but you know how it is when a cat is loose on city streets, with the traffic and all. Anything can happen. Besides, it isn't like she would be a total loss. How about that hundred grand you get if she is dead?"

"You don't understand," said Knight. "That cat is part of me. I wouldn't sell her for a million bucks. As far as the insurance goes, it only covers death under certain conditions. It does not apply if she is lost."

"Is she lost?"

"I don't know. I can't understand it." He kept run-

ning his hand through his thatch of sandy hair. "You
don't know how I watch over that cat. She is hardly
ever out of my sight. She sleeps in my bed, and we
even eat together."

"Maybe she's just taking a day off," I said, trying
to encourage him. "We've got a female cat, and she
likes to go out on the town now and then."

"Dizzy has never done that," said Knight, shaking
his head.

I said, "Have you thought about offering a reward?"

"There is a tag on Dizzy's collar," he explained,
"giving my name and offering five hundred dollars to
anyone who finds her if she is lost and returns her to
me or to the police. And I have checked with the
police—they are keeping a lookout for her."

I had been sizing him up. He did not strike me as
the type who would get rid of his cat for the insurance.
I knew my wife would never forgive me if I did not try
to find Dizzy for him, so although I was not hopeful, I
said, "Let's leave it like this. If I find her alive and
in good shape, we can talk about a bonus. If she is
dead, I get only my regular fee and expenses. Okay?
Now tell me exactly what happened. How did you lose
her?"

Knight said, "It was last night, in the theater. I was
waiting in the wings for McIntyre the Magician to finish. I always stand there for maybe ten minutes before
I go on, with Dizzy in my arms, so she can get used
to the noise and lights."

He was pretty emotional, you could tell, but he gave
me the facts straight and fast. "Then Barton—that's
Bill Barton, he's the Disgrace in Maribeth's act—he
called to me. He wanted to show me a loose piece of
rope that was hanging down just over where Dizzy

does her hoop act. He was afraid it might make her nervous. You couldn't see it from where I was standing, so I put Dizzy in her box, and walked back to where Bill was."

"Wait a second. Did you leave the box open?"

"No, I latched it. It is really a big leather traveling case that I had specially built for her. She couldn't get out. Not unless somebody opened the box."

"Then somebody did," I said. "Well, go on."

"Bill was right. The rope was swaying just enough so it might have distracted Dizzy. I went after a stage-hand and got him to go up and pull the rope out of the way."

"If you were on the stage," I said, "how come the audience couldn't see you?"

"McIntyre does the first part of his act before a close backdrop. I was behind the backdrop."

"How long were you away from Dizzy's box, all told?" I asked him.

"Not more than three minutes. At first I thought maybe some busybody had unlatched the box to look at her."

Maribeth said, "People are always trying to pet her."

"But," said Knight, "if Dizzy had jumped out of the box, she would have come to me. She always does. She just wasn't around. We searched everywhere—backstage, the wings, the dressing rooms. I called to her—she always comes running when I call, but she didn't show up. After McIntyre finished his act, I had to tell Mr. Thompson I couldn't go on. He explained to the audience what had happened, and asked them to let us know if any of them saw the cat—thinking it might have got out front somehow. But nobody had seen it."

I said, "You figure she was taken out of the box deliberately—stolen, is that it?"

"That's what must have happened," Knight said. "But who would do a thing like that? Everybody in the theater loves that cat, and is my friend. And where could they have hidden her? How could they have got her out of the theater without somebody noticing? It just doesn't make sense."

I chewed that over for a minute, and then I said, "Excuse me for getting personal—but did you and Miss Lewis just happen to come here at the same time?"

They looked at each other, and Knight said, "It's no secret. We're engaged. At least—" He stopped.

"Dave!" said Maribeth. "You know perfectly well we could make out." She turned to me. "We're going to get married when we finish our current bookings. But now he keeps saying that without Dizzy he doesn't amount to anything in the profession, and he has no right to ask me to team up with him. As if a cat— even Dizzy—should be allowed to decide how people should live their lives. Isn't that ridiculous, Mr. Terry?"

"Ridiculous," I agreed, looking her over—a really sumptuous dish. "How long have you known each other?"

"Oh," she said, "for several months. We have been traveling on the same circuit. It was in New Orleans that we really knew—wasn't it, darling?"

Knight nods, and says, "Yesterday the world looked wonderful. Today—" He didn't finish.

"Well," I said, "let me think aloud for a minute,

and don't hold it against me if I say something wrong. I'm just groping, you understand. You really love that cat, don't you? You think about her as if she was human."

"She is practically human. Of course I love her."

I put a cigar in my mouth, and lighted it, thinking hard. Then I said, "My wife once made me read a novel by a Frenchwoman—Colette, her name was—where a dame is so jealous of her husband's cat that she tries to kill it."

A second went by before Knight reacted. Then he exploded. "I thought you had some sense. You're crazy!"

But it was Maribeth I was watching. Her big, dark eyes flashed, but she only said, very quiet, "Mr. Terry, you're wrong. I love Dizzy, and I love Dave, and I'm not a murderess—or a kidnapper."

"Just testing," I said. I figured she was O.K. A woman who would consider killing a cat murder wouldn't kill it—or kidnap it. "Excuse it, please. Now let's get back to the facts. Knight, when you were standing in the wings with Dizzy, did you see anyone hanging around?"

"Not a soul. Nobody came near us."

"After you told the stagehand to take care of the rope, you went back to the box. You still didn't see anybody nearby?"

He shook his head.

"Everybody was backstage. They were just lifting the backdrop for the last part of McIntyre's act. The only person I could see from where I stood was McIntyre."

Something clicked in my mind. "How about the

midget? The leprechaun? Doesn't he go offstage a couple of times?"

"Little Pat? Wait. You're right. He does go off once or twice to bring in little props for McIntyre. I suppose he must have passed Dizzy's box a couple of times. I guess I was so used to him, I didn't pay any attention."

"But surely," said Maribeth, "Pat wouldn't steal the cat."

This seemed like a good chance to make like Sherlock Holmes, which always impresses the clients, so I said, "When you have eliminated the impossible, that which remains—no matter how improbable—must be the truth. The way I see it, Pat the midget is it. He was near the cat's box. He could have stooped down, unlatched the box, and taken the cat out."

"But what would he have done with it?" Knight said. "He had to be back on stage in a minute."

I cleared my throat—for my big idea. "Doesn't McIntyre put the leprechaun in a cabinet and make him disappear, the last part of his act?"

Knight jerked up straight. "You're right!" he said.

"Look at the facts. You are off looking for a stagehand. The cabinet that McIntyre uses for the disappearance trick is behind the backdrop—out of sight of the audience, and out of your sight, too. Nobody is around. It probably wouldn't take Pat more than a couple of seconds to carry the cat to the cabinet and put her inside. Let's say he knows how to work the trick. The cat disappears. Then he simply picks up his prop and goes on stage again with McIntyre."

Maribeth said, "But in that case, wouldn't Dizzy have come out when McIntyre opened the cabinet?"

Knight jumped to his feet. "No, that trick is just a new version of an old gag—works with a trapdoor.

I've seen it. The trap goes down to a room in the basement. That's what must have happened!"

He was starting for the door. "Take it easy," I said. "Do you know where we could find the midget now?"

"I saw him in the hotel this morning," said Maribeth. "And—oh! I just thought of something. He had a piece of sticking plaster on his face. I thought he had cut himself shaving."

"That does it," I said. "Let's go."

"The hell with the midget," said Knight. "Let's find Dizzy. She may still be down in that basement."

I agreed we should go to the theater first, and we piled into my car. There was a watchman on duty at the theater, and he let us in. Knight was so impatient he wanted to run. Right under the stage there was a big room with several ladders leading to trapdoors above. It was empty, though.

There was one window in the room, at the back, and it was open. Knight swore and looked sick. "She could have got out that way," he said.

The window opened on a narrow alley. We went out there and walked up and down, while Knight called, "Dizzy! Dizzy, baby!" No use. Not a sign of a cat. "This is terrible," he said. "Somebody must have taken her away. If she was loose, she would still be here. She has a wonderful homing sense."

I said, "Let's go to the hotel. I want to talk to the little leprechaun."

We found Pat in the Coffee Shop of the hotel, having lunch alone. Steak, no less. He was only about three feet high, and dressed very dapper. Sure enough, he had a big piece of adhesive on his face.

I didn't waste any time. "Pat," I said, "what's under the plaster?"

He turned pale and said in his piping voice, "A cut. I cut myself."

"Mind if I look?" I said.

He tried to get away, but Knight held him, and I pulled off the tape. There was no mistaking the marks—three short parallel scratches, deep enough to draw blood. Dizzy was evidently a lady who didn't like to be roughhoused.

At first, Pat clammed up—wouldn't say a word. So, sitting there at the luncheon table, I reconstructed what must have happened—everything he had done, step by step. "You don't even have to tell us who put you up to it," I said.

"McIntyre," Knight said, real grim.

"No," I said. "Your friend Bill Barton. How much did he pay you, Pat?"

The midget called Barton several words, and said, "He talked!"

Maribeth and Knight looked stunned. She said, "I can't believe it."

"Obvious, my dear Watson," I said, "from the first. Barton got Knight out of the way with that prearranged business about the rope while Pat made the snatch. And Barton has a motive. If you marry Knight, you break up his act. And maybe," I added, "he has other ideas about who you ought to marry, Miss Lewis."

Her face showed she thought I was right.

"He said," squeaked the midget, opening up at last and talking to Knight, "he just wanted to keep the cat for a little while to get you out of his hair. So you couldn't finish your bookings. He thought if Maribeth didn't see you for a while, he might be able to beat your time."

"We'll see you later," I told the midget. "Enjoy your ill-gotten steak while you can. Do you know the penalty for kidnapping? And don't try to tell me it was only catnapping."

We had Maribeth call Barton on the hotel house-phone to make sure he was in his room. She didn't say we were with her. When he opened his door to her knock and saw the three of us, he didn't like it. On stage, he had been made up as a bum, but standing there in his dressing gown he looked very distinguished—one of the tall, dark, and handsome boys.

Knight didn't stand on ceremony. He pushed Barton into a chair and stood over him, yelling, "You skunk, give me back my cat or I'll break your neck."

It took Barton only a few seconds to realize there was no use trying to lie out of it. Either he delivered the cat, I told him, or we would put him behind bars. That reached him. "I haven't got her," he said. "Believe me, I haven't. It was just a wild impulse. I'm in love with Maribeth, too. And I had to try to protect my act. You know the old saying—all's fair in love and war."

I hate guys who talk like that. "All right," I said, "then this is war." With that I cuffed him, hard, on the side of his head. "Spill it," I said. "Where's the cat?"

He rubbed his head and said, "She got away."

"What do you mean she got away?" Knight shouted.

Barton told us that after Pat had dropped the cat through the trapdoor under the magic cabinet, and Knight had gone to look for a stagehand, he had rushed down to the basement to get Dizzy. It was his idea to smuggle her out of the theater and keep her somewhere for a while. But she wasn't there. Somebody had left the basement window open, and she had got out. He had never seen her.

I believed him, and so did Knight, who started running his hand through his hair again. "Something must have happened to her," he groaned. "Otherwise she would have been reported by now."

Maribeth said, "Oh, Dave, darling," and he put his arms around her. I thought that was a good moment to give Barton a brief description of his ancestry and his future. Then we left him sitting there, crushed, and went back to the theater. I asked Knight again about his insurance policy. The way it was written, the company wasn't responsible if the cat was stolen or ran away while unguarded. Technically, that was what had happened, so it didn't seem as if Knight had a chance to collect. The only thing that could help him was to find Dizzy—pronto.

I didn't see much that I could do, but I felt I ought to try to earn my day's pay. When we reached the alleyway next to the theater, I stopped and said, "What we need now is psychology—cat psychology. Where would a cat go that jumped out of that basement window? I am assuming Dizzy is alive and able to navigate. Then she must be at a place where she is out of sight—because otherwise someone would have found her and brought her back for the reward. And it is probably a place that she likes—because otherwise she would have tried to come back to the theater and to Knight."

Knight nodded. "Yes," he said. "That makes sense." He was so eager to hope, it was pathetic.

"Now," I said, "what is it that would attract a cat like Dizzy so much that she would be content to stay away?"

"Could it be food?" Maribeth said.

"No," said Knight. "She is a dainty eater, and always gets her meals on schedule, and she never lets anybody else feed her. You couldn't keep her away just with food—not even caviar, which she loves."

"Look," I said. "She may have aristocratic tastes, but she is still a cat. What is the main interest of a female cat—especially one that has never had a boy friend?"

"Of course!" Maribeth said. "I bet that's it."

"I don't believe it," said Dave.

"You're just jealous," said Maribeth. "What could be more natural? I'm female myself. I know."

"Tomcats like alleys," I pointed out. "And if they are off somewhere holding paws, that would explain why nobody has seen her. I have noticed that cats like to keep to themselves at such times."

"But that would be ruinous!" said Knight.

"What's so terrible about it? It goes on all the time," I said.

"You don't understand," he said. "I had a talk with a cat authority about it. He said Dizzy's unusual intelligence shows that the ordinary cat instincts are not fully developed in her. He said if she were to—uh—have an affair with a male cat, she would probably revert to type, and then would not respond to me the way she does now."

"Maybe not," I said. "But you still want to find her, don't you?"

"Of course I do. Even if she never acts again, I've got to find her," he said.

"Then my hunch," I said, "I mean my deduction, is to look for a tomcat. And where would you be likely to find a tomcat in a business section like this?

There are no homes around here. And stray cats do not often come into streets full of traffic. No—the chances are that any cat you would see in this alley comes from some store or restaurant."

I looked down the alley. A few buildings beyond the theater was a door with a few crates stacked outside. "We'll start there," I said.

It was the back door of a restaurant called The Rendezvous. "This is the most likely place," I said, "because it's the closest. Let's go around front."

I got hold of the proprietor—a fat, friendly Italian named Pirelli—and asked him if he had a cat.

"Yes," he said, looking around. "Somewhere. Maybe in the kitchen. Maybe in the cellar. Maybe outside. He comes. He goes. What do you want with my cat?"

I said, "Look. This is important. We are trying to find a girl-cat who has got lost. We have an idea that she may be hiding out with some tomcat in this neighborhood. Could we look around your place for your cat, just in case the other one has sneaked in here too?"

When Pirelli got the idea, he laughed, and said, "Why, sure. My cat, Tommy, he is a great one with the ladies. You should hear the noise sometimes in the alley. Go ahead, look. I will go with you."

Tommy wasn't in the dining room or the kitchen. "Only one other place," Pirelli said. "Maybe down cellar."

Down cellar we went. When he switched on a light, we heard a miaow. Out from behind some barrels came a big, black, tough-looking tom, and rubbed against Pirelli's legs. Pirelli said, "Hello, Tommy. You got a lady friend down here, maybe?"

The tomcat looked at him and miaowed deeply.

From behind the barrels came another, more musical miaow, and Dave Knight yelled, "Dizzy!"

There she was, stretched out on an old piece of burlap. Knight picked her up and kissed her, and Maribeth made a big fuss over her, too. They both told me I was the greatest detective in the world, which is probably an exaggeration, and Pirelli congratulated us, while the tomcat and Dizzy miaowed. All of a sudden, Dizzy jumped out of Knight's arms, went to the tom, and rubbed against him.

"Aha!" said Pirelli. "You see? He is a great one with the ladies, that Tommy."

It was pretty plain that Dizzy thought so, too. When Knight reached for her, she drew back and spat at him. He stared at her in horror. Then she touched noses with Tommy. He licked himself, the way cats do when they are embarrassed by people looking at them. Finally, Dizzy turned around three times, and lay down on her side, stretching out her paws, purring like a little steam engine, and looking at Tommy with big, soulful eyes.

Knight looked absolutely crushed, and I didn't blame him. Dizzy had ceased to be a trained performing cat. She was just a female in love, and nobody could come between her and her mate—not even the man she had been sleeping with.

Maribeth said, "Dave, perhaps if the tom came along."

His face lighted up. "That's an idea," he said. "Mr. Pirelli, will you sell me your cat?"

Pirelli did not like it and held out for a while, but $25 finally convinced him. We got a big box, put both cats into it, loaded it into a taxi, and got it up to Knight's apartment in the hotel. The cats didn't seem to mind—they were so wrapped up in each other, a mere change of residence hardly mattered. Knight looked at the tom the way an outraged father might look at the scoundrel who has seduced his daughter, but what could he do?

What he wanted to know, of course, was whether Dizzy would do her tricks. He played a recording and tried to get her to dance and jump through a hoop, but all she did was turn her back, miaow, and sidle up to Tommy. When we put the tom out of the room, she scratched at the door and yelled until we had to let him in again.

Knight gave up. "Well," he said, "I have lost my meal ticket, but anyway, I've got my cat back."

"You have got your girl, too, in case you have forgotten," said Maribeth. "And don't think you can shake me with any excuse about poverty. Look at Dizzy and Tommy. You don't see them worrying about the future, do you?"

Knight kissed her. Finally I coughed and said, "Well, I guess the case is closed. I'll be going along."

They remembered me then, and began to shake my hand and thank me. Knight said, "About that five thousand. You've earned it. I haven't got it all in the bank, but I'll give you a check for a thousand right now, and the rest in a couple of days. Okay?"

"No," I said. "Forget it. What kind of a heel do you think I am? If Dizzy was still worth a thousand a week to you it might be different. This way, you will be needing all the money you have. This has been good fun, and you owe me exactly one day's pay— fifty dollars. The other four thousand, nine hundred and fifty is my wedding present to the two of you. Now don't argue about it!"

And that's the way we left it. When I asked Knight what we wanted to do about Barton and the midget, he said, "What's the use of making trouble? Their punishment won't get Dizzy to perform again—and the publicity would hurt McIntyre and Maribeth's sisters, who are innocent."

He was a good kid. So was Maribeth. They went to New York to try to work up a husband-and-wife act, and I didn't hear from them for more than two months. Then a postcard came from Maribeth, saying they were happy, and still hopeful of getting somewhere with their act. Also, Dizzy had produced six adorable kittens—three like herself, two like Tommy, and one white one that they couldn't account for. They had named the white one Terry, after me.

She sounded as if they were having a struggle, but not minding it too much. A few more months went by. Then, just yesterday, I got a letter from them. When I opened it, a check fell out. It was for $4,950. The letter said:

About this check. It is not your wedding present to us. No, we have been living on that, and blessing you for it. This is something else again. It is what we owe you, according to our original agreement, and if we did not pay it we would never feel right. So please take it—because we can afford it now. Besides, our agent says we can charge it off on our income tax.

You see, some time back we went into the little room where Dizzy was playing with her kittens. There she was, turning somersaults again. And then it happened. *One after another, all of the kittens turned somersaults, too!*

Inherited aptitude, they call it. We spent endless

hours making sure, and training them. Today we signed a contract, with a big advance, for a full season's bookings and movie and television appearances. Fifteen hundred a week. We're going to be rich.

We open at the Palace. The act is terrific. We have got a trapeze number with all six kittens flying through the air at the same time while Dizzy stands there like a ringmaster, with a little whip in her paw. There is no doubt about it. Every one of those kittens is a genius, just like Dizzy. Tommy, of course, is not in the act. But he does not have to do tricks. He has other gifts.

We're billed as *Those Wonderful Cats—and the Knights*. When we come your way, there will be tickets at the box office for you and Mrs. Terry. Bless you.

Love from Dave, Maribeth, Dizzy, Tommy, and The Six.

My wife can hardly wait to see the act. As a matter of fact, neither can I.

MISS PHIPPS
AND THE SIAMESE CAT

by Phyllis Bentley

"Original plus two copies, double spacing, margins twelve and twenty-two, fresh page for each chapter, French words underlined—" began Miss Phipps.

"Punctuation to be followed exactly," concluded Mrs. Norton with a prim cough.

"Just so."

"It's a long time since you've visited the Norton Agency for typing, Miss Phipps," said Mrs. Norton, her tone slightly acid. "I thought perhaps you'd obtained a permanent secretary again."

"Oh, I have. A very nice girl. Very accurate. But at the moment she's *hors de combat*. Having a baby."

"Married, I hope," said Mrs. Norton with a sniff.

"Of course," replied Miss Phipps staunchly. "Now when can I have my finished typescript, please?"

"Well, you can't."

How she enjoys saying that, thought Miss Phipps, vexed. "Shall I take it elsewhere, then?" she said coolly, rising.

"No, no! I mean you can't have it done by me until the week after next."

"Oh, dear," fretted Miss Phipps.

"There's Maureen, however, or Bertha."

"Who's Maureen? Who's Bertha?"

"Bertha is my senior girl. Maureen did your last one."

"Oh, well, her work was satisfactory."

"Maureen, come here a moment."

A small slender girl with remarkably long golden hair rose from one of the desks in the crowded room a-clatter with typewriters. Miss Phipps noted with pleasure that this golden mane was beautifully brushed.

"You've nearly finished that report, Maureen?" said Mrs. Norton in a voice which would have frozen a polar bear.

"On the last page, Mrs. Norton."

"We'd better just look at your work together," suggested Mrs. Norton, holding out a hand to Miss Phipps for the script. "Is it a full-length novel, dear?"

"Just a short children's book," deprecated Miss Phipps, blushing and feeling embarrassed and inferior, as she always did when her writing was mentioned.

She reluctantly laid the script on the table in its folder, which she had tied round with string two ways to keep the pages within from slipping. If asked, Miss Phipps would have admitted frankly that while all the literary work on the script was as good as she could make it, the outside appearance was not altogether prepossessing, the folder being slightly dirty and dog-eared and the string knotted in several places.

Mrs. Norton, with her rather pompous little cough, advanced long-nailed fingers toward it, with an air of trying, for friendship's sake, not to show disdain. Miss Phipps hated to see those mercenary hands take hold of her precious writing—But that's not fair, she re-

buked herself. She's a professional in her own line
and proud of it, just as I am in mine.

While Miss Phipps was thinking this, the group had
been joined by a new member. A Siamese cat, slim,
brownish, young and handsome, had leaped onto the
table and was now devoting tooth and claw to the
dismemberment of the folder's string.

"No, no," said Miss Phipps mildly, gently laying
aside a smooth brown paw.

The cat promptly scratched her.

"I don't mind a scratch or two," said Miss Phipps.
"But not the string, please. *PLEASE!* No, pussy! No.
I shall be cross!"

"She doesn't understand," purred Mrs. Norton.
"She lives here, you see. This office is her home and
she thinks she can do as she pleases. Now, Edith,
dear."

"Who is Edith?" inquired Miss Phipps, looking in-
terrogatively at Maureen, who was standing patiently
by the table.

"The cat, of course. Called after my aunt, who gave
her to me."

"Edith!" said Miss Phipps sternly. "Paws off, please!"

Edith bit the bow of the string, rolled over with
that beautiful feline grace which is the admiration and
despair of humans, and lying on her back, waving a
couple of paws, seemed to invite praise. Since she had
contrived to untie the string and wind it about herself
in complex trails, Miss Phipps did not feel the slightest
bit laudatory.

"You're a naughty cat, Edith," Miss Phipps said,
snatching the precious folder from the table.

Edith scowled ferociously from yellow eyes.

"Well, really!" exclaimed Mrs. Norton. "Don't blame the cat! Maureen spoils her."

Indeed Maureen, smiling, had extended loving arms toward Edith.

"*You'd* better take her, Bertha," commanded Mrs. Norton.

A rather handsome girl, tall, with a composed face and a stack of fair curls piled up on her head, approached from her front-row desk with dignity, raised the bestringed Edith distastefully into her arms, and walked away.

"Let Bertha finish that report, Maureen," instructed Mrs. Norton, having flicked Miss Phipps's pages. "Begin Miss Phipps's script at once. I know she's always in a hurry."

Bertha, having detached the string, put Edith outside the door of the room, closed the door, and came back, walking with measured tread. Meanwhile Maureen retrieved Miss Phipps's script. She handled it respectfully, and Miss Phipps felt somewhat mollified.

"I'll give you a ring when it's done," offered Mrs. Norton.

They parted on cool but friendly terms.

The Norton Typing Agency occupied an office-apartment on the first floor of a large Victorian house. Outside the room Miss Phipps found Edith, glowering, seated at the head of the steps leading to the street. Miss Phipps was not at all disposed to let the cat approach within range of her typescript, so she took some pains to close the office door promptly. Edith tripped down the steps gracefully in front of her and sat at the foot, still glowering.

"Beautiful animal," conceded Miss Phipps. "Fine coat."

At the foot of the steps, leaning against the wall, was Geoffrey, Mrs. Norton's son, now an engineer apprentice. Mrs. Norton was a widow, and Geoffrey could have used a father, Miss Phipps thought, surveying his beads and style of dress. She had known Geoffrey since he was an infant, and greeted him in familiar tones.

"Hullo, Geoff. You've grown a good deal lately, I see."

"Hullo, Miss Phipps. Edith doesn't seem to like you, *I* see."

"We had a bit of a tiff upstairs," admitted Miss Phipps, noting the cat's still furious glaring and the lashing of her slender tail. "She's vexed."

"Well, wouldn't you be vexed if *you* were thrown out on your paws?"

"She wasn't exactly thrown out," objected Miss Phipps.

"That's what you think," said Geoffrey. "Now purr nicely for Miss Phipps, Edith."

Edith, in the haughty manner peculiar to cats, raised her head and stalked slowly off in the opposite direction.

Miss Phipps and Geoffrey laughed together. "Cats know how to administer the snub direct," said Geoff.

"None better. How's life, Geoff?"

"*Comme ci comme ca,*" said Geoff without enthusiasm, scowling.

"If only all this hoo-ha nowadays made the young happier, I shouldn't mind," reflected Miss Phipps, moving toward a bus. "But it doesn't seem to, you know."

Three days later Miss Phipps, hearing the bell ring

in her flat one evening, found Geoffrey, Maureen, and a neatly packed parcel at her door.

"Your script, Miss Phipps," said Maureen meekly, offering the parcel.

"Come in, come in!" exclaimed Miss Phipps, delighted. "Have some coffee." She tore off the wrapping hastily and gloated over the neat, professionally typed script. "You type very well, Maureen," she said with pleasure.

She was particularly enthusiastic because she thought Maureen looked rather downcast, indeed almost ready to cry. Of course it was obvious these children were madly in love with each other. They were both good-looking, even handsome. Geoffrey with fine dark eyes and masses of thick dark curls—pity he didn't cut them! And Maureen with that really glorious golden hair. A sweet face, too. They sat down. Miss Phipps gave them coffee. Nobody spoke.

"Is anything wrong?" asked Miss Phipps at length.

Maureen at once burst into tears. Geoffrey blushed.

"Oh, dear, oh, dear, I'm terribly sorry," apologized Miss Phipps.

"It's Mother," said Geoffrey with disgust. "She doesn't want us to get married."

"Aren't you perhaps a little—young?"

"Why should we waste all these years?" demanded Geoffrey, almost savagely.

"Well," began Miss Phipps. But on thinking it over, she couldn't find a particularly good reason, so she said nothing.

"Will you say a word to Mother? Persuade her?" urged Geoffrey.

"I don't think your mother would like that, Geoffrey," said Miss Phipps nervously.

"Oh, yes, she would."

"She thinks the world of you, Miss Phipps," said Maureen. "She's proud of typing your stories and all that. Isn't she, Geoffrey?"

"Yes. I don't read them myself, of course," said Geoffrey flatly.

Somehow this touch of honesty cheered Miss Phipps.

"When will you be out of your apprenticeship, Geoffrey?" she inquired.

"Next spring."

"Why not wait till then?"

"Yes, if we can have a firm promise from Mum for then. But to go on just hanging around isn't good enough. And she seems set against it. She prefers Bertha," concluded Geoffrey in a tone of disgust.

"The trouble is, you see," said Maureen sadly, "Mrs. Norton thinks I'm a bad worker—careless, you know—and so I should be a careless unreliable wife for Geoff. But I wouldn't," she protested, weeping again.

"Look, Maureen," said Miss Phipps, kind but firm. "You've just said two things to me. Since they contradict each other, one of them must be untrue."

Maureen looked up, horrified. "Oh, Miss Phipps! I wouldn't say anything untrue to you, truly, I wouldn't."

"You said Mrs. Norton is proud of typing my stories, and you said she thinks you're a careless worker. But she gives my stories to you to type. Don't you see? Either she doesn't care a button about me, or she doesn't think you're a careless worker."

"I'm not a careless person, Miss Phipps," said Maureen raising her head, with spirit.

"I believe you."

"Will you come and see Mum and put in a word for us, then?" pleaded Geoff.

"Perhaps."

"Tomorrow?"

"Well—I'll see."

As it turned out, the next morning Miss Phipps visited the Norton Typing Agency, but in a very different mood and on a very different errand. She raged up to Mrs. Norton's table, threw down the parcel of typing, and shouted, "That abominable cat!"

"What do you mean, Miss Phipps?" asked Mrs. Norton in her most genteel voice.

"If you will examine my original script, pages thirty through thirty-six, chapter four, and then examine your own typed version of chapter four, you will see that pages thirty through thirty-six have been omitted in your version. I have marked the passage with strips of paper."

"Maureen!" cried Mrs. Norton. Miss Phipps with regret could not help but detect an undercurrent of satisfaction in Mrs. Norton's voice. Maureen, pale and anguished, approached. "The carelessness can easily be remedied," said Mrs. Norton stiffly.

"It can, if my original pages are not lost," said Miss Phipps.

"What are you suggesting, Miss Phipps?"

"That abominable Edith tore them to shreds."

To Miss Phipps's astonishment Mrs. Norton burst into tears.

"I never typed those pages," said Maureen quickly. "I noticed they weren't there. But some writers make gaps, you know. It was the end of one section and the beginning of another, so I thought—"

Mrs. Norton continued to weep.

"Well, never mind, don't cry. I must rewrite that chapter, that's all. It's tiresome, but I daresay I can manage," said Miss Phipps, furious.

"You don't understand," wept Mrs. Norton.

"She's lost," whispered Maureen in Miss Phipps's ear. "Edith, I mean. She's disappeared. Last night, perhaps—she wasn't here this morning. We've searched the whole house. It's awful. Come with me."

She led the mystified Miss Phipps to the communal bathroom-cum-lavatory in the rear of the agency. The sash window was slightly raised. The bath was spattered with splashes of red oily liquid which Miss Phipps observed with horror.

"We don't like to clear it away," murmured Maureen. "Mrs. Norton doesn't know whether to send for the police."

"You don't think—" began Miss Phipps, aghast.

"Well, yes, we do really. Edith has vanished. She used to go down to the housekeeper in the basement, you see, at night, but the housekeeper hasn't seen her."

"But, my dear child—" began Miss Phipps. She wanted to ask where, if these were splashes of Edith's blood, was Edith's body? Nerving herself to a great effort of courage, she bent over the bathtub, dipped one finger in a crimson splash, and raised the finger to her nose. Then, to Maureen's exclamation of horror, she actually put the stained finger in her mouth.

"This, my dear Maureen," she announced triumphantly, "is cough medicine. It probably comes," she went on, raising her eyes to the glass shelves in the corner, "from that bottle up there."

"But how—but why—but where is she now?" objected

Maureen, accepting the bottle of sticky red medicine as the obvious but still mysterious explanation.

"She was shut in here and was frightened and leaped about and knocked over the bottle."

"How could she get shut in here?"

"That is what we must find out."

"Where is Edith now?"

Miss Phipps strode to the window, threw up the sash, and gazed out. The landscape visible from this back window, as is true so often in central London, consisted of an architectural chaos—walls, mostly blank, roofs, chimneys, houses, snug little secret yards, with here and there one or two lean but courageous trees. Edith was not visible.

"She wriggled out of the window and fell down there."

"We must ask at every house in that back street, Miss Phipps," urged Maureen. "Come along."

As they proceeded down the street, building by building, Miss Phipps was struck by the kindliness and good humor shown to them. Some of the buildings were occupied by offices filled with clerks, some were still private homes. All the inhabitants looked rather cross when first summoned from their occupations to seek a lost cat, but then Miss Phipps had an inspiration.

"You see, the cat belongs to the mother of this young lady's boyfriend," she explained.

They all melted at once, perceiving the romantic importance of the cat to Maureen. They smiled sympathetically. "Really!" they said. "Well, come in, dear. She may be in the backyard, you know. We don't often go out there."

And that was just where Edith was, when at last they found her. In a corner of a dismal little yard,

surrounded by high windowless walls, Edith lay on her
front, with her paws neatly tucked in beneath her. The
moment she saw Maureen, she sprang toward her, and
safe in the girl's arms nestled against her neck, kneading her over and over with her paws and giving her
loud, raucous purr.

"Fond of you, I daresay," said the elderly clerk with
them.

"I hope so."

"She'll be hungry, poor thing. I'll get a drop of
milk. I wonder how she got down here, I must say."

"She fell out of our bathroom window, I expect,
and then made her way along, looking for a way out."

"That'll be it. Here you are, pussy. Lap this up."

"But how did Edith get shut into the bathroom?"
queried Mrs. Norton, stroking the cat with the passion
of a lonely woman. "I suppose the door must have
slammed."

"I think Bertha slammed the door," said Miss
Phipps, giving Bertha an accusing look.

"Why should I lock up Edith?" demanded Bertha.

"You destroyed my pages, you wanted Edith to be
blamed for that, and Maureen to be blamed for
allowing it to happen. For obvious reasons," added
Miss Phipps.

"Nonsense," snapped Bertha. But she had crimsoned.

"Edith was frightened and rushed round the bathroom and upset the cough-mixture bottle. *You* re-
corked the bottle and replaced it on the upper shelf.
After you had contrived that she fell out of the
window."

"I didn't mean her any harm," cried Bertha. "She
wriggled suddenly out through the open part of the

window. I couldn't stop her. You know how quick cats are."

"Some cats I know are rather too clever for their own good," said Miss Phipps.

"If you don't care for cats, Bertha, you had perhaps better give your notice at once," said Mrs. Norton coldly. "I must get your replacement settled in before Maureen leaves to get married, in the spring."

"I should like to continue working for you after our marriage, Mrs. Norton," said Maureen mildly.

"Very well, dear, agreed Mrs. Norton.

CAT BURGLAR

by Gene DeWeese

"Come on, Uncle Clay, you're the sheriff," the twenty-four-year-old voice on the phone whined. "Mom will listen to *you*."

"If she listened to me, Jerry," Clayton Barlow said, resisting an almost overwhelming urge to shout, "she and your stepfather would've cut you off cold a year ago. If you think I'm going to help you milk them for even *more* money—"

"But if my car gets repossessed, how can I get to work?"

"You live in the big city. Springfield has bus service. And *you* had feet the last time I looked. According to your mother, you live only a mile and a half from your job. Now if there's nothing else, things are busy around here."

"I'm sorry." The boy's voice was suddenly filled with sympathy and insincerity. "Any idea who the burglar is yet? Mom said you'd been getting pressure from the mayor."

"No, no idea, but we'll get him. He'll make a mistake, they always do."

"I hope so, Uncle Clay. But look, about what we were talking about, maybe if I drove down this evening so I could explain my situation to everyone all at once—are you all having dinner at the usual place?"

"Yes, we are, and you stay away. I mean it, Jerry. Stay away!"

Slamming the receiver down, Barlow leaned back in the swivel chair and pulled in a deep breath, hoping he could get rid of the knot of anger in his stomach before the monthly ritual of dinner with his sister and her husband. All he needed was for his ulcer to start acting up at the restaurant. Claudia would want to know what was wrong, and he'd have to either lie or tell her about Jerry's call, and that would just start the same old argument all over again. Not as bad as if Jerry showed up himself, but bad enough. She'd say he was her son and she had to see him through this latest self-generated crisis, and Clayton would tell her she was just making things worse, that the boy would never learn to stand on his own two feet as long as she kept bailing him out every time he came to her with a new sob story.

Grimacing, he checked his shirt pocket to be sure he had a full packet of antacid tablets.

To his relief, he didn't need them. The rash of burglaries—a dozen in the last month and a half—was all Claudia and her husband Martin wanted to talk about. Each time it looked as if they were about to start on something else, someone else would stop by the table and start it all up again by asking Barlow how the investigation was going.

It wasn't until they were in Martin's air-conditioned car on the way home that Jerry's name was mentioned. "You'll never guess the stunt he pulled the last time he was down," Martin said, ignoring Claudia's fluttering efforts to shush him. "He purposely let Mordecai out. We were lucky it was so warm and Jeff next door had his car windows down. You know how Mordecai loves cars."

Smiling in spite of himself, Barlow remembered how he'd found the cat two winters before in an abandoned car a few miles outside town. The car—and probably Mordecai—had been there at least a month before a farmer had called about having it towed away. Mordecai had obviously once been someone's pet and, unlike the feral cats the department occasionally got calls about, was on his best behavior when Barlow pried open the door. The cat had jumped down from the seat, next to the hole in the floorboards through which he had doubtless entered, and waited, apprehensive but not frightened. When Barlow had tentatively reached out, the animal, instead of retreating, had come forward and started rubbing against his outstretched fingers.

After that, it had been only a matter of showing the cat to Claudia, and when it took to her as quickly as it had to him, the matter was all settled. The only problem was, the cat refused to quit thinking of cars as homes away from home and was as likely to hop into the first one he found as he was to come back to the house. This made taking him to the vet a cinch, but it also made it impossible to let him outside. If he got into the wrong car, he could be miles away before the driver noticed him, curled up and sleeping in the back seat.

"Now, Martin," Claudia objected, "he didn't do it on purpose. The screen door just didn't close all the way."

"Oh, he did it on purpose all right," Martin said, shaking his head. "The little freeloader's jealous."

"Martin, please! You mustn't talk about the boy that way. And he's getting better. He hasn't asked for a cent for at least a month now."

"Face it, Claudia. I've seen the way he looks at the cat. And I've heard—we've both heard—the cracks he makes about how soft a life he has."

"But he's just *joking,* Martin."

"He wants you to *think* he's joking, that's all. I'll give you ten to one that behind that twinkly little smile of his, he's deadly serious."

Sighing, Clayton settled back for the rest of the drive. At the house, after turning down Claudia's half-hearted invitation to come in out of the muggy evening air for awhile, he walked to his squad car, still at the curb where he'd left it three hours before. He was just getting in when Claudia came running across the lawn.

"Clay! The house—someone's broken in!"

His instant reaction was to smile and tell her not to let her imagination run away with her. All the burglaries had been in the middle of the night, not the evening, and in houses where the owners were out of town for at least the night, not just out for dinner at a local restaurant. But when he got inside, he saw it was real, and except for the odd timing, it was identical to all the others. Entry through a basement window, nothing disturbed or torn up, VCR and TV sets missing along with Martin's laptop computer and Claudia's few pieces of jewelry.

Barlow was just hanging up after phoning his office when Claudia let out an anguished shriek. "Mordecai!"

Hurrying to the kitchen, he found his sister on the

back steps looking frantically around the yard in the harsh glare of the outdoor lights.

"The back door was open," Claudia almost wailed. "He's gone."

Barlow blinked, remembering Martin's words about his stepson's latest stunt. Suddenly it all made sense. The different time, the fact that Claudia and Martin hadn't been out of town, the fact that Jerry hadn't mooched any money recently.

And especially that seemingly pointless call—the boy wasn't stupid enough to think he could talk Barlow into pleading his case with his mother. He had simply called to verify that she and Martin would be out of the house for the evening.

And he hadn't been able to resist leaving the door ajar so Mordecai could get out. In all the other houses, the doors had been carefully closed, so that everything would seem perfectly normal from the outside.

"A couple of deputies will be here in a few minutes, sis," he said. "I have somewhere to go."

Without waiting for a reply, he stalked to his squad car. Forty-five minutes later, he was jabbing the bell at the front door of his nephew's ten-unit apartment building. The boy's car, its hood still warm, sat at the curb in front of the squad car a few yards away.

"Who is it?" Jerry's voice came tinnily through the intercom.

"Your uncle. Open up."

"Uncle Clay? What are *you* doing here?"

"Open up and I'll tell you."

There was no reply.

"Open up, Jerry!"

"No."

"I haven't told the Springfield police yet, Jerry, but I will if you don't open up—now!"

"The police? Why would you—"

"Because you just burglarized your parents' house—and probably a dozen others the last six weeks."

For a moment there was only silence, but then the boy's voice came back, harsh and filled with infuriating confidence. "You're out of your jurisdiction, Uncle Clay, and even if you weren't, you'd need a warrant."

"I'll get one, and—"

"You need evidence for that. Probable cause, they call it, or something like that. Now beat it."

The crackle of the intercom died. Barlow jabbed at the button again, but there was no response.

Swearing under his breath, he turned from the door, realizing the boy was right. With nothing more than a sudden hunch, compounded by dislike, he'd never get a judge to sign a warrant.

And by the time he got proof—*if* he got proof—it would be too late. Now that the boy knew Barlow was onto him, he'd ditch whatever was still in the apartment. If only he'd waited, acted more calmly. If only—

As he walked angrily past Jerry's car, something meowed.

Stiffening, he glanced around.

It meowed again. This time, listening, he caught the direction it was coming from. Leaning close and cupping his hands on either side of his eyes, he looked through the closed back window of the car.

"Mordecai!"

The cat, apparently searching the floorboards for a

nonexistent exit, looked up, saw Clayton, and hopped up on the seat.

Clayton laughed suddenly as he turned to glance up at the lighted windows of his nephew's apartment.

"You want probable cause, Jerry," he breathed grimly as he walked to the squad car, "you got probable cause—unless you can think of some way a cat could cover thirty miles on his own in less than four hours."

Taking the microphone from its clip under the dash, he switched to the channel used by the Springfield police.

CAT OF DREAMS

by Frances & Richard Lockridge

Ann Notson was nine years old; she had eyes which in certain lights looked green; there was a kind of glow in her soft brown hair. Her mother had had such eyes and hair, and so Philip Notson, when he looked at his daughter, must often—too often—have been reminded of his wife.

Ann Notson was an imaginative child—a "very" imaginative child, her teacher in Van Brunt District School had written, underlining the word "very." This, decided Captain M. L. Heimrich of the New York State Police, meant that Ann sometimes saw things which were not there or, perhaps, saw what was there in a more interesting form than was entirely real.

There was, however, no doubt of the very ugly reality of what she saw at about eight thirty of a bright, cold Saturday morning in mid-December—saw behind the garage of her father's house on Brickhouse Road in the town of Van Brunt, County of Putnam. She had gone out of the house to find a "kitty." "May I be excused, please?" she said to her father, who was lingering over breakfast coffee, as a man may on Saturday morning. "I want to go out and see if the kitty is all right."

"Um-mm," Philip Notson said. "Bundle up, kitten."

He heard the front door slam and stopped, coffee cup halfway between saucer and lips, and expression drained out of his eyes. It was the little, meaningless things which now were the worst things. Jean had always closed doors more firmly than necessary. . . . He wrenched his mind from memory.

What "kitty" did Ann expect to find? A cat of dreams, probably, since they had no cat; a "kitty" who frisked, chased his tail, only in a child's quick mind.

He picked up the newspaper. He made himself read it.

The door slammed again. She hadn't stayed long. No kitty to be found, he supposed. However imaginative a child . . .

"Daddy," Ann said, almost before she was in the dining room. "Daddy! There's a man out there. Lying right on the ground. Is he asleep, Daddy? Because it's cold. It's—*awful* cold."

There was urgency in the clear voice; there was something—fear? shock?—in the child's greenish eyes. Philip Notson said, "Where?" and, on being told, went to see. The man who lay on the ground behind the garage, between it and the bank which broke sharply down from the field above, was not asleep.

Captain Heimrich, whose chief concern is with murder, drove up the driveway from Brickhouse Road to Philip Notson's white and gray house at a little after nine. Fortunately he had been nearby.

There were police cars already in the driveway and in the turnaround in front of the garage. He went around the garage and looked down at the body of Malcolm Arthur Bell.

Just two days before, on Thursday, Heimrich had heard Bell called "a very fortunate man" by County Judge Davies, who had just accepted a verdict of Not Guilty from a jury in the Carmel courthouse. Not guilty, that was, of manslaughter in connection with the death of one Jean Notson, thirty-one years old, at about one thirty-five o'clock on the morning of Sunday, the twenty-first of September. Bell's luck had now run out.

"Oh," Philip Notson said to Heimrich. "I see how it looks. He killed my wife. The jury says he's not guilty of anything. And—I said some bitter things and was heard saying them. I see how it looks. All the same—"

All the same, he knew nothing of Bell's death. Murder, if they were so sure it was that. He himself had thought that Bell had stumbled on the rough steps leading down from the upper field, pitched headlong, and landed on a rock. Which, he said with some savagery, would have been appropriate.

Heimrich, a notably solid man, sat and watched and listened to Philip Notson—a slim, quick man, tall and with just a suggestion of the tall man's stoop. Notson walked back and forth in the living room and made quick motions with his hands. He was in his middle thirties; his hair was beginning to recede a little; the summer's tan had not quite faded from his mobile face.

"No," Heimrich said, "he didn't fall, Mr. Notson. He was struck. Several times, probably with an iron bar. Sometime yesterday evening. Between five and nine, at a guess—a wide guess, admittedly. He would have come that way, coming here?"

"Across the field? Yes. They used to. He and his wife. Not since Jean died. Since—he killed her."

But it had not been like that—not as Phil Notson said it now, looking down, his eyes angry, at Heimrich. The jury had said it was an accident—an accident in the early hours of a Sunday morning, after a dance.

"Come on and ride in a real car," Mal Bell had said to Jean Notson, a pretty, slender woman in a gray-green party dress, and patted the hood of his sports car. "Just try it and you'll make old stick-in-the-mud get you one."

They had all laughed, not that there was anything especially funny, but because they were young enough, and gay, and had had a good time at the country club dance.

They had all had drinks, but nobody—and specifically, of course, Malcolm Bell—had had too many. Bell said that it was a blown front tire that sent the hurrying little car into a tree, and Jean out of the car—far, far out of it, until a stone fence stopped her diving flight.

"As to yesterday evening, Mr. Notson," Heimrich said. "You got home about when?"

"A little after seven."

Heimrich raised his eyebrows and waited. Van Brunt is an express-train hour from Grand Central. Most commuters manage to make the 5:06.

Notson had missed the usual train, he told Heimrich. He had telephoned Mrs. Billings, who was the housekeeper, and caught the 5:58. Heimrich could ask Mrs. Billings. "Oh," Heimrich said. "Yes, naturally. You came home, had dinner. Then?"

"Read to my daughter. Saw she got to bed—about

eight thirty. Read a little longer and went to bed myself. Didn't take time out to kill Mal Bell.''

Heimrich said, "Now, Mr. Notson," and then Sergeant Forniss opened the door from the hall and made a motion with his head. Heimrich went out into the hall and closed the door behind him.

A little girl, with very wide greenish eyes and very soft brown hair and wearing a snow suit, was sitting on the third step of the stairs which led up from the hall, and looking out through the front door.

Heimrich smiled at her and Ann Notson said, "I saw a man." She had, Heimrich knew. That she would forget seeing him, after time enough, Heimrich hoped. He said, "Yes, dear," and listened to Forniss.

Then he smiled again at the little girl and went back into the living room, and told Philip Notson that the people across the road had seen the floodlight come on at the Notson place about nine o'clock the previous evening, and said that it had stayed on for about a quarter of an hour. Could Mr. Notson—

"Oh," Phil Notson said, and was very quick in speaking. "That. People looking for the Blakes. Live on Van Brunt Lane, the Blakes do. Next road up. They'd turned off too soon. Told them how to get there."

He looked at Heimrich with challenge. Heimrich told Philip Notson that he saw.

"No reason we would have heard anything," Notson said. "Unless Bell shouted. Maybe not even then. We'd have been in the dining room, the kitten—Ann, that is—and I, and Mrs. Billings in the kitchen."

"No," Heimrich said. "Killing that way doesn't make a lot of noise. Well—"

"You know about the Perkins kid?" Notson said. "What Perkins said he'd do?"

"I know," Heimrich said. "We'll talk to Mr. Perkins."

"Kid of twelve," Notson said. "Crippled now. Who knows when he'll walk again? Because a louse doesn't look where he's going, where he's driving his car. The kid was a pitcher."

"I know," Heimrich said. But he also knew, and supposed that Philip Notson knew—but a bitter mind cannot be predicted—that Bell had not been at fault that time, either; that Jimmy Perkins had been on a bicycle, and had wobbled into the road too far, and that Bell had been driving within the limit, which was forty, through the place they called The Flats, and had done all that could be expected of a driver. (Except, possibly, to drive below the posted speed, which was too high, considering the number of kids, and dogs, on the highway where it ran through The Flats.)

The boy's father, a short and powerfully built man who was a yardman for the Van Brunt Supply Company, had said a lot of things which, it was to be presumed, he hadn't meant. At any rate, that had been a year ago and Perkins had not done anything. Except, of course, to collect a modest sum—modest since Bell had done all that could, officially, be asked—from Bell's insurance company.

Heimrich said, "Well, thanks, Mr. Notson," and went out into the hall. Forniss raised his eyebrows in inquiry and Heimrich shrugged in answer.

The little girl was still on the third step. She said, "You're a policeman, aren't you?"

"Yes, Ann," Heimrich said and smiled down at the little girl—the pretty little girl who, they said, looked so much like her mother. "I'm a policeman."

"I saw a man," Ann said. "When I turned the lights on. He was running. And a kitty."

"Yes," Heimrich said, but sat down on his heels so that he was level with the little girl. "Running?"

"A funny man," Ann said. "Thick. He ran funny. Why don't you wear clothes like the other policemen?"

Heimrich explained about that. He said, "When did you see the funny man, Ann?"

She had seen him the previous evening. When it was time for Daddy to come home—Mrs. Billings had said he was going to be late, but you couldn't tell— she turned on the floodlights over the garage. "It's my—perogative." She stopped and looked at Heimrich with doubt. He nodded his head. "Since Mamma went away," Ann said. "So Daddy won't bump into anything."

She had turned the light on at ten minutes after six—"precisely"—and she had seen the funny man running away from the house, toward the road. (He was funny, Heimrich decided, because he was a grown person and was running. Which was quite reasonable.) Ann didn't know who he was. He wasn't Mr. Bell. Of course she knew Mr. Bell. He wasn't Daddy. "Don't be so silly."

"And," Ann Notson said, "there was a kitty. Just where the light stops. It had shiny eyes. Like tail lights."

That was unexpected. In semidarkness, but with light on them, the eyes of cats shine—shine green, shine yellow.

"Like tail lights?" Heimrich said. "How like tail lights, dear?"

"Red," Ann said. "Red as anything. Like in the fireplace sometimes."

"Oh," Heimrich said. "Did you tell Daddy about the kitty with red eyes? And about the man?"

"Of course," Ann said. "He said I shouldn't make up things. *Every*body says that." She paused. "All the *time*," she said. "He said cats never have red eyes. But this"—

Heimrich touched the soft brown hair, smiled at her, stood up, and supposed that people did, all the *time*, tell Ann not to make things up.

A man running.

A red-eyed cat.

For a moment Heimrich wished that, just this once at any rate, a cat's eyes would glow red in semidarkness, with a light on them, instead of green or yellow; that such a glow, and a man running, would prove not to be merely things a little girl had made up. It would be bad for the soft-haired child if something happened to Daddy . . .

Things are collected, are put together. This takes time, since the collection must extend to byways. It takes more men than two. A trooper had been sent to talk to James Perkins, and by no means only to carry out Heimrich's assurance to Philip Notson.

Perkins was to be asked—was asked—whether he still had borne a grudge against the man who had maimed his son. He was also to be asked—was asked—where he had been the previous evening . . . between the hours of five, say, and nine.

The trooper had found Perkins loading sand into a burlap bag in the yard of the Van Brunt Supply Company. Perkins stuck his shovel in the sand and said that, hell, he bore no grudge, hadn't since he had had time to think it over. A kid on a bicycle—well, Perkins drove a car himself. Things happen before you know it; things you can't do anything about. Bell had been decent enough about it—or his insurance company had.

As for the previous evening, Perkins had got home from work a little after five, had had dinner around six, and had stayed home until bedtime, looking at TV. And they could ask his wife. His wife had been asked; had said he certainly had. Wives have been known to alibi for husbands. And it could not be denied that Perkins might, by a child, well be called a "thick" man.

But Malcolm Bell's body had not been found in Perkins's back yard. It had been found behind Philip Notson's garage. So Heimrich and Sergeant Forniss concentrated, most logically, on Bell himself and on Philip Notson.

Bell, on the last day of his life, had driven his wife to New York and put her on a plane for Palm Beach. He had driven back and had a drink at the Old Stone Inn, and told a friend he met there he was thinking about going around to see old Phil Notson and try to get things straightened out.

Half a dozen men had got off the 5:58 local-express at Van Brunt, and one of them might have been Notson, but they had not proved it by late afternoon.

Nobody had seen Notson on the 5:06, and since that was his regular train he probably would have been noticed and spoken to if he had been on it. Which did not prove much, since the most likely thing was that Notson had turned the garage floodlight on at a little after nine to see who had come to the door, and when he found out, killed him. . . .

Nobody had showed up at the Blake house on Van Brunt Lane to say that they had had to stop to ask directions. Of course, the prospective droppers-in might merely have changed their minds . . . Ann's teacher said the poor little thing was a dear, but that she was a *most* imaginative child.

And—the eyes of cats do not shine red when light strikes them out of darkness. Heimrich had been sure of that, but all the same—since a policeman can never be too sure of anything—he had talked to an eye specialist he knew. "Nope," the ophthalmologist said, "not that I ever heard of. Oh—I suppose an albino cat's might. No pigment on the tapetum lucidum."

"The what?"

"Layer in the chorioid," the eye man said. "Back part of the eye. What reflects light. Good many mammals have it. We don't, more's the pity."

"Are there," Heimrich asked, "many albino cats?"

"One in a million, at a guess. I never saw one. Never met anybody who had seen one. They'd have pink eyes, of course. White cats with pink eyes."

A cat like that would be noticeable, Heimrich thought, and he asked around. Nobody had ever seen one. Not around there or anywhere else. So—Ann had not seen a red-eyed cat. A million to one she hadn't. And hence—not a man running, either, since the two things went together—went together in a child's imagination.

Heimrich turned his car off NY 11-F into Brickhouse Road. It was time to get to work on Philip Notson—to get really to work on him. It was dusk, then.

Heimrich switched the headlights on—and jammed his brakes on; and Sergeant Forniss, sitting beside him, put hands out to brace himself and said, "What the *hell*?"

"Look," Heimrich said, and they both looked—looked at two tiny lights by the road's edge; lights which glowed like coals in a fireplace, like the twin tail lights of a car. Red lights.

The little red lights went out. But then they were glowing from the top of a stone fence. They went out again, but by then Heimrich had the car off the road and they were out of it at a driveway.

There was enough light to see a cat streak toward a house. A woman stood on the porch. The woman called, *"Boots! Here,* Boots. *Here—"* and then said to the arriving cat. *"You!* Again. *Again!"*

The woman was Mrs. Burnett—Mrs. Harry Burnett. Of course the cat belonged to her. "Come here, Boots," she said again, and Boots came to prove it.

"Oh," Heimrich said, and looked at Boots, who was certainly not a white cat with pink eyes; he was a cat with a black face and deep blue eyes and a black tail. "Oh," Heimrich said. "Siamese. We were looking for an albino cat." He could not remember that, as a policeman, he had ever made a sillier remark. "A cat with red eyes," he added, and felt sillier than ever, looking down at the blue-eyed cat.

"With red—" Mrs. Burnett said. "Oh—you mean with a light on them? Of course. They always are. Siamese eyes, I mean. Because Siamese are part albino, you know. Even if you'd never guess it to look at them."

It proved fortunate for Philip Notson—and for a little girl with greenish eyes and an imagination not quite, this time, as fervid as people were always saying—that Boots was a cat who led a somewhat circumscribed life; was a young female who, particularly at the moment, had her own idea about things, and hence was not let roam at large. But a cat who got out anyway, now and again, as she had this Saturday evening, but only for a few minutes.

The night before, however, Boots had got out at five thirty in the evening, Mrs. Burnett confided, and had been gone for an hour or more, and goodness knew where, and one could only hope.

Since two things were linked in the mind of a child, Heimrich and Forniss did not go on to the Notson house, but drove the other way—drove to The Flats and, with not much trouble found a "thick" man standing at the bar of the Three Oaks Tavern.

James Perkins did not seem surprised to see them, but then James Perkins was drunk now—mumbling drunk.

He mumbled a good deal about a so-and-so who thought he could get away with anything, and about bought-off so-and-sos who would let him. And about that so-and-so Bell, who knew better now, knew you couldn't cripple a kid and get off for a few measly dollars. Some drunken men talk a lot.

If Perkins talked enough, Heimrich thought, they might never have to ask a little girl if this was the man—the thick man—she had seen running.

But he would, he thought, some day make a point of telling a little girl that some cats do too have red eyes.

DEATH AT THE EXCELSIOR

by P. G. Wodehouse

The room was the typical bedroom of the typical boardinghouse, furnished, insofar as it could be said to be furnished at all, with a severe simplicity. It contained two beds, a pine chest of drawers, a strip of faded carpet, and a wash basin. But there was that on the floor which set this room apart from a thousand rooms of the same kind. Flat on his back, with his hands tightly clenched and one leg twisted oddly under him and with his teeth gleaming through his gray beard in a horrible grin, Captain John Gunner stared up at the ceiling with eyes that saw nothing.

Until a moment before, he had had the little room all to himself. But now two people were standing just inside the door, looking down at him. One was a large policeman, who twisted his helmet nervously in his hands. The other was a tall gaunt old woman in a rusty black dress, who gazed with pale eyes at the dead man. Her face was quite expressionless.

The woman was Mrs. Pickett, owner of the Excelsior boardinghouse. The policeman's name was Grogan. He was a genial giant, a terror to the riotous element of the waterfront, but obviously ill at ease in the presence of death. He drew in his breath, wiped his forehead, and whispered, "Look at his eyes, ma'am!"

Mrs. Pickett had not spoken a word since she had brought the policeman into the room, and she did not do so now. Constable Grogan looked at her quickly. He was afraid of Mother Pickett, as was everybody else along the waterfront. Her silence, her pale eyes, and the quiet decisiveness of her personality cowed even the tough old salts who patronized the Excelsior. She was a formidable influence in that little community of sailormen.

"That's just how I found him," said Mrs. Pickett. She did not speak loudly, but her voice made the policeman start.

He wiped his forehead again. "It might have been apoplexy," he hazarded.

Mrs. Pickett said nothing. There was a sound of footsteps outside, and a young man entered, carrying a black bag.

"Good morning, Mrs. Pickett. I was told that— good Lord!" The young doctor dropped to his knees beside the body and raised one of the arms. After a moment he lowered it gently to the floor and shook his head in grim resignation.

"He's been dead for hours," he announced. "When did you find him?"

"Twenty minutes back," replied the old woman. "I guess he died last night. He never would be called in the morning. Said he liked to sleep on. Well, he's got his wish."

"What did he die of, sir?" asked the policeman.

"It's impossible to say without an examination," the

doctor answered. "It looks like a stroke, but I'm pretty sure it isn't. It might be a coronary attack, but I happen to know his blood pressure was normal, and his heart sound. He called in to see me only a week ago and I examined him thoroughly. But sometimes you can be deceived. The inquest will tell us."

He eyed the body almost resentfully. "I can't understand it. The man had no right to drop dead like this. He was a tough old sailor who ought to have been good for another twenty years. If you want my honest opinion—though I can't possibly be certain until after the inquest—I should say he had been poisoned."

"How would he be poisoned?" asked Mrs. Pickett quietly.

"That's more than I can tell you. There's no glass about that he could have drunk it from. He might have got it in capsule form. But why should he have done it? He was always a pretty cheerful sort of man, wasn't he?"

"Yes, sir," said the constable. "He had the name of being a joker in these parts. Kind of sarcastic, they tell me, though he never tried it on me."

"He must have died quite early last night," said the doctor. He turned to Mrs. Pickett. "What's become of Captain Muller? If he shares this room he ought to be able to tell us something?"

"Captain Muller spent the night with some friends at Portsmouth," said Mrs. Pickett. "He left right after supper, and hasn't returned."

The doctor stared thoughtfully about the room, frowning.

"I don't like it. I can't understand it. If this had happened in India I should have said the man had died from some form of snake bite. I was out there two years, and I've seen a hundred cases of it. The poor devils all looked just like this. But the thing's ridiculous. How could a man be bitten by a snake in a Southampton waterfront boardinghouse? Was the door locked when you found him, Mrs. Pickett?"

Mrs. Pickett nodded. "I opened it with my own key. I had been calling to him and he didn't answer, so I guessed something was wrong."

The constable spoke, "You ain't touched anything, ma'am? They're always very particular about that. If the doctor's right and there's been anything up, that's the first thing they'll ask."

"Everything's just as I found it."

"What's that on the floor beside him?" the doctor asked.

"Only his harmonica. He liked to play it of an evening in his room. I've had some complaints about it from some of the gentlemen, but I never saw any harm, so long as he didn't play it too late."

"Seems as if he was playing it when—it happened," Constable Grogan said. "That don't look much like suicide, sir."

"I didn't say it was suicide."

Grogan whistled. "You don't think—"

"I'm not thinking anything—until after the inquest. All I say is that it's queer."

Another aspect of the matter seemed to strike the policeman. "I guess this ain't going to do the Excelsior any good, ma'am," he said sympathetically.

Mrs. Pickett shrugged.

"I suppose I had better go and notify the coroner," said the doctor.

He went out, and after a momentary pause the policeman followed. Constable Grogan was not greatly troubled with nerves, but he felt a decided desire to be where he could not see the dead man's staring eyes.

Mrs. Pickett remained where she was, looking down at the still form on the floor. Her face was expressionless, but inwardly she was tormented and alarmed. It was the first time such a thing as this had happened at the Excelsior, and, as Constable Grogan had suggested, it was not likely to increase the attractiveness of the house in the eyes of possible boarders. It was not the threatened pecuniary loss which was troubling her. As far as money was concerned, she could have lived comfortably on her savings, for she was richer than most of her friends supposed. It was the blot on the escutcheon of the Excelsior, the stain on its reputation, which was tormenting her.

The Excelsior was her life. Starting many years before, beyond the memory of the oldest boarder, she had built up a model establishment. Men spoke of it as a place where you were fed well, cleanly housed, and where petty robbery was unknown.

Such was the chorus of praise that it is not likely that much harm could come to the Excelsior from a single mysterious death, but Mother Pickett was not consoling herself with that.

She looked at the dead man with pale grim eyes. Out in the hallway the doctor's voice further increased her despair. He was talking to the police on the telephone, and she could distinctly hear his every word.

The offices of Mr. Paul Snyder's Detective Agency in New Oxford Street had grown in the course of a dozen years from a single room to an impressive suite bright with polished wood, clicking typewriters, and other evidences of success. Where once Mr. Snyder had sat and waited for clients and attended to them himself, he now sat in his private office and directed eight assistants.

He had just accepted a case—a case that might be nothing at all or something exceedingly big. It was on the latter possibility that he had gambled. The fee offered was, judged by his present standards of prosperity, small. But the bizarre facts, coupled with something in the personality of the client, had won him over. He briskly touched the bell and requested that Mr. Oakes should be sent in to him.

Elliott Oakes was a young man who both amused and interested Mr. Snyder, for though he had only recently joined the staff, he made no secret of his intention of revolutionizing the methods of the agency. Mr. Snyder himself, in common with most of his assistants, relied for results on hard work and common sense. He had never been a detective of the showy type. Results had justified his methods, but he was perfectly aware that young Mr. Oakes looked on him as a dull old man who had been miraculously favored by luck.

Mr. Snyder had selected Oakes for the case in hand principally because it was one where inexperience could do no harm, and where the brilliant guesswork which Oakes preferred to call his inductive reasoning might achieve an unexpected success.

Another motive actuated Mr. Snyder. He had a strong suspicion that the conduct of this case was going to have the beneficial result of lowering Oakes's self-esteem. If failure achieved this end, Mr. Snyder felt that failure, though it would not help the agency, would not be an unmixed ill.

The door opened and Oakes entered tensely. He

did everything tensely, partly from a natural nervous energy, and partly as a pose. He was a lean young man, with dark eyes and a thin-lipped mouth, and he looked quite as much like a typical detective as Mr. Snyder looked like a comfortable and prosperous stockbroker.

"Sit down, Oakes," said Mr. Snyder. "I've got a job for you."

Oakes sank into a chair like a crouching leopard and placed the tips of his fingers together. He nodded curtly. It was part of his pose to be keen and silent.

"I want you to go to this address"—Mr. Snyder handed him an envelope—"and look around. The address is of a sailors' boardinghouse down in Southampton. You know the sort of place—retired sea captains and so on live there. All most respectable. In all its history nothing more sensational has ever happened than a case of suspected cheating at halfpenny nap. Well, a man has died there."

"Murdered?" Oakes asked.

"I don't know. That's for you to find out. The coroner left it open. 'Death by Misadventure' was the verdict, and I don't blame him. I don't see how it could have been murder. The door was locked on the inside, so nobody could have got in."

"The window?"

"The window was open, granted. But the room is on the second floor. Anyway, you may dismiss the window. I remember the old lady saying there were bars across it, and that nobody could have squeezed through."

Oakes's eyes glistened. "What was the cause of death?" he asked.

Mr. Snyder coughed. "Snake bite," he said.

Oakes's careful calm deserted him. He uttered a cry of astonishment. "Why, that's incredible!"

"It's the literal truth. The medical examination proved that the fellow had been killed by snake poison—cobra, to be exact, which is found principally in India."

"Cobra!"

"Just so. In a Southampton boardinghouse, in a room with a door locked on the inside, this man was stung by a cobra. To add a little mystification to the limpid simplicity of the affair, when the door was opened there was no sign of any cobra. It couldn't have got out through the door, because the door was locked. It couldn't have got out through the window, because the window was too high up, and snakes can't jump. And it couldn't have got up the chimney, because there was no chimney. So there you have it."

He looked at Oakes with a certain quiet satisfaction. It had come to his ears that Oakes had been heard to complain of the infantile nature of the last two cases to which he had been assigned. He had even said that he hoped someday to be given a problem which should be beyond the reasoning powers of a child of six. It seemed to Mr. Snyder that Oakes was about to get his wish.

"I should like further details," said Oakes, a little breathlessly.

"You had better apply to Mrs. Pickett, who owns the boardinghouse," Mr. Snyder said. "It was she who put the case in my hands. She is convinced that it is murder. But if we exclude ghosts, I don't see how any third party could have taken a hand in the thing at all. However, she wanted a man from this agency, and was prepared to pay for him, so I promised her I would send one. It is not our policy to turn business away."

He smiled wryly. "In pursuance of that policy I want you to go and put up at Mrs. Pickett's boarding-house and do your best to enhance the reputation of our agency. I would suggest that you pose as a ship's chandler or something of that sort. You will have to be something maritime or they'll be suspicious of you. And if your visit produces no other results, it will, at least, enable you to make the acquaintance of a very remarkable woman. I commend Mrs. Pickett to your notice. By the way, she says she will help you in your investigations."

Oakes laughed shortly. The idea amused him.

"It's a mistake to scoff at amateur assistance, my boy," said Mr. Snyder in the benevolently paternal manner which had made a score of criminals refuse to believe him a detective until the moment when the handcuffs snapped on their wrists. "Crime investigation isn't an exact science. Success or failure depends in a large measure on applied common sense and the possession of a great deal of special information. Mrs. Pickett knows certain things which neither you nor I know, and it's just possible that she may have some stray piece of information which will provide the key to the entire mystery."

Oakes laughed again. "It is very kind of Mrs. Pickett," he said, "but I prefer to trust to my own methods." Oakes rose, his face purposeful. "I'd better be starting at once," he said. "I'll send you reports from time to time."

"Good. The more detailed the better," said Mr. Snyder genially. "I hope your visit to the Excelsior will be pleasant. And cultivate Mrs. Pickett. She's worthwhile."

The door closed, and Mr. Snyder lighted a fresh cigar. Dashed young fool, he thought and turned his mind to other matters.

A day later Mr. Snyder sat in his office reading a typewritten report. It appeared to be of a humorous nature, for, as he read, chuckles escaped him. Finishing the last sheet he threw his head back and laughed heartily. The manuscript had not been intended by its author for a humorous effect. What Mr. Snyder had been reading was the first of Elliott Oakes's reports from the Excelsior. It read as follows:

"I am sorry to be unable to report any real progress. I have formed several theories which I will put forward later, but at present I cannot say that I am hopeful.

"Directly I arrived I sought out Mrs. Pickett, explained who I was, and requested her to furnish me with any further information which might be of service to me. She is a strange silent woman, who impressed me as having very little intelligence. Your suggestion that I should avail myself of her assistance seems more curious than ever now that I have seen her.

"The whole affair seems to me at the moment of writing quite inexplicable. Assuming that this Captain Gunner was murdered, there appears to have been no motive for the crime whatsoever. I have made careful inquiries about him, and find that he was a man of 55; had spent nearly 40 years of his life at sea, the last dozen in command of his own ship; was of a somewhat overbearing disposition, though with a fund of rough humour; he had travelled all over the world, and had been a resident of the Excelsior for about ten months.

He had a small annuity, and no other money at all, which disposes of money as the motive for the crime.

"In my character of James Burton, a retired ship's chandler, I have mixed with the other boarders, and have heard all they have to say about the affair. I gather that the deceased was by no means popular. He appears to have had a bitter tongue, and I have not met one man who seems to regret his death. On the other hand, I have heard nothing which would suggest that he had any active and violent enemies. He was simply the unpopular boarder—there is always one in every boardinghouse—but nothing more.

"I have seen a good deal of the man who shared his room—another sea captain named Muller. He is a big silent person, and it is not easy to get him to talk. As regards the death of Captain Gunner he can tell me nothing. It seems that on the night of the tragedy he was away at Portsmouth. All I have got from him is some information as to Captain Gunner's habits, which leads nowhere.

"The dead man seldom drank, except at night when he would take some whisky. His head was not strong, and a little of the spirit was enough to make him semi-intoxicated, when he would be hilarious and often insulting. I gather that Muller found him a difficult roommate, but he is one of those placid persons who can put up with anything. He and Gunner were in the habit of playing draughts together every night in their room, and Gunner had a harmonica which he played frequently. Apparently he was playing it very soon before be died, which is significant, as seeming to dispose of any idea of suicide.

"As I say, I have one or two theories, but they are in a very nebulous state. The most plausible is that on one of his visits to India—I have ascertained that he made several voyages there—Captain Gunner may in some way have fallen foul of the natives. The fact that he certainly died of the poison of an Indian snake supports this theory. I am making inquiries as to the movements of several Indian sailors who were here in their ships at the time of the tragedy.

"I have another theory. Does Mrs. Pickett know more about this affair than she appears to? I may be wrong in my estimate of her mental qualities. Her apparent stupidly may be cunning. But here again, the absence of motive brings me up against a dead wall. I must confess that at present I do not see my way clearly. However, I will write again shortly."

Mr. Snyder derived the utmost enjoyment from the report. He liked the substance of it, and above all he was tickled by the bitter tone of frustration which characterized it. Oakes was baffled, and his knowledge of Oakes told him that the sensation of being baffled was gall and wormwood to that high-spirited young man. Whatever might be the result of this investigation, it would teach him the virtue of patience.

He wrote his assistant a short note:

"Dear Oakes,

"Your report received. You certainly seem to have got the hard case which, I hear, you were pining for. Don't build too much on plausible motives in a case of this sort. Fauntleroy, the London murderer, killed a woman for no other reason than that she had thick ankles. Many years ago I myself was on a case where a man murdered an intimate friend because of a dispute about a bet. My experience is that five murderers out of ten act on the whim of the moment, without anything which, properly speaking, you could call a motive at all.

Yours very cordially,
Paul Snyder

P.S. I don't think much of your Pickett theory. However, you're in charge. I wish you luck."

Young Mr. Oakes was not enjoying himself. For the first time in his life that self-confidence which characterized all his actions seemed to be failing him. The change had taken place almost overnight. The fact that the case had the appearance of presenting the unusual had merely stimulated him at first. But then doubts had crept in and the problem had begun to appear insoluble.

True, he had only just taken it up, but something told him that, for all the progress he was likely to make, he might just as well have been working on it steadily for a month. He was completely baffled. And every moment which he spent in the Excelsior boardinghouse made it clearer to him that that infernal old woman with the pale eyes thought him an incompetent fool. It was that, more than anything, which made him acutely conscious of his lack of success.

His nerves were being sorely troubled by the quiet scorn of Mrs. Pickett's gaze. He began to think that perhaps he had been a shade too self-confident and abrupt in the short interview which he had had with her on his arrival.

As might have been expected, his first act, after his brief interview with Mrs. Pickett, was to examine the room where the tragedy had taken place. The body was gone, but otherwise nothing had been moved.

Oakes belonged to the magnifying-glass school of detection. The first thing he did on entering the room was to make a careful examination of the floor, the walls, the furniture, and the window sill. He would have hotly denied the assertion that he did this because it looked well, but he would have been hard put to it to advance any other reason.

If he discovered anything, his discoveries were entirely negative and served only to deepen the mystery. As Mr. Snyder had said, there was no chimney, and nobody could have entered through the locked door.

There remained the window. It was small, and apprehensiveness, perhaps, of the possibility of burglars had caused the proprietress to make it doubly secure with two iron bars. No human being could have squeezed his way through.

It was late that night that he wrote and dispatched to headquarters the report which had amused Mr. Snyder . . .

Two days later Mr. Snyder sat at his desk, staring with wide unbelieving eyes at a telegram he had just received. It read as follows:

HAVE SOLVED GUNNER MYSTERY.

RETURNING. OAKES.

Mr. Snyder narrowed his eyes and rang the bell.

"Send Mr. Oakes to me directly he arrives," he said.

He was pained to find that his chief emotion was one of bitter annoyance. The swift solution of such an apparently insoluble problem would reflect the highest credit on the agency, and there were picturesque circumstances connected with the case which would make it popular with the newspapers and lead to its being given a great deal of publicity.

Yet, in spite of all this, Mr. Snyder was annoyed. He realized now how large a part the desire to reduce Oakes's self-esteem had played with him. He further realized, looking at the thing honestly, that he had been firmly convinced that the young man would not come within a mile of a reasonable solution of the mystery. He had desired only that his failure would prove a valuable educational experience for him. For he believed that failure at this particular point in his career would make Oakes a more valuable asset to the agency.

But now here Oakes was, within a ridiculously short space of time, returning to the fold, not humble and defeated, but triumphant. Mr. Snyder looked forward with apprehension to the young man's probable demeanor under the intoxicating influence of victory.

His apprehensions were well grounded. He had barely finished the third of the series of cigars which, like milestones, marked the progress of his afternoon, when the door opened and young Oakes entered. Mr. Snyder could not repress a faint moan at the sight of him. One glance was enough to tell him that his worst fears were realized.

"I got your telegram," said Mr. Snyder.

Oakes nodded. "It surprised you, eh?" he asked.

Mr. Snyder resented the patronizing tone of the question, but he had resigned himself to be patronized, and managed to keep his anger in check.

"Yes," he replied, "I must say it did surprise me. I didn't gather from your report that you had even found a clue. Was it the Indian theory that turned the trick?"

Oakes laughed tolerantly. "Oh, I never really believed that preposterous theory for one moment. I just put it in to round out my report. I hadn't begun to think about the case then—not really think."

Mr. Snyder, nearly exploding with wrath, extended his cigar case. "Light up and tell me all about it," he said, controlling his anger.

"Well, I won't say I haven't earned this," said Oakes, puffing away. He let the ash of his cigar fall delicately to the floor—another action which seemed significant to his employer. As a rule his assistants, unless particularly pleased with themselves, used the ashtray.

"My first act on arriving," Oakes said, "was to have a talk with Mrs. Pickett. A very dull old woman."

"Curious. She struck me as rather intelligent."

"Not on your life. She gave me no assistance whatever. I then examined the room where the death had taken place. It was exactly as you described it. There was no chimney, the door had been locked on the inside, and the one window was too high up. At first sight it looked extremely unpromising. Then I had a chat with some of the other boarders. They had nothing of any importance to contribute. Most of them simply gibbered. I then gave up trying to get help from the outside and resolved to rely on my own intelligence."

He smiled triumphantly. "It is a theory of mine, Mr. Snyder, which I have found valuable, that in nine cases out of ten remarkable things don't happen."

"I don't quite follow you there," Mr. Snyder interrupted.

"I will put it another way, if you like. What I mean is that the simplest explanation is nearly always the right one. Consider this case. It seemed impossible that there should have been any reasonable explanation of the man's death. Most men would have worn themselves out guessing at wild theories. If I had started to do that, I should have been guessing now. As it is—here I am. I trusted to my belief that nothing remarkable ever happens, and I won out."

Mr. Snyder sighed softly. Oakes was entitled to a certain amount of gloating, but there could be no doubt that his way of telling a story was downright infuriating.

"I believe in the logical sequence of events. I refuse to accept effects unless they are preceded by causes. In other words, with all due respect to your possibly contrary opinions, Mr. Snyder, I simply decline to believe in a murder unless there was a motive for it. The first thing I set myself to ascertain was—what was the motive for the murder of Captain Gunner? And after thinking it over and making every possible inquiry, I decided that there was no motive. Therefore, there was no murder."

Mr. Snyder's mouth opened, and he obviously was about to protest. But he appeared to think better of it and Oakes proceeded: "I then tested the suicide theory. What motive was there for suicide? There was no motive. Therefore, there was no suicide."

This time Mr. Snyder spoke. "You haven't been spending the last few days in the wrong house by any chance, have you? You will be telling me next that there wasn't any dead man."

Oakes smiled. "Not at all. Captain John Gunner was dead, all right. As the medical evidence proved, he died of the bite of a cobra. It was a small cobra which came from Java."

Mr. Snyder stared at him. "How do you know?"

"I do know, beyond any possibility of doubt."

"Did you see the snake?"

Oakes shook his head.

"Then, how in heaven's name—"

"I have enough evidence to make a jury convict Mr. Snake without leaving the box."

"Then suppose you tell me this. How did your cobra from Java get out of the room?"

"By the window," replied Oakes impassively.

"How can you possibly explain that? You say yourself that the window was too high up."

"Nevertheless, it got out by the window. The logical sequence of events is proof enough that it was in the room. It killed Captain Gunner there and left traces of its presence outside. Therefore, as the window was the only exit, it must have escaped by that route. Somehow it got out of that window."

"What do you mean—it left traces of its presence outside?"

"It killed a dog in the back yard behind the house," Oakes said. "The window of Captain Gunner's room projects out over it. It is full of boxes and litter and there are a few stunted shrubs scattered about. In fact, there is enough cover to hide any small object like the body of a dog. That's why it was not discovered at first. The maid at the Excelsior came on it the morning after I sent you my report while she was emptying a box of ashes in the yard. It was just an ordinary stray dog without collar or license. The analyst examined the body and found that the dog had died of the bite of a cobra."

"But you didn't find the snake?"

"No. We cleaned out that yard till you could have eaten your breakfast there, but the snake had gone. It must have escaped through the door of the yard, which was standing ajar. That was a couple of days ago, and there has been no further tragedy. In all likelihood it is dead. The nights are pretty cold now, and it would probably have died of exposure."

"But I just don't understand how a cobra got to Southampton," said the amazed Mr. Snyder.

"Can't you guess it? I told you it came from Java."

"How did you know it did?"

"Captain Muller told me. Not directly, but I pieced it together from what he said. It seems that an old shipmate of Captain Gunner's was living in Java. They corresponded, and occasionally this man would send the captain a present as a mark of his esteem. The last present he sent was a crate of bananas. Unfortunately, the snake must have got in unnoticed. That's why I told you the cobra was a small one. Well, that's my case against Mr. Snake, and short of catching him with the goods, I don't see how I could have made out a stronger one. Don't you agree?"

It went against the grain for Mr. Snyder to acknowledge defeat, but he was a fair-minded man, and he was forced to admit that Oakes did certainly seem to have solved the impossible.

"I congratulate you, my boy," he said as heartily as he could. "To be completely frank, when you started out, I didn't think you could do it. By the way, I suppose Mrs. Pickett was pleased?"

"If she was, she didn't show it. I'm pretty well convinced she hasn't enough sense to be pleased at anything. However, she has invited me to dinner with her tonight. I imagine she'll be as boring as usual, but she made such a point of it I had to accept."

For some time after Oakes had gone, Mr. Snyder sat smoking and thinking, in embittered meditation. Suddenly there was brought the card of Mrs. Pickett, who would be grateful if he could spare her a few moments. Mr. Snyder was glad to see Mrs. Pickett. He was a student of character, and she had interested him at their first meeting. There was something about her which had seemed to him unique, and he welcomed this second chance of studying her at close range.

She came in and sat down stiffly, balancing herself on the extreme edge of the chair in which a short while before young Oakes had lounged so luxuriously.

"How are you, Mrs. Pickett?" said Mr. Snyder genially. "I'm very glad that you could find time to pay me a visit. Well, so it wasn't murder after all."

"Sir?"

"I've been talking to Mr. Oakes, whom you met as James Burton," said the detective. "He has told me all about it."

"He told *me* all about it," said Mrs. Pickett dryly.

Mr. Snyder looked at her inquiringly. Her manner seemed more suggestive than her words.

"A conceited, headstrong young fool," said Mrs. Pickett.

It was no new picture of his assistant that she had drawn. Mr. Snyder had often drawn it himself, but at the present juncture it surprised him. Oakes, in his hour of triumph, surely did not deserve this sweeping condemnation.

"Did not Mr. Oakes's solution of the mystery satisfy you, Mrs. Pickett?"

"No."

"It struck me as logical and convincing," Mr. Snyder said.

"You may call it all the fancy names you please, Mr. Snyder. But Mr. Oakes's solution was not the right one."

"Have you an alternative to offer?"

Mrs. Pickett tightened her lips.

"If you have, I should like to hear it."

"You will—at the proper time."

"What makes you so certain that Mr. Oakes is wrong?"

"He starts out with an impossible explanation and rests his whole case on it. There couldn't have been a snake in that room because it couldn't have gotten out. The window was too high."

"But surely the evidence of the dead dog?"

Mrs. Pickett looked at him as if he had disappointed her. "I had always heard *you* spoken of as a man with common sense, Mr. Snyder."

"I have always tried to use common sense."

"Then why are you trying now to make yourself believe that something happened which could not possibly have happened just because it fits in with something which isn't easy to explain?"

"You mean that there is another explanation of the dead dog?" Mr. Snyder asked.

"Not *another*. What Mr. Oakes takes for granted is not an explanation. But there is a common-sense explanation, and if he had not been so headstrong and conceited he might have found it."

"You speak as if you had found it," said Mr. Snyder.

"I have." Mrs. Pickett leaned forward as she spoke, and stared at him defiantly.

Mr. Snyder started. "*You* have?"

"Yes."

"What is it?"

"You will know before tomorrow. In the meantime try and think it out for yourself. A successful and prosperous detective agency like yours, Mr. Snyder, ought to do something in return for a fee."

There was something in her manner so reminiscent of the schoolteacher reprimanding a recalcitrant pupil that Mr. Snyder's sense of humor came to his rescue. "We do our best, Mrs. Pickett," he said. "But you mustn't forget that we are only human and cannot guarantee results."

Mrs. Pickett did not pursue the subject. Instead, she proceeded to astonish Mr. Snyder by asking him to swear out a warrant for the arrest of a man known to them both on a charge of murder.

Mr. Snyder's breath was not often taken away in his own office. As a rule he received his clients' communications calmly, strange as they often were. But at her words he gasped. The thought crossed his mind that Mrs. Pickett might be mentally unbalanced.

Mrs. Pickett was regarding him with an unfaltering stare. To all outward appearances she was the opposite of unbalanced. "But you can't swear out a warrant without evidence," he told her.

"I have evidence," she replied firmly.

"Precisely what kind of evidence?" he demanded.

"If I told you now you would think that I was out of my mind."

"But, Mrs. Pickett, do you realize what you are asking me to do? I cannot make this agency responsible for the arbitrary arrest of a man on the strength of a single individual's suspicions. It might ruin me. At the least it would make me a laughingstock."

"Mr. Snyder, you may use your own judgment whether or not to swear out that warrant. You will listen to what I have to say, and you will see for yourself how the crime was committed. If after that you feel that you cannot make the arrest I will accept your decision. I know who killed Captain Gunner," she said. "I knew it from the beginning. But I had no proof. Now things have come to light and everything is clear."

Against his judgment Mr. Snyder was impressed. This woman had the magnetism which makes for persuasiveness.

"It—it sounds incredible." Even as he spoke, he remembered that it had long been a professional maxim of his that nothing was incredible, and he weakened still further.

"Mr. Snyder, I ask you to swear out that warrant." The detective gave in. "Very well," he said.

Mrs. Pickett rose. "If you will come and dine at my house tonight I think I can prove to you that it will be needed. Will you come?"

"I'll come," promised Mr. Snyder.

Mr. Snyder arrived at the Excelsior and shortly after he was shown into the little private sitting room where he found Oakes, the third guest of the evening unexpectedly arrived.

Mr. Snyder looked curiously at the newcomer. Captain Muller had a peculiar fascination for him. It was not Mr. Snyder's habit to trust overmuch to appearances. But he could not help admitting that there was something about this man's aspect, something odd— an unnatural aspect of gloom. He bore himself like one carrying a heavy burden. His eyes were dull, his face haggard. The next moment the detective was reproaching himself with allowing his imagination to run away with his calmer judgment.

The door opened and Mrs. Pickett came in.

To Mr. Snyder one of the most remarkable points about the dinner was the peculiar metamorphosis of Mrs. Pickett from the brooding silent woman he had known to the gracious and considerate hostess.

Oakes appeared also to be overcome with surprise,

so much so that he was unable to keep his astonishment to himself. He had come prepared to endure a dull evening absorbed in grim silence, and he found himself instead opposite a bottle of champagne of a brand and year which commanded his utmost respect. What was even more incredible, his hostess had transformed herself into a pleasant old lady whose only aim seemed to be to make him feel at home.

Beside each of the guest's plates was a neat paper parcel. Oakes picked his up and stared at it in wonderment. "Why, this is more than a party souvenir, Mrs. Pickett," he said. "It's the kind of mechanical marvel I've always wanted to have on my desk."

"I'm glad you like it, Mr. Oakes," Mrs. Pickett said, smiling. "You must not think of me simply as a tired old woman whom age has completely defeated. I am an ambitious hostess. When I give these little parties, I like to make them a success. I want each of you to remember this dinner."

"I'm sure I will."

Mrs. Pickett smiled again. "I think you all will. You, Mr. Snyder." She paused. "And you, Captain Muller."

To Mr. Snyder there was so much meaning in her voice as she said this that he was amazed that it conveyed no warning to Muller. Captain Muller, however, was already drinking heavily. He looked up when addressed and uttered a sound which might have been taken for an expression of polite acquiescence. Then he filled his glass again.

Mr. Snyder's parcel revealed a watch charm fashioned in the shape of a tiny candid-eye camera. "That," said Mrs. Pickett, "is a compliment to your profession." She leaned toward the captain. "Mr. Snyder is a detective, Captain Muller."

He looked up. It seemed to Mr. Snyder that a look of fear lit up his heavy eyes for an instant. It came and went, if indeed it came at all, so swiftly that he could not be certain. "So?" said Captain Muller. He spoke quite evenly, with just the amount of interest which such an announcement would naturally produce.

"Now for yours, Captain," said Oakes. "I guess it's something special. It's twice the size of mine, anyway."

It may have been something in the old woman's expression as she watched Captain Muller slowly tearing the paper that sent a thrill of excitement through Mr. Snyder. Something seemed to warn him of the approach of a psychological moment. He bent forward eagerly.

There was a strangled gasp, a thump, and onto the table from the captain's hands there fell a little harmonica. There was no mistaking the look on Muller's face now. His cheeks were like wax, and his eyes, so dull till then, blazed with a panic and horror which he could not repress. The glasses on the table rocked as he clutched at the cloth.

Mrs. Pickett spoke. "Why, Captain Muller, has it upset you? I thought that, as his best friend, the man who shared his room, you would value a memento of Captain Gunner. How fond you must have been of him for the sight of his harmonica to be such a shock."

The captain did not speak. He was staring fascinated at the thing on the table. Mrs. Pickett turned to Mr. Snyder. Her eyes, as they met his, held him entranced.

"Mr. Snyder, as a detective, you will be interested

in a curious and very tragic affair which happened in this house a few days ago. One of my boarders, Captain Gunner, was found dead in his room. It was the room which he shared with Mr. Muller. I am very proud of the reputation of my house, Mr. Snyder, and it was a blow to me that this should have happened. I applied to an agency for a detective, and they sent me a stupid boy, with nothing to recommend him except his belief in himself. He said that Captain Gunner had died by accident, killed by a snake which had come out of a crate of bananas. I knew better. I knew that Captain Gunner had been murdered. Are you listening, Captain Muller? This will interest you, as you were such a friend of his."

The captain did not answer. He was staring straight before him, as if he saw something invisible in eyes forever closed in death.

"Yesterday we found the body of a dog. It had been killed, as Captain Gunner had been, by the poison of a snake. The boy from the agency said that this was conclusive. He said that the snake had escaped from the room after killing Captain Gunner and had in turn killed the dog. I knew that to be impossible, for, if there had been a snake in that room it could not have made its escape."

Her eyes flashed and became remorselessly accusing. "It was not a snake that killed Captain Gunner. It was a cat. Captain Gunner had a friend who hated him. One day, in opening a crate of bananas, this friend found a snake. He killed it, and extracted the poison. He knew Captain Gunner's habits. He knew that he played a harmonica. This man also had a cat. He knew that cats hated the sound of a harmonica. He had often seen this particular cat fly at Captain

Gunner and scratch him when he played. He took the cat and covered its claws with the poison. And then he left the cat in the room with Captain Gunner. He knew what would happen."

Oakes and Mr. Snyder were on their feet. Captain Muller had not moved. He sat there, his fingers gripping the cloth. Mrs. Pickett rose and went to a closet. She unlocked the door. "Kitty!" she called. "Kitty! Kitty!" A black cat ran swiftly out into the room. With a clatter and a crash of crockery and a ringing of glass the table heaved, rocked, and overturned as Muller staggered to his feet. He threw up his hands as if to ward something off. A choking cry came from his lips. "Gott! Gott!"

Mrs. Pickett's voice rang through the room, cold and biting. "Captain Muller, you murdered Captain Gunner!"

The captain shuddered. Then mechanically he replied, "Gott! Yes, I killed him."

"You heard, Mr. Snyder," said Mrs. Pickett. "He has confessed before witnesses."

Muller allowed himself to be moved toward the door. His arm in Mr. Snyder's grip felt limp. Mrs. Pickett stopped and took something from the debris on the floor. She rose, holding the harmonica.

"You are forgetting your souvenir, Captain Muller," she said.

SPECTRE IN BLUE DOUBLEKNIT

by Bruce Bethke

As his eyes adjusted to the darkness, he found Richard and Louisa sprawled on the bed, asleep. Quietly, so as not to disturb them, he stepped out of the bedroom and wandered through the apartment, correlating.

The tattered green easy chair, the cigarette-scarred sofa; the disorganized heap of textbooks on the coffee table; good. The pint mason jar of marijuana, the pyramid of empty Schmidt "Sportspak" beer cans, the cold half-cup of coffee etching a ring on the top of the stereo speaker; all was exactly as he had pictured it. He headed for the kitchen, for the final test.

Blue mercury streetlight spilled through the uncurtained windows, allowing him to clearly read the date of the *Tribune* sports section lying on the radiator. May 6, 1975. Perfect. He'd manifested right on target.

He stepped back into the bedroom, and took a gentle moment to compare the dozing man to himself. The sleeper had a full head of thick, curly, brown hair, a smooth, clear, untroubled face, and a trim, muscular, one-hundred-seventy-pound physique. His own body was another story; his hairline had receded clear back to the crown of his head, his ulcer was developing a resistance to Maalox, and he couldn't keep his weight under two forty on a bet.

A small twinge of sympathy passed through him as he looked down at the man on the bed. Twenty-two-year-old Richard Luck had such *possibilities* ahead of him. And he was about to toss them all away . . . That thought choked off the sympathy. He leapt up on the bed and kicked young Richard hard in the ribs.

His foot passed right through, of course.

With a modest sigh of disappointment, he lay down through the sleeper and started insinuating himself into the dream.

Richard and Carynne go to Marty's Deli for lunch, and as soon as they get inside the door he sees Louisa working behind the counter. He yells, "I can explain!" but she picks up that enormous knife she uses to slice the French bread, so he grabs Carynne's hand and starts running.

They run across the street, jump the fence, and start through the railroad tunnel, but when they get about halfway he sees his mother coming from the other end. "It's okay, Mom," he says, "I know what I'm doing." She just stands there blocking the end of the tunnel (which has become so narrow he's got to stoop to stand in it), and he can hear Louisa coming up behind, so he turns and drags Carynne down a side passage he hadn't noticed before. They emerge into the corridor by the physics classrooms in the basement of North Hall and round the corner to find the stair-well door locked from the other side, so Carynne pulls him into one of the dark classrooms and—my God, how'd she get to be so naked?—and pulls him tight against her smooth, cool skin, and pulls him down, and pulls him—

The fluorescent lights flare on; he and Carynne are entwined, naked, on the sofa in his parents' basement, and his father is standing there scowling. Except it isn't his father, it's the pudgy guy in the navy blue doubleknit suit! The pudgy guy walks over, picks up Richard's jeans off the floor, throws them at him, and says, "Wake up, dirtball. We need to talk."

"Dammit, you again? Bug off!"

"You can chase wet dreams later. This is important."

"Who *are* you?" Richard demands. "What are you doing here?" Carynne has vanished.

" 'Is it bigger than a breadbox?' " the pudgy guy mocks him. "What do you *think* I'm doing here? This is a premonition. I'm you from twenty years in the future."

"I'm going to look like *that* when I'm forty?" Richard wakes with a start, and finds himself drenched in cold sweat.

No, as Richard lay in the dark thinking about it, maybe he hadn't waked up. He was in his bedroom for sure, in his bed, staring at the ceiling; everything *seemed* real enough, but he was utterly unable to move. He believed the woman sleeping next to him was Louisa, but an effort to roll over and confirm that got him nowhere.

And then there was this curious sense of *detachment*, he felt. He was lying on the bed, and at the same time lying under the bed among the old sneakers and dust bunnies, and sitting perched like a cat on the windowsill, and gently floating up near the ceiling, noting that the lintel moldings hadn't been cleaned in years. He thought his eyes were open, but the multiple viewpoints cast some doubt on that.

Deep in the back of his head, his rational daytime self panicked and started screaming something about being dead or paralyzed or at the very least psychotic, but Richard ignored the noise. His windowsill self (which was looking more like a cat with every passing moment) had spotted a sort of umbilical cord between his bedded and ceiling selves, and ambled over to investigate. The thought occurred to him then that if he could just get a window open, he'd be able to fly his ceiling self like a kite.

Whatever state his mind was in, it certainly wasn't awake.

"It's called lucid sleep," someone suggested, helpfully. "Your forebrain is awake, but your voluntary nervous system doesn't know that yet."

Richard managed to round up most of his attention and become aware of another presence in the room. A presence sitting on the foot of his bed, to be exact.

"Hello!" the spectre in the blue polyester suit said cheerfully.

With an unpleasant lack of startle reflex, Richard's eyes didn't snap open. "Omigod," Richard . . . *said*, for lack of a better word. His lips barely moved, no sound came out, and yet the thought was expressed. "Naw. Don't hallucinate like this from pot. Must be still dreaming." He turned his attention out to graze and tried to slide back into deep sleep.

"Stop it!" said the apparition. "Don't drag me back into dreamstate again."

"Give me two good reasons," Richard mumbled.

"Lucid sleep is the only state I can reliably communicate with you in. If you go back to normal sleep I'm just a nightmare."

"A nightmare with lousy timing," Richard corrected. "I was finally going to score with Carynne."

"You want to go back to sleep? Never see me again?"

"Who, *me*?" Richard said, as sarcastically as possible. "Did *I* say that?"

The apparition leaned in close to bedded Richard's face. "Well, then get *this* through your little pea-sized brain, boy! You won't be rid of me until you hear me out. You don't know *half* the nightmare I can be!"

With the equivalent of a resigned sigh, Richard turned back from deep sleep. "Okay. Accepting—just for the moment—that this isn't some bizarre twist in the dream, how do you do it? I mean, you've been invading my sleep all week."

"Sympathetic resonance. My consciousness resonates inside your empty head."

"Insults from hallucinations I don't need," Richard snarled. The tiny flare of anger led to a twitch in his leg, which disturbed Louisa. She rolled a bit, *mmphed* something, and put an arm across Richard's chest.

The apparition bit his lip. "I'm pre-memory, okay? I'm an up-town projection of your own future consciousness. Look, it's all in the Muldoon book; read about it later. I can only hyperdynamize like this for about thirty minutes, so you'll excuse me if I get to the point."

"Aha!" Richard gleefully seized an idea. "*I* know where you come from. It's that silly parapsychology course, isn't it? I skipped the readings and now my subconscious is punishing me for it." He wished he were awake enough to resolutely cross his arms.

"Well, I don't care if I get a Z-minus on the final. I got a B on the mid-term and an A on my paper, so I pass no matter what. I am *not* going to read any more of that garf; I've got a marketing final to worry about."

"Gah!" The pudgy spectre slapped himself on the forehead. "You *jerk*! Sure, there's so much fluff in the course it says *Do Not Remove Tag Under Penalty of Law* in the syllabus. Some of it is still true. If you—but no, all *you* can think about is Louisa's breasts and Carynne's tight jeans. *I* had to start studying projection all over again when I was thirty-five because *you* took such lousy notes. It took me six years to get here."

Louisa dragged an arm up, pushed a few strands of her long brown hair out of her face, and whimpered, "Whasmatter honey?" before nodding off again.

Richard focused on her, then on the spectre sitting across his knees. "Can she hear?" he whispered.

The pudgy man paled. "Jeez, I hope not. I'm supposed to be manifesting to you only. Maybe there's some spillover."

"Well, try to keep it down, will you?"

"Okay." They stared at each other in uneasy silence until Richard realized the older man was composing himself to deliver a lecture, just as Richard's father used to.

Richard quickly spoke first. "So you're my future, huh? How's IBM doing?" It had the desired effect; he totally blew away the older man's composure. "Y'see, I figure I can borrow another three grand at two points on my tuition loan and invest—"

"Kid!" the older man barked. "I came here to pre-

vent the biggest mistake in your life. Not to turn a
few lousy bucks."

"Slack off, okay?" Richard said defensively. "I
mean, I'm having some trouble dealing with this,
y'know? It's not every day my future pops in for a
chat." Richard let his viewpoint drift back to the cat.
He felt comfortable being a cat. "But I do know that
if this were *really* happening, I wouldn't miss an opportunity like this. You sure you're my future?" The
man just glared.

"Okay. Accepting for the sake of argument that
you're who you say you are, don't you know that coming back is absurd? If you convince me to change my
future, then the thing you say came back to warn me
about doesn't happen, so you don't—"

"I'm trying to save his life," the older man growled
under his breath, "and he wants to argue jerk-off phi-
losophy with me." He pointed at Richard and raised
his voice. "Look, kid, every time you say causality
paradox I'll say branching alternate time-line. Person-
ally, I think you get premonitions from unchosen fu-
tures all the time; you're just too dimwitted to notice
them. It took me five tries to get you lucid."

"But if this works, won't you disintegrate or something?"

"I don't know. And frankly I don't care."

Richard whistled low. "That bad, huh?" and watched
as the pudgy man slowly, portentously, nodded.
"There you go, getting all ominous again. You came
back from the future, didn't you? That means the
world doesn't get nuked into slag in the next twenty
years. Hey, I feel better already!"

"Worse things can happen than the end of the
world."

"You out of a job?" Richard suggested. "Economy collapse in the late eighties like Greenburg says it will?"

The older man angrily dug his ghost fingers into sleeping Richard's leg. "Is that all you want from the future? Money? Kid, your priorities are *all* screwed up. 'Am I successful?' Sure, I'm successful. I'm national sales manager for IMDC; I make—"

Richard interrupted. "Who?"

"Integrated Micro Data Corp. They don't exist yet."

"Damn." Cat/Richard twitched his tail with vexation. "And how much did you say you earn?" His interest perked up.

"For chrissakes, what difference does it make?!"

"I only ask," Richard pointed out, "because I want to know why a successful man wears such an ugly suit."

"It's part of the projection," the older man explained, patience struggling with exasperation. "I'm not physically here, of course. I can only travel by avatar—symbol—and my avatar is a sweaty guy in a cheap suit. It's not a true image; in the real world I wouldn't be caught dead wearing white patent leather loafers and a matching vest."

"Sure," said the cat, dubiously, "and—"

"Dammit, stop changing the subject! I'm trying to tell you about real happiness!"

"Ah," Richard said, with dawning comprehension. "Now we come to the point. You advise choosing spiritual fulfillment over material success, right? Thanks, I'll think it over, good night."

"Louisa's a nice girl. Marry her."

Richard licked a paw, rubbed his ear, and then sat

in thoughtful silence. At last he spoke. "You traveled twenty years to tell me *that*?"

"She's a sweet kid. The two of you could be very happy."

"That's *it*?"

"No, there's one thing more. You're so worried about this marketing final, you've talked Carynne Reichmann into giving you some coaching this weekend. Break the date."

"But if I do that," Richard protested, "I'll flunk. And if I flunk marketing, how do I get to be a national sales manager?"

"Come off it," the older man said, annoyed. "You've had the hots for Carynne all year; this is just an excuse to take one last crack at her before she graduates."

Richard looked chagrined. "Okay, I admit I was dreaming about her. But hey, she's the original Snow Queen. Nothing will happen."

"Dickie boy," the older man said, clucking his tongue, "you forget who you're lying to. I *remember* what you're thinking. And right now, you're thinking that if you were getting somewhere with Carynne you'd toss Louisa out the door in a minute." The older man suddenly grabbed cat/Richard roughly by the neck, held him nose-to-nose, and spoke in low, dark tones. *"So get this straight, pinhead!* This Saturday, Carynne not only coaches you for the exam, but she also invites you into her bed. You'll come dragging your lethargic ass home Sunday at six in the morning to find Louisa already packed."

The cat stopped squirming. "Oh?"

"Of all the things you could possibly do in this universe, I promise you, you do *not* want to do that."

"Are you out of your mind?" Richard shrieked.

"Carynne's beautiful! Brilliant! Everything I ever wanted in a woman!"

"Including selfish? Demanding? Manipulative?"

Richard fastened on an idea. "That's it. You're right about alternate time-lines; I'm the wrong past for you. *My* Carynne's nothing like—"

"Of course she isn't. Now."

Richard paused. "Okay, tell you what. If it turns out you're right, I'll dump her in a few years."

"Idiot!" the older man thundered, "in six months you marry her! In a year she pushes you into going back to school full-time—while holding down a full-time job—to get your MBA. In five years she's into leased BMW's and semiannual vacations in the Virgin Islands, neither of which you can afford; by the time you're thirty your hairline's back *here,*" the older man karate-chopped himself on the crown of his head, "your stomach's in real trouble, and Carynne has realized you aren't half as ambitious as she is."

"So? Lots of people survive divorce."

"You, unfortunately, stay married. Always hoping things will improve, and always getting affection from her the same way Muffy gets dog yummies: only when you roll over and beg."

"Muffy?"

The older man dropped the cat on the bed. "Her lhasa apso."

"You mean one of those small, yapping . . . ? Eesh," said Richard, disgusted. He jumped down to the floor, sniffed at his self lying under the bed, then looked up at the older man and cocked his head quizzically. Somehow, no matter how hard he tried, he found it hard to accept such grim portents from a caricature of a salesman. "So it won't work, huh?"

"It can't work," the spectre explained. "You two are incompatible at the most primal level. I mean—look, you've got three avatars now, right? That's 'cause your life path isn't decided yet.

"That inert spud under the bed—that's *me*. Or rather what Carynne will make out of me. And that one up there," he gestured at the Richard floating near the ceiling, "I don't know what future he represents.

"But right now, your primary manifestation is as a cat. That's your favorite avatar; the tomcat.

"She can't stand cats unless they're neutered, de-clawed, and kept in the house. Even then she prefers docile, obedient, nearly asexual dogs. You're a cat person. She's a dog person. It's that basic."

Richard began pacing back and forth between the bed and the radiator, twitching his tail anxiously. "Look, there's got to be something redeeming about the marriage. Kids?" he suggested, hopefully.

"Two daughters who are carbon copies of their mother. They're into horses. You have any idea how much a ten-year-old who wants a horse can whine?"

"Friends, then?"

"Hers. Frank and Gordy are too plebeian for her tastes and you won't see them again after '77."

Richard looked up, into the older man's face. There was tremendous bitterness and inner-directed anger there, eating away at the man like a cancer. And yet, there was something else. A soft—wistfulness? Ignor-ing the cat for the moment, the older man had turned and was watching Louisa sleep. Hesitantly, tenderly, he reached out a ghost hand and touched her leg. She didn't stir. Quickly, as if she were a delicate treasure he feared his rude touch would ruin, he pulled his hand away and turned around, to find the cat looking straight into his eyes.

"Anyway, that's what I came here to tell you," the older man said softly. "It's your decision now." He turned to look at Louisa again. "I'll be snapping back to my own time in a minute or two."

That, at last, was what touched cat/Richard. For all the bluster, it was the brief, unguarded slice of tenderness that convinced Richard the older man was telling the truth. Unable to think of anything more comforting, he rubbed up against the man's legs. Older Richard noticed, reached down to scratch him behind the ears, and whispered, "Take good care of her, okay?" Before cat/Richard could answer, older Richard suddenly sat up straight, blanched white with pain, and clamped his fists to the sides of his head.

"What's wrong?" the cat mewed. "Can I help?"

"Weird!" gasped the older man. "Like—*hot maggots* in my brain! Snapback never felt like this be . . ." In that instant, both of them became aware of another presence in the room.

"I thought I'd find you here."

"Carynne!" older Richard shouted. Cat/Richard spun around to find a thin, deeply wrinkled, ascetic old woman wearing an elegant white dress and sitting stiffly erect in a Louis Quatorze armchair (which she had apparently brought with her), holding a lhasa apso in her lap. "And your little dog, too!" At that moment the dog spotted cat/Richard and, with a pugnacious yap, jumped out of the woman's arms.

"Muffy the fourth!" she commanded. "Heel!"

Instinctively, cat/Richard leapt up onto the bed, turned to face the dog, and let out his most vile and guttural hiss. The dog stopped short, considered the *very* sharp claws Richard had extended, and dutifully trotted back to Carynne. "I'm sorry," she said, addressing the cat. "Muffy's so excitable." She lifted the dog into her lap, then turned to older Richard. "Now, if you're done lying to this young man . . ."

"You can't be here!" older Richard gasped.

"Don't look so surprised, dear," the woman said. "If you can learn projection, I can."

"But—time transference only works between the same mind!"

"Dickie," she admonished, "as usual you're too stubborn to admit you're wrong. I *am* here; therefore I *can* be." She glanced at cat/Richard. "I only hope I'm in time."

"In time for what?" cat/Richard asked, suspiciously.

"I don't know what he's told you so far," Carynne explained, smiling, "but Dickie was going through a premature mid-life crisis when he started this projection business. Seems he had a habit of picking up teenage bimbos on his sales trips, and when his weight hit two fifty they started laughing in his face. Gave his poor little male ego a terrible shock."

Cat/Richard turned sharply on older Richard, forming the question.

"She isn't *my* Carynne," older Richard protested.

"I certainly am!" she countered.

"But you're so—"

"*Old?*" she completed. "Did you think you had a monopoly on projecting into your past? All this—" she pointed a long, polished fingernail at older Richard, "including *your* present, is *my* past!"

"How did you—"

"You hid your notes well, Dickie. I didn't find out

about this projection nonsense until I went through your papers after you died."

"Died!" cat/Richard yowled.

"Don't listen to her," the older man said quickly. "She's trying to get you rattled."

"And so I've come back to provide some balance," Carynne continued, addressing the cat. "Not that it really matters what he tells you. He can't possibly succeed—causality paradox, you know—I'm just disappointed that he spent years trying."

"Kid?" the older man prompted, panic rising in his voice. Cat/Richard found himself wishing Carynne had flown in, cackling, on a broomstick; it would've made things so much easier. Instead, the glimpse of his own mortality had triggered a surge of guilt, and he was busy remembering just how convincingly he could lie to himself when he wanted something. "Listen, she's . . ." older Richard started, then paused when he saw the way the cat was glaring, first at him, then at Carynne.

"He's trying to decide who to believe," Carynne observed.

Older Richard turned on her. "You'll ruin *every-thing*!" he hissed. "You weren't satisfied with making *my* life miserable; you're trying to screw up all my *possible* lives." Closing his eyes, he sat up rigidly and grimaced with fierce concentration. "I won't let you do it," he whispered. "I'll force you out."

"Really, Dickie dear," Carynne said, shaking her head slowly, "I should think by now you'd know better than to try a contest of wills with me."

"I am restructuring the projection . . ." he muttered.

"And I'm still here," she said nonchalantly. "At the risk of reminding you of our sex life: are you finished?"

With a gasp, older Richard broke concentration and staggered to his feet, defiantly facing Carynne. "You think you've won, don't you?" he snarled. "I'll be back!"

"No, you won't," Carynne stated flatly.

"Stop me!"

Carynne shrugged. "If you insist. Dickie dear, do you understand how dreamstate time is purely subjective? I can control my projections far better than you ever could." She rapped her knuckles on the arm of the chair for emphasis. "In a month of real time I can haunt you for the rest of your sad little life, if you force it on me."

"No!" shouted cat/Richard. "Don't give in, Dickie!" He urgently tried to pull his selves together and focus all his awareness through the cat. "We can beat her! If we unite—"

"Goodbye, Dickie," Carynne smiled. A silvery umbilicus snaked down from somewhere and started entwining older Richard. Cat/Richard leapt at it, claws flailing, but the cord was unyielding as cold marble. It fell about older Richard in heavy loops; he struggled briefly, but when the end dropped down and the whole mass began constricting, he gave up.

"Dickie?" the cat screamed.

"I'm sorry," came a muffled voice from inside the coils. "I can't hold off snapback any longer." In the space of a few seconds, the coils tightened to a mass the size of a fist and then abruptly vanished, leaving a momentary pucker in the air.

On the night of June 27th, 1995, Richard Luck woke up at two A.M. with a start so sudden it disturbed his wife, Carynne.

"What's the matter, Dickie?" she asked.

"Oh . . . just had a *weird* dream."

"That's all right," she mumbled. Pulling him close, she gave him a peck on the cheek, then rolled over and turned her back to him. "Go back to sleep, dear. And no more dreaming about Louisa."

He was awake for hours, wondering.

"My, that was easy," Carynne said smugly. "Now, as for *you*," she took a step towards cat/Richard, who crouched low, raised his hackles, and bared his teeth. "Oh, very well. Go ahead and have your little tantrum; you won't escape me, dear." She lifted the lhasa apso into her arms and began spinning the same glossy cord about herself, slipping into the coils with practiced ease. "See you Saturday!" she called out gaily.

Cat/Richard frantically nudged at his sleeping self, trying to wake up. He had a feeling it was critically urgent that he wake up; he desperately needed to tell the whole story to his rational daytime self, which was still asleep. If he could just remember every detail; if he could just see Carynne with his waking eyes before she vanished—

As she spun the last loops about herself, Carynne cocked her head at Louisa's sleeping form. "Dickie dear, you always had such cheap taste in women. Whatever do you see in *her*?"

Cat/Richard was getting through. Slowly, his sleeping self was beginning to rouse. Slowly, *very* slowly, his daytime mind was grinding into gear. And then—

Carynne vanished. Richard sat up straight in bed. The disturbance woke Louisa. She rolled over, brushed a few strands of her long brown hair out of her face, and mumbled, "Whasmatter, honey? How come you're awake?"

"Damn cat was licking my face."

"Don't *have* a cat," Louisa noted.

"Then we'll get one. I want a cat."

"Silly boy," Louisa murmured. Richard realized that, as was often the case, when he woke up in the middle of the night, he needed to go to the bathroom. He slid out of bed.

"Honey?" Louisa called out as he pulled on the terrycloth bathrobe they shared. "Come back to bed?"

"In a minute." He had this odd, nagging feeling in the back of his head, like there was something he needed to remember.

"Don't stay up late reading again. You need sleep, too."

"I know." Something *important,* and it was just beyond his grasp.

"Don't want to fall asleep during your marketing exam." He stopped short at the bedroom door. He *remembered.* Turning around, he came back to the bed, and kissed Louisa.

"Lou, sweetheart," he said gently, "I think it's time we talked about getting married."

"Inna morning, honey," she mumbled. Then, as the words soaked in, her eyes snapped wide open. "Did you say married?" she whispered. He nodded. Louisa threw her arms around Richard and hugged so hard his ribs ached. "I thought you'd *never* ask!"

Somewhere down the twisting braided streams of time, a different Richard began chuckling in his sleep again, which woke his wife one more time. It annoyed Carynne no end when it happened, but there was nothing she could do about it.

At that moment.

ANIMALS

by Clark Howard

As Ned Price got off the city bus at the corner of his block, he saw that Monty and his gang of troublemakers were, as usual, loitering in front of Shavelson's Drugstore. A large portable radio—they called it their "ghetto blaster"—was sitting atop a newspaper vending machine, playing very loud acid rock. The gang, six of them, all in their late teens, appeared to be arguing over the contents of a magazine that was circulating among them.

Ned started down the sidewalk. An arthritic limp made him favor his right leg. That, coupled with lumbago and sixty-two years of less than easy living, gave him an overall stooped, tired look. A thrift-shop sportcoat slightly too large didn't help matters. Ned could have crossed the street and gone around Monty and his friends, but he lived on this side of the street so he would just have to cross back again farther down the block. It was difficult enough to get around these days without taking extra steps. Besides, he figured he had at least as much right to walk down the sidewalk as they did to obstruct it.

When Ned got closer, he saw the magazine the gang was passing around was *Ring* and that their argument had to do with the relative merits of two boxers named

Hector "Macho" Camacho and Ray "Boom Boom" Mancini. Maybe they'd be too caught up in their argument to hassle him today. That would be a welcome change. A day without having to match wits with this year's version of the Sharks.

But no such luck.

"Hey, old man, where you been?" Monty asked as Ned approached. "Down to pick up your check?" He stepped in the middle of the sidewalk and blocked the way.

Ned stopped. "Yes," he said, "I've been down to pick up my check."

"You're one of those old people who don't let the mailman bring their check, huh?" Monty asked with a smile. "You know there's too many crooks in this neighborhood. You're smart, huh?"

"No, just careful," Ned said. If I was smart, he thought, I would have crossed the street.

"Hey, lemme ask you something," Monty said with mock seriousness. "I seen on a TV special where some old people don't get enough pension to live on an' they eat dogfood and catfood. Do you do that, old man?"

"No, I don't," Ned replied. There was a slight edge to his answer this time. He knew several people who *did* resort to the means Monty had just described.

"Listen, old man, I think you're lying," Monty said without rancor. "I myself have seen you in Jamail's Grocery buying catfood."

"That's because I have a cat." Ned tried to step around Monty but the youth moved and blocked his way again.

"You got a cat, old man? Ain't that nice?" Monty feigned interest. "Wha' kind of cat you got, old man?"

"Just an ordinary cat," Ned said. "Nothing special."

"Not a Persian or a Siamese or one of them expensive cats?"

"No. Just an ordinary cat. A tabby, I think it's called."

"A tabby! Hey, tha's really nice."

"Can I go now?" Ned asked.

"Sure!" Monty said, shrugging elaborately. "Who's stopping you, old man?"

Ned stepped around him and this time the youth did not interfere with him. As he walked away, Ned heard Monty say something in Spanish and the others laughed.

A regular Freddie Prinze, Ned thought.

As Ned entered his third-floor-rear kitchenette, he said, "Molly, I'm back." Double-locking the door securely behind him, he hung his coat on a wooden wall peg and limped into a tiny cluttered living room. "Molly!" he called again. Then he stood still and a cold feeling came over him that he was alone in the apartment. "Molly?"

He stuck his head in the narrow Pullman kitchen, then pushed back a curtain that concealed a tiny sleeping alcove.

"Molly, where are you?"

Even as he asked the question one last time, Ned knew he would not find her. He hurried into the bathroom. The window was open about three inches. Ned raised it all the way and stuck his head out. Three stories below, in the alley, some kids were playing Kick-the-Can. A ledge ran from the window to a backstairs landing.

"Molly!" Ned called several times.

Moments later, he was out in front looking up and down the street. Monty and his friends, seeing him, sauntered down to where he stood.

"What's the matter, old man?" Monty asked. "You lose something?"

"My cat," Ned said. He turned suspicious eyes on Monty and his friends. "You wouldn't have seen her, by any chance, would you?"

"Is there a reward?" Monty inquired.

Ned gave the question quick consideration. There was an old watch of his late wife's he could probably sell. "There might be, if the cat isn't harmed. Do you know where she is?"

Monty turned to the others. "Anybody see this old man's cat?" he asked with a total absence of concern. When they all shrugged and declared ignorance, he said to Ned, "Sorry, old man. If you'd let the mailman deliver your check, you'd have been home to look after your cat. See the price you pay for being greedy?" He strutted off down the street, his followers in his wake. Feeling ill, Ned watched them all the way to the corner, where they turned out of sight. Pain from an old ulcer began as acid churned in his stomach.

"Molly!" he called and started walking down the block. "Molly! Here, kitty, kitty."

He searched for her until well after dark.

Ned was up early the next morning and back outside looking. He scoured the block all the way to the corner, then came back the other way. In front of the drugstore, he encountered Monty again. The youth was alone this time, leaning up against the building, eating a jelly doughnut and drinking milk from a pint carton.

"You still looking for that cat, old man?" Monty asked, his tone a mixture of incredulity and irritation.

"Yes."

"Man, why don't you go in the alley and get another one? There mus' be a dozen cats back there."

"I want this cat. It belonged to my wife when she was alive."

"Hell, man, a cat's a cat," Monty said.

Shavelson, the drugstore owner, came out, broom in hand. "Want to make half a buck sweeping the sidewalk?" he asked Monty, who looked at him as if he were an imbecile, then turned away disdainfully, not even dignifying the question with an answer. Shavelson shrugged and began sweeping debris toward the curb himself. "You're out early," he said to Ned.

"My cat's lost," Ned said. "She may have got out the bathroom window while I was downtown yesterday."

"Why don't you go back in the alley—"

Ned was already shaking his head. "I want _this_ cat."

"Maybe the pound got her," Shavelson suggested. "Their truck was all over this neighborhood yesterday."

The storekeeper's words sent a chill along Ned's spine. "The pound?"

"Yeah. You know, the city animal shelter. They have a truck comes around—"

"It was here yesterday? On this block?"

"Yeah."

"Where do they take the animals they catch?" Ned asked out of a rapidly drying mouth.

"The animal shelter over on Twelfth Street, I think. They have to hold them there seventy-two hours to see if anybody claims them."

Too distressed by the thought to thank Shavelson, Ned hurried back up the street and into his building. Five minutes later, he emerged again, wearing a coat, his city bus pass in one hand. Crossing the street, he went to the bus stop and stood peering down the street, as if by sheer will he could make a bus appear.

Monty, having finished his doughnut and milk, sat on the curb in front of Shavelson's, smoking a cigarette and reading one of the morning editions from the drugstore's sidewalk newspaper rack. From time to time he glanced over at Ned, wondering at his concern over a cat. Monty knew a few back yards in the neighborhood that were knee-deep in cats.

Presently it began to sprinkle light rain. Monty stood up, folding the newspaper, and handed it to Shavelson as the storekeeper came out to move his papers inside.

"You sure you're through with it?" Shavelson asked. "Any coupons or anything you'd like to tear out?"

Monty's eyes narrowed a fraction. "Someday, man, you're gonna say the wrong thing to me," he warned. "Then you're gonna come to open up your store and you gonna find a pile of ashes."

"You'd do that for *me*?" Shavelson retorted.

The sprinkle escalated to a drizzle as the storekeeper went back inside. From the doorway, Monty looked over at the bus stop again. Ned was still standing there, his only concession to the rain being a turned-up collar. I don't believe this old fool, Monty thought. He goes to more trouble for this cat than most people do for their kids.

Tossing his cigarette into the gutter, he trotted

down the block and got into an old Chevy that had a pair of oversize velvet dice dangling from the rearview mirror. Revving the engine a little, he listened with satisfaction to the rumble of the car's gutted muffler, then made a U-turn from the curb and drove to the bus stop.

"Get in, old man," he said, leaning over to the passenger window. "I'm going past Twelfth Street— I'll give you a lift."

Ned eyed him suspiciously. "No, thanks. I'll wait for the bus."

"Hey, man, waiting for a bus in this city at your age ain't too smart. An old lady over on Bates Street *died* at a bus stop last week, she was there so long. Besides, in case you ain't noticed, it's raining." Monty's voice softened a touch. "Come on, get in."

Ned glanced up the street one last time, saw that there was still no bus in sight, thought of Molly caged up at the pound, and got in.

As they rode along, Monty lighted another cigarette and glanced over at his passenger. "You thought me and my boys did something with your cat, didn't you?"

"The thought did cross my mind," Ned admitted.

"Listen, I got better things to do with my time than mess with some cat. You know, for an old guy you ain't very smart."

Ned grunted softly. "I won't argue with you there," he said.

On Twelfth, Monty pulled to the curb in front of the animal shelter. "I got to go see a guy near here, take me about fifteen minutes. I'll come back and pick you up after you get your cat."

Ned studied him for a moment. "Is there some kind of Teenager of the Year award I don't know about?"

"Very funny, man. You're a regular, what's-his-name, Jack Albertson, ain't you?"

At the information counter in the animal shelter a woman with tightly styled hair and a superior attitude asked, "Was the animal wearing a license tag on its collar?"

"No, she—"

"Was the animal wearing an ID tag on its collar?"

"No, she wasn't wearing a collar. She's really an apartment cat, you see—"

"Sir," the woman said, "our animal enforcement officers don't go into apartments and take animals."

"I think she got out the bathroom window."

"That makes her a street animal, unlicensed and unidentifiable."

"Oh, I can identify her," Ned assured the woman. "And she'll come to me when I call her. If you'll just let me see the cats you picked up yesterday—"

"Sir, do you have any idea how many stray animals are picked up by our trucks every day?"

"Why, no, I never gave—"

"*Hundreds,*" he was told. "Only the ones with license tags or ID tags are kept at the shelter."

"I thought all animals had to be kept here for three days to give their owners time to claim them," Ned said, remembering what Shavelson had told him.

"You're not listening, sir. Only the animals with license or ID tags are kept at the shelter for the legally required seventy-two hours. Those without tags are taken directly to the disposal pound."

Ned turned white. "Is that where they—where they—?" The words would not form.

"Yes, that is where stray animals are put to sleep." She paused a beat. "Either that or sold."

Ned frowned. "Sold."

"Yes, sir. To laboratories. To help offset the overhead of operating our department." Her eyes flicked over Ned's shabby clothing. "Tax dollars don't pay for *everything*, you know." But she had unknowingly given Ned an ember of hope.

"Can you give me the address of this—disposal place?"

The woman scribbled an address on a slip of paper and pushed it across the counter to him. "Your cat might still be there," she allowed, "if it was picked up late yesterday. Disposal hours for cats are from one to three. If it was a dog you'd be out of luck. They do dogs at night, eight to eleven, because there are more of them. That's because they're easier to catch. They trust people. Cats, they don't trust—"

She was still talking as Ned snatched up the address and hurried out.

Monty was waiting at the curb.

"I didn't think you'd be back this quick," Ned said, getting into the car.

"The guy I went to see wasn't there," Monty told him. It was a lie. All he had done was drive around the block.

"They've taken my cat to be gassed," Ned said urgently, "but if I can get there in time I might be able to save her." He handed Monty the slip of paper. "This is the address. It's way out at the edge of town, but if you'll take me there I'll pay you." He pulled out a pathetically worn billfold, the old-fashioned kind that zipped around three sides. When he opened it, Monty could see several faded cellophane inserts with photographs in them. The photographs were old, all in black-and-white except for a paper picture of June Allyson that had come with the billfold.

From the currency pocket Ned extracted some bills, all of them singles. "I don't have much because I haven't cashed my check yet. But I can at least buy you some gas."

Monty pushed away the hand with the money and started the car. "I don't *buy* gas, man," he scoffed, "I quit buying it when it got to a dollar a gallon."

"Where do you get it?" Ned asked.

"I siphon it. From police cars parked behind the precinct station. It's the only place where cars are left on a lot unguarded." He flashed a smile at Ned. "That's because nobody would *dare* siphon gas from a cop car, you know what I mean?"

They got on one of the expressways and drove toward the edge of the city. As Monty drove, he smoked and kept time to rock music from the radio by drumming his fingers on the steering wheel. Ned glanced at a scar down the youth's right cheek. Thin and straight, almost surgical in appearance, it had probably been put there by a straight razor. Ned had been curious about the scar for a long time. Now would be an opportune time to ask how he got it, but Ned was too concerned about Molly. She was such an old cat, nearly fourteen. He hoped she hadn't died of a stroke from the trauma of being captured and caged. If she was still alive, she was going to be so glad to see him Ned doubted she would ever climb out the bathroom window again.

After half an hour on the expressway, Monty exited and drove them to a large warehouselike building at the edge of the city's water-treatment center. A sign above the entrance read simply: *Animal Shelter—Unit F.*

F for final, Ned thought. He was already opening his door as Monty brought the car to a full stop.

"Want me to come in with you?" Monty asked.

"What for?" Ned wanted to know, frowning.

The younger man shrugged. "So's they don't push you around. Sometimes people push old guys around."

"Really?" Ned asked wryly.

Monty looked off at nothing. "You want me to come in or not?"

"I can handle things myself," Ned told him gruffly.

The clerk at this counter, a thin gum-chewing young man with half a dozen ballpoints in a plastic holder in his shirt pocket, checked a clipboard on the wall and said, "Nope, you're too late. That whole bunch from yesterday was shipped out to one of our lab customers early this morning."

Ned felt warm and slightly nauseated. "Do you think they might sell my cat back to me?" he asked. "If I went over there?"

"You can't go over there," the clerk said. "We're not allowed to divulge the name or address of any of our lab customers."

"Oh." Ned wet his lips. "Do you suppose you could call them for me? Tell them I'd like to make some kind of arrangements to buy back my cat?"

The clerk was already shaking his head. "I don't have time to do things like that, mister."

"A simple phone call," Ned pleaded. "It'll only take—"

"Look, mister, I said no. I'm a very busy person."

Just then someone stepped up to the counter next to Ned. Surprised, Ned saw that it was Monty. He had his hands on the counter, palms down, and was smiling at the clerk.

"What time you get off work, Very Busy Person?" he asked.

The clerk blinked rapidly. "Uh, why do you want to know?"

"I'm jus' interested in what kind of hours a Very Busy Person like you keeps." Monty's smile faded and his stare grew cold. "You don't have to tell me if you don't want to. I can wait outside and find out for myself."

The clerk stopped chewing his gum; the color disappeared from his face, leaving him sickly pale. "Why, uh—why would you do that?"

" 'Cause I ain't got nothing better to do," Monty replied. "I *was* gonna take this old man here to that lab to try and get his cat back. But if he don't know where it is, I can't do that. So I'll just hang around here." He winked at the clerk without smiling. "See you later, man."

Monty took Ned's arm and started him toward the door.

"Just—wait a minute," the clerk said.

Monty and Ned turned back to see him rummaging in a drawer under the counter. He found a sheet of paper with three names and addresses mimeographed on it. With a ballpoint from the selection in his shirt pocket, he circled one of the addresses. Monty stepped back to the counter and took the sheet of paper.

"If it turns out they're expecting us," Monty said, "I'll know who warned them. You take my meaning, man?"

The clerk nodded. He swallowed dryly and his gum was gone.

At the door, looking at the address circled on the paper, Monty said, "Come on, old man. This here place is clear across town. You positive one of them cats in the alley wouldn't do you?"

On their way to the lab, Ned asked, "Why are you helping me like this?"

Monty shrugged. "It's a slow Wednesday, man."

Ned studied the younger man for a time, then observed, "You're different when your gang's not around."

Monty tossed him a smirk. "You gonna, what do you call it, analyze me, old man? You gonna tell me I got 'redeeming social values' or something like that?"

"I wouldn't go quite that far," Ned said dryly. "Anyway, sounds to me like you've *been* analyzed."

"Lots of times," Monty told him. "When they took me away from my old lady because it was an 'unfit environment,' they had some shrink analyze me then. When I ran away from the foster homes I was put in, other shrinks analyzed me. After I was arrested and was waiting trial in juvenile court for some burglaries, I was analyzed again. When they sent me downstate to the reformatory, I was analyzed. They're very big on analyzing in this state."

"They ever tell you the results of all that analyzing?"

"Sure. I'm incorrigible. And someday I'm supposed to develop into a sociopath. You know what that is?"

"Not exactly," Ned admitted.

Monty shrugged. "Me neither. I guess I'll find out when I become one."

They rode in silence for a few moments and then Ned said, "Well, anyway, I appreciate you helping me."

"Forget it," Monty said. He would not look at Ned; his eyes were straight ahead on the road. After several seconds, he added, "Jus' don't go telling nobody about it."

"All right, I won't," Ned agreed.

Their destination on the other side of the city was a large square two-story building on the edge of a forest preserve. It was surrounded by a chain-link fence with an entrance gate manned by a security guard. A sign on the gate read: *Consumer Evaluation Laboratory*.

Monty parked outside the gate and followed Ned over to the security-guard post. Ned explained what he wanted. The security guard took off his cap and scratched his head. "I don't know. This isn't covered in my guard manual. I'll have to call and find out if they sell animals back."

Ned and Monty waited while the guard telephoned. He talked to one person, was transferred to another, then had to repeat his story to still a third before he finally hung up and said, "Mr. Hartley of Public Relations is coming out to talk to you."

Mr. Hartley was a pleasant but firmly uncooperative man. "I'm sorry, but we can't help you," he said when Ned had told him of Molly's plight. "We have at least a hundred small animals in there—cats, dogs, rabbits, guinea pigs—all of them undergoing scientific tests. Even the shipment we received this morning has already been processed into a testing phase. We simply can't interrupt the procedure to find one particular cat."

"But it's *my* cat," Ned insisted. "She's not homeless or a stray. She belonged to my late wife—"

"I understand that, Mr. Price," Hartley interrupted, "but the animal *was* outside with no license or ID tag around its neck. It was apprehended legally and sold to us legally. I'm afraid it's just too late."

As they were talking, a bus pulled up to the gate. Hartley waved at the driver, then turned to the security guard. "These are the people from Diamonds-and-Pearls Cosmetics, Fred. Pass them through and then call Mr. Draper. He's conducting a tour for them."

As the bus passed through, Hartley turned back to resume the argument with Ned, but Monty stepped forward to intercede.

"We understand, Mr. Hartley," Monty said in a remarkably civil tone. "We're sure you'd help us if you could. Please accept our apology for taking up your time." Monty offered his hand.

"Quite all right," Hartley said, shaking hands.

Ned was staring incredulously at Monty. Macho had suddenly become Milquetoast.

"Come along, old fellow," Monty said, putting an arm around Ned's shoulders. "We'll go to a pet store and buy you a new kitty."

Ned allowed himself to be led back to the car, then demanded, "What the hell's got into you?"

"You're wasting your time with that joker," Monty said. "He's been programmed to smile and say no to whatever you want. We got to find some other way to get your cat."

"What other way?"

Monty grinned. "Like using the back door, man."

Driving away from the front gate, Monty found a gravel road and slowly circled the fenced-in area of the Consumer Evaluation Laboratory. On each side of the facility, beyond its fence, were several warehouses and small plants. In front, beyond a feeder road, was a state highway. Growing right up to its rear fence was the forest preserve: a state-protected wooded area.

Monty made one full circuit of the complex occupied by the laboratory and its neighbors, then said, "I think the best plan is to park in the woods, get past the fence in back, and sneak in that way."

"You mean slip in and *steal* my cat?" Ned asked.

Monty shrugged. "They stole her from you," he said.

Ned stared at him. "I'm sixty-two years old," he said. "I've never broken the law in my life."

"So?" said Monty, frowning. He did not see any relevance. The two men, one young, one old, each so different from the other, locked eyes in a silent stare for what seemed like a long time.

They were parked on the shoulder of the gravel road, the car windows down. The air coming into the car was fresh from the morning rain. Ned detected the scent of wet earth. Some movement a few yards up the road caught his eye and he turned his attention away from Monty. The movement was a gray squirrel scurrying across the road to the safety of the nearby woods. Watching the little animal, wild and free, made Ned think of the animals in the laboratory that were not free—the dogs and rabbits and guinea pigs.

And cats.

"All right," he told Monty. "Let's go in the back way."

Monty parked in one of the public picnic areas. From the trunk, he removed a pair of chain cutters and held them under his jacket with one hand.

"What do you carry those things for?" Ned asked, and realized at once that his question was naive.

"To clip coupons with, man," Monty replied. "Coupons save you money on everyday necessities."

The two men made their way through the trees to the rear of the laboratory's chain-link fence. Crouching, they scrutinized the back of the complex. Monty's eyes settled immediately on a loading dock served by a single-lane driveway coming around one side of the building. "We can go in there," he said. "Overhang doors are no sweat to open. But first let's see if there's any juice in this fence." Keeping his hands well on the rubber-covered handles, he gently touched the metal fence with the tip of the chain cutters. The contact drew no sparks. "Nothing on the surface," he said. "Let's see if there's anything inside. Some of these newer chain-links have an insulated circuit running through them." Quickly and expertly, he spread the cutters and snipped one link of the metal. Again there were no sparks. "This is going to be a breeze."

With a practiced eye, he determined his pattern and quickly snipped exactly the number of links necessary to create an opening large enough for them to get through. Then he gripped the cut section and bent it open, like a door, about eight inches. The chain cutters he hid nearby in some weeds.

"Now here's our story," he said to Ned. "We was walking through the public woods here and saw this hole cut in the fence, see? We thought it was our civic duty to tell somebody about it, so we came inside looking for somebody. If we get caught, stick to that story. Got it?"

"Got it," Ned confirmed.

Monty winked approval. "Let's do it, old man."

They eased through the opening and Monty bent the cut section back into place. Then they started toward the loading dock, walking upright with no attempt at hurrying or hiding. Ned was nervous but Monty remained very cool; he even whistled a soft little tune. When he sensed Ned's anxiety, he threw him a grin.

"Relax, old man. It'll take us forty, maybe fifty seconds to reach that dock. The chances of somebody seeing us in that little bit of time are so tiny, man. And even if they do, so what? We got our story, right?"

"Yeah, right," Ned replied, trying to sound confident.

But as Monty predicted, they reached the loading dock unobserved and unchallenged. Once up on the dock, Monty peered through a small window in one of the doors. "Just a big room with a lot of work tables," he said quietly. "Don't look like nobody's around. Hey, this service door's unlocked. Come on."

They moved inside into a large room equipped with butcher-block tables fixed to a tile floor. A number of hoses hung over each table, connected to the ceiling. As the two men stood scrutinizing the room, they suddenly heard a voice approaching. Quickly they ducked behind one of the tables.

An inner door opened and a man led a group of people into the room, saying, "This is our receiving area, ladies and gentlemen. The animals we purchase are delivered here and our laboratory technicians use these tables to wash and delouse them. They are then taken into our testing laboratory next door, which I will show you next. If you would, please take a smock from the pile there, to protect your clothes from possible contact with any of the substances we use in there."

Peering around the table, Ned and Monty watched as the people put on smocks and regrouped at the door. As they were filing out, Ned nudged Monty and said, "Come on."

Monty grinned. "You catching on, old man."

The two put on smocks and fell in at the rear of the group. They followed along as it was led through the hall and into a much larger room. This one was set up with a series of aisles formed by long work counters on which stood wire-grille cages of various sizes. Each cage was numbered and had a small slot containing a white card on its door. In each cage was a live animal.

"Our testing facility, we feel, is the best of its kind currently in existence," the tour guide said. "As you can see, we have a variety of test animals: cats, dogs, rabbits, guinea pigs. We also have access to larger animals, if a particular test requires it. Our testing procedures can be in any form. We can force-feed the test substance, introduce it by forced inhalation, reduce it to a dermal form and apply it directly to an animal's shaved skin, or inject it intravenously. Over here, for instance, are rabbits being given what is known as a Draize test. A new hairspray is being sprayed into their very sensitive eyes in order to gauge its irritancy level. Just behind the rabbits you see a group of puppies having dishwashing detergent introduced directly into their stomachs by a syringe with a tube attached to a hand pump. This is called an Internal LD-50 test; the LD stands for lethal dose and the number fifty represents one-half of a group of one hundred animals on which the test will be conducted. When half of the test group has died, we will have an accurate measurement of the toxity level of this product. This will provide the company marketing the product with evidence of safety testing in case it is later sued because some child swallows the detergent and dies. During the course of the testing, we also learn exactly how a particular substance will affect a living body, by observing whatever symptoms the animal exhibits: convulsions, paralysis, tremors, inability to breathe, blindness as in the case of the rabbits there—"

Ned was staring at the scene around him. As he looked at the helpless, caged, tortured animals, he felt his skin crawl. Which were the animals, the ones in the cages, or the ones outside the cages? Glancing at Monty, he saw the younger man reacting the same way—his eyes were wide, his expression incredulous, and his hands were curled into fists.

"We can test virtually any substance or product there is," the guide continued. "We test all forms of cosmetics and beauty aids, all varieties of detergents and other cleaning products, every food additive, coloring, and preservative, any new chemical or drug product—you name it. In addition to servicing private business, we test pesticides for the Environmental Protection Agency, synthetic substances for the Food and Drug Administration, and a variety of products for the Consumer Product Safety Commission. Our facility is set up so that almost no lead time is required to service our customers. As an example of this, a dozen cats brought in this morning are already in a testing phase over here—"

Ned and Monty followed the group to another aisle where the guide pointed out the newly arrived cats and explained the test being applied to them. Ned strained to see beyond the people in front of him, trying to locate Molly.

Finally the tour guide said, "Now, ladies and gentlemen, if you'll follow me, I'll take you to our cafeteria, where you can enjoy some refreshments while our testing personnel answer any questions you have about how we can help Diamonds-and-Pearls Cosmetics keep its products free of costly lawsuits. Just drop your smocks on the table outside the door."

Again Ned and Monty ducked down behind a workbench to conceal themselves as the people filed out of the room. When the door closed behind the group, Ned rose and hurried to the cat cages. Monty went over to lock the laboratory door.

Ned found Molly in one of the top cages. She was lying on her side, eyes wide, staring into space. The back part of her body had been shaved and three intravenous needles were stuck in her skin and held in place by tape. The tubes attached to the needles ran out the grille and up to three small bottles suspended above the cage. They were labeled: FRAGRANCE, DYE, and POLYSORBATE 93.

Ned wiped his eyes with the heel of one hand. Unlatching the grille door, he reached in and stroked Molly. "Hello, old girl," he said. Molly opened her mouth to meow, but no sound came.

"Dirty bastards," Ned heard Monty whisper. Turning, he saw the younger man reading the card on the front of Molly's cage. "This is some stuff that's going to be used in a hair tint," he said. "This test is to see if the cat can stay alive five hours with this combination of stuff in her."

"I can answer that," Ned said. "She won't. She's barely alive now."

"If we can get her to a vet, maybe we can save her," Monty suggested. "Pump her stomach or something." He bobbed his chin at the back wall. "We can get out through one of those windows—they face our hole in the fence."

"Get one open," Ned said. "I'll take Molly out."

Monty hurried over to the window while Ned gently unfastened the tape and pulled the hypodermic needles out of Molly's flesh. Once again the old cat looked at him and tried to make a sound, but she was too weak and too near death. "I know, old girl," Ned said softly. "I know it hurts."

Near the window, after opening it, Monty noticed several cages containing puppies that were up and moving around, some of them barking and wagging their tails. Monty quickly opened their cages, scooped them out two at a time, and dropped them out the window.

"Lead these pups to the fence, old man," he said as Ned came over with Molly.

"Right," Ned replied. He let Monty hold the dying cat as he painfully got his arthritic legs over the ledge and lowered himself to the ground. "What about you?" he asked as Monty handed down the cat.

"I'm gonna turn a few more pups loose, an' maybe some of those rabbits they're blinding. You head for the fence—I'll catch up."

Ned limped away from the building, calling the pups

to follow him. He led them to the fence, bent the cut section open again, and let them scurry through. As he went through himself, he could feel Molly becoming ever more limp in his hands. By the time he got into the cover of the trees, her eyes had closed, her mouth had opened, and she was dead. Tears coming again, he knelt and put the cat up against a tree trunk and covered her with an old red bandanna he pulled out of his back pocket.

Looking through the fence, he saw that Monty was still putting animals out the window. Two dozen cats, dogs, rabbits, and guinea pigs were moving around tentatively on the grass behind the laboratory. He's got to get out of there or he'll get caught, Ned thought. Returning through the opening in the fence, he hurried back to the window.

"Come on," he urged as the younger man came to the window with a kitten in each hand.

"No—" Monty tossed the kittens to the ground "—I'm going to turn loose every animal that can stand!"

Old man and young man fixed eyes on each other as every difference there had ever been between them faded.

"Give me a hand up, then," Ned said.

Monty reached down and pulled him back up through the window.

As they worked furiously to open more cages and move their captives out the window, they became aware of someone trying the lab door and finding it locked. Several moments later, someone tried it again. A voice outside the door mentioned a key. The two inside the lab worked all the faster. Finally, a sweating

Monty said, "I think that's all we can let go. The rest are too near dead. Let's get out of here!"

"I'm going to do one more thing first," Ned growled.

Poised by the open window, Monty asked, "What?"

Ned walked toward a shelf on which stood several plastic gallon jugs of isopropyl alcohol. "I'm going to burn this son-of-a-bitch down."

Monty rushed over to him. "What about the other animals?"

"You said yourself they were almost dead. At least this will put them out of their misery without any more torture." He opened a jug and started pouring alcohol around the room. After a moment of indecision, Monty joined him.

Five minutes later, just as someone in the hall got the lab door open and several people entered, Ned and Monty dropped out the open window and tossed a lighted book of matches back inside.

The laboratory became a ball of flame.

While the fire spread and the building burned, Ned and Monty managed to get the released animals through the fence and into the woods. Sirens of fire and police emergency vehicles pierced the quiet afternoon. There were screams and shouts as the burning building was evacuated. Monty retrieved the chain cutters and ran toward the car. Ned limped hurriedly after him, but stopped when he got to where Molly was lying under the red bandanna. I can't leave her like that, he thought. She had been a good, loving pet to Ned's wife, then to Ned after his wife died. She deserved to be buried, not left to rot next to a tree. Dropping to his knees, he began to dig a grave with his hands.

Monty rushed back and saw what he was doing. "They gonna catch you, old man!" he warned.

"I don't care."

Ned kept digging as Monty hurried away.

He had barely finished burying Molly a few minutes later when the police found him.

Ned's sentence, because he was a first offender and no one had been hurt in the fire, was three years. He served fourteen months. Monty was waiting for him the day he came back to the block.

"Hey, old man, ex-cons give a neighborhood a bad reputation," Monty chided.

"You ought to know," Ned said gruffly.

"You get the Vienna sausages and crackers and stuff I had sent from the commissary?"

"Yeah." He did not bother to thank Monty; he knew it would only embarrass him.

"So how you like the joint, old man?"

Ned shrugged. "It could have been worse. A sixty-two-year-old man with a game leg, there's not much they could do to me. I worked in the library, checking books out. Did a lot of reading in between. Mostly about animals."

"No kidding?" Monty's eyebrows went up. "I been learning a little bit about animals, too. I'm a, what do you call it, volunteer down at the A.S.P.C.A. That's American Society for the Prevention of Cruelty to Animals."

"I know what it is," said Ned. "Good organization. Say, did that Consumer Evaluation Laboratory ever rebuild?"

"Nope," Monty replied. "You put 'em out of business for good, old man."

"Animal shelter still selling to those other two labs?"

"Far as I know."

"Still got their addresses?"

Monty smiled. "You bet."

"Good," Ned said, nodding. Then he smiled, too.

THE CAT AND
FIDDLE MURDERS

by Edward D. Hoch

The strange chain of events that carried Sir Gideon
Parrot and myself to England in the autumn of last
year need not be recounted here. Suffice it to say
that upon completion of the business at hand we were
invited to spend a few days at a little island off the
Devon Coast. Our host was to be Archibald Knore,
the department-store heir who'd spent ten years and
countless thousands of pounds assembling a private
zoo for the amusement of himself and his friends.

"How do you happen to know Knore?" I asked
Gideon as we made our way across the strip of water
that separated the mainland from Placid Island. Knore's
was one of the largest department-store chains in Brit-
ain, and the invitation to spend a few days in such
illustrious company was most impressive.

"I did the man a favor once," Gideon explained.
"It's not the sort of favor one mentions in polite conversation, and I doubt if he will do so. He was visiting
a young lady of dubious reputation and I helped him
escape just before her apartment was raided by the
police. But this was years ago. I dare say Archibald

has settled down now and devotes his full energies to this private zoo of his."

Right on cue there came a loud trumpeting from the island just ahead. The little mail boat bucked in the water as if startled by the noise and I fastened a grip on Gideon's arm. "What was that?"

"Sounded like an elephant to me. We'll see soon enough—there's the dock straight ahead."

I'd expected Archibald Knore himself to be waiting for us at dockside, but although he wasn't there it was no disappointment. In his stead was as lovely a young woman as I'd ever had the pleasure to meet since leaving New York. She reached down a firm hand to help us onto the dock, then introduced herself with a sunny smile. "I'm Lois Lanchester, Mr. Knore's secretary. Welcome to Placid Island."

"What a nice name for it," Gideon said, bowing to kiss her hand.

She laughed and tossed her mane of yellow hair with one hand. "During the winter storms we sometimes suspect the prior owners chose that name to enhance its value as real estate."

"This is a year-round home, then?" I asked.

She turned, as if noticing me for the first time, and Gideon hurried to introduce me. "Yeah," she said. "Mr. Knore devotes his full time to the zoo these days. The family business is handled by others."

She led the way up to the house, the fit of her designer jeans over her perfectly formed hips snug. When the great house itself came into full view, my gaze was distracted elsewhere. It was a magnificent place, a sprawling English country house that seemed oblivious to its somewhat cramped island setting. And on the lawn to greet us was a strutting peacock, its iridescent tail-feathers erect.

"He's quite a sight," I remarked.

"King Jack is our official greeter. But you'll be seeing more animals soon." As if to confirm her words the trumpet of the distant elephant sounded again.

We entered the house and passed down an oak-paneled corridor to a grimly masculine study where Archibald Knore awaited us. I'd seen newspaper pictures of him once or twice, but they hadn't prepared me for the overwhelming presence of the man himself. He was tall and large without seeming overweight, and his voice seemed to boom across the room. "Sir Gideon! A pleasure to see you again! Come right in!"

He shook my hand vigorously as Gideon introduced me. "He spent a great deal of time in your London store this week," Gideon said.

Knore smiled broadly. "Spending money, I hope. These animals seem to eat more every year."

"We're anxious to see your zoo," I told him. "But isn't a private zoo unusual these days?"

"No. There are privately owned wildlife habitats in several countries. My friend Gerald Durrell, the author, has a very fine zoo on the island of Jersey. Only government regulation prevents many others from existing. I firmly believe that the task of preserving certain rare species could be carried out much more efficiently in private hands. As long as zoos remain dependent upon public funds, those funds are often the first items to be cut in a budget crunch. The point that feeding people is more important than feeding animals is too easily made."

"Why don't I get you two settled," Lois Lanchester suggested, "and then we can show you around?"

"Do that, Lois," Archibald Knore agreed, "and then bring them back downstairs to meet the other guests for cocktails."

On the way up to our rooms Gideon asked about the other guests. "Mr. Knore often has weekend visitors," Lois said. "This weekend it's a cousin, Bertie Foxe, his wife, and a close friend of theirs, the Czech violinist Jan Litost."

Our adjoining rooms were all we could have desired, with comfortable beds and leaded glass windows looking out on the sea. I was thankful the zoo itself was on the other side of the house where the nocturnal noises of the animals were less likely to disturb our sleep.

We'd barely had time to unpack when Lois Lanchester was tapping on our doors with all the exuberance of a shipboard cruise director. "If you're ready I can give you a quick look at the zoo before cocktails," she told us. "Sylvia Foxe wants to come along too."

"It will be a pleasure," Gideon said. "I've always had a great love for animals."

We met the wife of Knore's cousin in the downstairs hall. She was a tall dark-haired woman dressed in riding britches and leather boots. She had no doubt been pretty once but middle age had turned her face hard and stern. "Are there bridle paths on the island?" I asked after Lois had introduced us.

"No," Sylvia replied. "I simply find this costume more suitable for prowling around the animals. I wouldn't want some little creature taking a bite out of my leg."

"There's no danger of that," Lois told her sweetly. We left the house by a rear door and followed a covered walkway to a low cinder-block building. Already the scent of animals was heavy in the air, but Lois explained that only the smallest creatures and most dangerous species of snake were kept indoors.

Never having been one for snakes, I passed quickly by the glass cages with their traditional tree branch upon which a serpent lay sunning itself beneath the artificial light from above. The lizards I found a bit more interesting, especially when they were in motion. "The temperature is kept at eighty degrees for the reptiles," Lois explained as she walked us through. "Over there is the bird house with its new penguin pond. But let me show you some of the big cats first."

The lions and tigers were kept in large open pits, with plenty of space to roam about and trees for climbing. "In the coldest weather we take them indoors," Lois said.

"Who takes care of the animals?" Gideon Parrot asked, his eyes on a large tiger that seemed to be feasting on its afternoon meal.

"We have a full-time zookeeper on the staff. His name is Taupper. You'll meet him later. He—" She paused, watching the tiger now, along with Gideon. "My god! That looks like a human body in the tiger pit!"

"It most certainly does," Gideon confirmed. "You'd better call for help."

We were above it now, and as the tiger rolled it over with one powerful paw Sylvia Foxe gasped, "It's Jan! It's our friend Jan Litost!"

A burly man in work clothes I took to be the zookeeper came running in answer to Lois's summons. While he was lowering a ladder into the pit Gideon pulled me aside and pointed to a large sheet of paper that had been tacked to a nearby tree. In large child-like letters were printed some familiar words: HIGH DIDDLE, DIDDLE, THE CAT AND THE FIDDLE.

"He was murdered," Archibald Knore said some twenty minutes later. "There's no doubt in my mind."

"Murdered by someone on this island?" Lois Lanchester asked.

We were back at the main house, gathered about the big stone fireplace where cocktails were to have been served. Sylvia Foxe's husband Bertie had joined us, a slender man with thinning hair. "It *can't* be murder," he insisted. "Who on this island could have any possible motive for killing Jan?"

"The back of his skull was crushed," Knore argued. "He was hit very hard with a blunt instrument of some sort. And there are spots of blood on the railing surrounding the tiger pit. Someone killed him and dumped him in there. As to who would have a motive, that's for the police to discover."

"Have they been summoned?" Gideon asked.

"I'll do that now."

But his telephone call to the mainland didn't bring the prompt response we desired. The local constable informed Knore that all the boats were tied up with a rescue mission down the coast and with the winds increasing as darkness approached the police helicopter couldn't make the flight over to the island until morning. "Don't touch anything," his voice crackled. "We'll be there first thing in the morning."

Archibald Knore slammed down the telephone. "The old fool! If there's a murderer loose on this island we could all be dead by morning!"

"The winds are picking up outside," Sylvia Foxe said. "It looks like a storm."

"No storm," the zookeeper said. "The animals aren't that restless." It was the first time Peter Taupper had spoken since he'd lifted the body of Jan Litost from the pit. He was a burly, unkempt man with tufts of gray hair protruding from his ears. I wondered if Knore paid him as much as a municipal zoo would, though I had no idea what good public or private zookeepers earned.

At this point Gideon Parrot cleared his throat and the room fell silent. "In the absence of the official police I may be of some service," he announced. "I was invited here as a guest, but Archibald knows I've had some experience in matters of this nature. I propose we take a few moments to examine the facts."

"What facts?" Lois asked.

"Well, if someone on this island is a murderer we need to know exactly how many people are here."

"That's easy," she responded, counting them off on her fingers. "You two, myself, Mr. Knore, Mrs. Knore—"

"Wait a minute," Gideon interrupted. "Is your wife on the island, Archibald?"

"Dora has been crippled for some years now. She never leaves her room."

"I see. Go on, please, Miss Lanchester."

"O.K. Mrs. Knore, Mr. and Mrs. Foxe, Peter Taupper, his assistant Milo Lune who also tends to the gardening, and of course the butler, the maid, and the cook. There is also a nurse who tends to Mrs. Knore, but this is her day off."

"Then there are twelve people on the island at the present time, not counting the unforunate Mr. Litost."

"That's correct."

"Who tends to Mrs. Knore when the nurse is away?"

Knore answered the question. "The maid does. She's quite efficient."

"Mr. and Mrs. Foxe," Gideon said. "You brought the victim to this island. Suppose you tell me a bit about him."

Bertie Foxe snorted. "No one has to be told about Jan Litost. He was one of Europe's foremost violinists—he wasn't yet forty years old! It's a terrible loss to the world of music!"

"Had he a wife? A lover?"

"I believe he was married in his youth, but he'd been alone for many years. We met him in London last season and became fast friends. It was I who suggested he might want to visit Archibald's private zoo."

"When did you arrive?"

"Yesterday afternoon."

Gideon turned to Mrs. Foxe. "And how is it you hadn't viewed the animals until today?"

"I was indisposed when we arrived," Sylvia Foxe explained. "It was a rough crossing by boat just after lunch—my stomach was unprepared for it."

"But your husband and the late Mr. Litost had toured the zoo?"

"I took them around yesterday," Knore volunteered, "and Peter showed them the giraffe and the zebras this morning. They're kept farther out, away from the house."

Another man in work clothes, somewhat younger than Taupper, entered during the conversation. Taupper introduced him to Gideon and me. "This is my assistant, Milo Lune."

The man seemed unusually shy. He rubbed his dirty hands against the legs of his work pants as he answered Gideon's questions. "Did I see Mr. Litost this afternoon? No—well, yes, I think I did spot him strolling by the monkey cages but only at a distance. I didn't speak with him."

"Is something the matter?" Gideon asked. "You seem nervous."

"No, no—it's just I'm worried about the animals is all."

Gideon next produced the crudely printed note he'd discovered tacked to the tree. "Did any of you see this before? I found it on a tree near the scene."

"It looks like the work of a child," Lois Lanchester said.

"Are there any children on Placid Island?"

"No."

Archibald Knore came forward to study the message. "A child's nursery rhyme. What does it mean?"

"The cat and the fiddle could refer to the tiger and Jan Litost."

"The rhyme is believed to be a reference to Queen Elizabeth the First," Bertie Foxe said. "I've made a study of nursery rhymes."

"Notice the location of the commas in the message," Gideon said, holding it up again.

HIGH DIDDLE, DIDDLE, THE CAT AND THE FIDDLE,

"What about it?" Lois asked.

"Not many persons would place commas between those two 'diddles,' yet that is the correct version of the rhyme. The person who wrote this was no child.

Note too the comma at the end of the line. What does that tell us?"

"That there's more to come," Lois answered quietly.

There was always the possibility of another person on the island, perhaps an escaped convict who'd come out by boat from the mainland and remained hidden back there among the animals. Knore suggested a search party be organized and I readily agreed to be part of it. Gideon, who walked slowly at best, decided to stay behind and question the servants about anything unusual they might have seen.

I found myself with Bertie Foxe, Peter Taupper, and Milo Lune, making a sweep of the far end of the island. There was a dense wooded area here, with only a high fence to indicate the outer limits of the zoo itself. "No one's here," Milo Lune said. "I'm back here a few days a week and nothing's been disturbed. We're wasting our time."

"We should split up," Foxe suggested. "We'd cover the ground much quicker."

The zookeeper, Taupper, agreed readily enough. "Why don't we spread out and keep walking in a counter-clockwise direction? Then meet back at the house?"

I found myself on the far right of the sweep, close to the rocky shoreline with a view of the water. The others were out of sight within minutes and I eyed the setting sun uncertainly, hoping I'd make it back before dark. But the island wasn't as large as I'd feared and it took me only a quarter of an hour to circle around, following the shoreline until the big house was in sight once more.

But now there were only three of us.

Taupper's assistant, Milo Lune, was missing.

"Where the hell is he?" Taupper demanded, and tried shouting his name. There was no reply.

"Shall we go back?" Foxe suggested. "It'll be dark soon."

"He'll show up," Taupper said, a bit uncertainly.

We were standing, uncertain of our next move, when a window high in the house opened and Sylvia Foxe's head appeared. "There's someone in the elephant enclosure!" she shouted. "I can see him from here!"

I took a deep breath and followed quickly after the others. When we reached the elephant enclosure I saw at once what Sylvia had spotted from her window. Milo Lune was crumpled near the fence of the enclosure while one of the smaller elephants nudged the body with its trunk. The back of his head was battered and bloody, but I was beyond blaming the injury on an elephant's hoof. I wasn't even surprised a few minutes later when Gideon Parrot joined us and snatched another message off a nearby tree.

"THE COW JUMP'D OVER THE MOON," he read.

After a dinner eaten quickly in gloomy silence, we gathered in Archibald Knore's study to sort out what few facts we had in our possession. Knore himself had tried to reach the mainland again, but without success. "The phone is dead," he reported. "It may be because of the heavy winds, or—"

"Or the line may have been cut," Sylvia Foxe supplied. "God, we're trapped on this island with a madman!"

"We must all stay together," Knore agreed. He turned toward Gideon Parrot and said, "I think you and your friend had better double up for the night. Bertie and Sylvia will be together and I will be with my wife." He paused, trying to puzzle out the rest of it. "Lois, you'd better share a room with the maid and cook. And, Peter, you can sleep with the butler."

"Old Oakes?" the zookeeper snorted. "He snores so loud he keeps the animals awake! I'll take my chances alone, thanks!"

We'd already been over the timing of Milo Lune's killing and everyone agreed that either Bertie or Peter Taupper could have done it—or even myself, for that matter. But it was just as likely that someone from the house, or a hidden stranger, could have surprised him with that terrible blow to the head.

"But how could he let anyone approach him with a club or anything after what happened to Jan Litost?" Lois asked. "It doesn't make sense."

"The killer might have been well hidden and struck before he was seen," Gideon suggested.

"But he'd have to push the body into the elephant enclosure," I pointed out. "With the rest of us in the area, someone would be sure to see him."

"But no one did," Gideon replied. "So apparently it wasn't such a risk, after all." He turned to Sylvia Foxe. "You were watching from your window. Did you see anything?"

She shook her head. "Not until I noticed the body. But I wasn't at the window for very long. I'd just come up from downstairs. I went to see if Bertie was in sight anywhere and I spotted what looked like a body."

Gideon turned to Archibald Knore. "Where were you during this time?"

"Alone here in the study. You certainly can't suspect *me* of killing them!"

"I suspect everyone. It's the only way. In fact, I must ask you the same question, Miss Lanchester."

Lois flushed prettily and stammered a bit. "Well, I—well, I was using one of the upstairs bathrooms. My stomach's been in knots since Jan's body was found. I wasn't feeling well."

"Perfectly understandable," Gideon agreed.

Knore came out from behind his desk. "The killer is no one here. It's some madman who murders whoever he finds alone. Jan and Milo were simply unlucky."

But Gideon shook his head, like a professor correcting a wayward student. "No, they were the intended victims. We know that from the nursery rhyme. The cat was the tiger, and the fiddle was a reference to the violinist, Jan Litost."

"But how," Knore asked, "does this latest message pertain to Lune and the elephants?"

"Lune is the French word for moon, of course. I noticed some smaller elephants in that enclosure." He turned to the zookeeper. "Mr. Taupper, if male elephants are called bulls, what are the females called?"

"Cows," Taupper answered quietly. "Everyone knows that."

"Thus, the cow jumped over the moon—and crushed his skull while doing it."

"What's the rest of the rhyme?" Bertie Foxe asked after a moment's silence. "Nothing about foxes in it, is there?"

"No," Gideon answered seriously. "In its earliest version the verse reads, High diddle, diddle, The Cat and the Fiddle, The Cow jump'd over the Moon; The little Dog laugh'd To see such Craft, And the Dish ran away with the Spoon."

"You remember all that?" Lois asked.

"During this afternoon's search I looked it up in *The Oxford Dictionary of Nursery Rhymes*. There's a copy in the library."

"Where anyone else could have looked it up too," I observed. "That's how they got the punctuation right."

"Perhaps."

"The little Dog laugh'd To see such Craft," Knore repeated. "I don't see how that can apply to anyone here. And there are no dogs on the island.".

"We can't have them," Taupper explained. "They'd upset the animals with their barking."

"Then maybe the chain will be broken," Lois said. "Maybe the killer's work is finished."

Gideon Parrot said nothing. He was staring at a photograph on Knore's desk, obviously a portrait of Knore and his wife when they were much younger. "I think we must speak with Mrs. Knore," he said quietly.

"She knows nothing," Knore protested. "She never leaves her room."

"But things can be seen from a window. Sylvia Foxe saw a body from her window. Your wife might have seen the killer."

Archibald Knore was silent for a moment. Finally he said, "Very well. You and your friend can see her. But only for a few minutes. I'll take you up."

The upper reaches of the house seemed unusually dark, with only a dim bulb at the top of the stairs to light the way. The maid who'd been sitting with Dora

Knore rose as we entered and Archibald dismissed her with a wave of his hand.

The woman in the bed seemed about Knore's age but she was very thin and rather feeble in her gestures. "You've brought me visitors, Archie," she said in a soft voice. "How nice."

"This is Sir Gideon Parrot, dear. He's investigating the trouble I told you about."

"The killings?"

"Yes."

"Terrible things! We moved here to get away from crime in the cities. After my accident I couldn't walk any more—"

"Might I ask what caused it?" Gideon asked her.

"An auto crash. Archie was driving and the car went off the road. I think he was dozing a bit but I've never blamed him for what happened."

"Mrs. Knore," Gideon began, keeping his voice soft to match hers, "I was wondering if you might have seen anything today from your window at about the time either of those men were killed."

"Oh, no. I never get out of bed. The nurse or Winifred—the maid—tells me what I need to know, which is very little. The weather makes no impact on my life and the animals are Archie's hobby, not mine."

"So you saw or heard nothing?"

"Not a thing."

Her eyes closed for a moment and Knore took that as a signal she was tiring. "That's all," he said.

When we were in the hall Gideon asked, "Wouldn't she be more comfortable in a wheelchair, with the rest of us?"

"No, no," her husband said. "She's fine as she is. She wants it this way."

Back downstairs, plans were again made for the sleeping arrangements. Everyone would be safe through the remainder of the night. And in the morning the police would come.

That, at least, is what we thought.

But in the morning, as Gideon and I were arising before breakfast, Peter Taupper brought news of the latest outrage. The island's only boat had been scuttled at its dock and now lay in eight feet of water. Tacked to one of the mooring posts was the expected message: THE LITTLE DOG LAUGH'D TO SEE SUCH CRAFT,

The telephone was still dead and the winds were still high. We were cut off from the mainland with a killer who showed no sign of stopping.

Over breakfast Archibald Knore said, "At least no one was killed this time."

"No," Lois Lanchester murmured. "Not yet. But there's still one line of the nursery rhyme to go." She was helping to serve the breakfast and, taking a sip of Knore's hot porridge with a spoon before she placed the bowl in front of him, she said, "Tastes good."

The Foxes were together at the end of the table, looking unhappy, and Taupper stood in the doorway with a cup of coffee, explaining how he'd happened to find the damaged boat. "I went down to the dock to see if any boats were coming over from the mainland. That's when I saw her sunk in the water. Somebody whacked the side of it with an axe—below the water line, near as I could tell. It was probably done last night, before we all went to bed."

"But what sense does the message make?" Bertie

Foxe asked. "I understand that the craft refers to the boat, but there's still no dog on the island."

"Nor anyone whose name sounds like dog," Sylvia chimed in.

Knore looked unhappy. "My wife Dora. *Dora* and *dog* start with the same two letters, but that's a bit farfetched."

"It certainly is," Lois agreed. "Your wife is the one person on the island who *can't* be involved. She never leaves her *room.*"

"It's obvious the killer intends to complete the verse," Gideon said. "It's important that we anticipate his actions and beat him to it."

"What is it? *And the Dish ran away with the Spoon?* What could that possibly mean?" I asked.

"I think we're worrying needlessly," Taupper said. "As soon as the winds die down, the helicopter will be over from the mainland."

"Can the boat be repaired?" Knore asked.

"Certainly. Anything can be repaired."

"Can it be repaired by you?"

"I think so. I can patch it and pump out the water."

"Then do it, man! Quickly!"

Sylvia Foxe cleared her throat. "Might I suggest that someone should go with him? If he's down there alone the killer might get ideas."

"Good thinking," her husband said.

"Lois, how about you?" Sylvia suggested. "Or would you rather I go?"

Lois Lanchester finished her morning coffee and stubbed out her cigarette. "I'll be glad to go, but I don't know that I'll be of much help. What say, Peter? Do you need me?"

Taupper grinned. "You can hold my tools. Come along."

After they'd left, Gideon and I went for a walk outside. The unsettled weather had made the animals restless, and the camels shied away as we approached their pen. Over beyond it the zoo's young giraffe was romping in the tall grass and two zebras grazed nearby. "A peaceful place," Gideon said. "The peaceable kingdom—even with a killer loose."

"Gideon," I said, "I've got a theory. Suppose the animals really did kill Litost and Lune. Suppose those crazy notes were written afterward by Taupper to protect his precious animals."

"An interesting theory, but hardly a practical one. The rhyme doesn't fit the events perfectly, but there is some connection. It could hardly have been a spur-of-the-moment idea in the first case, and the coincidence of a second killing accidentally fitting the pattern is out of the question."

"What now?"

He'd turned to stare up at the great old house. "I think we should speak to Bertie Foxe."

We found Bertie and his wife upstairs in their room where they'd gone after breakfast. It was a big sunny bedroom, larger than the one Gideon and I were now sharing but similarly furnished. Bertie sat on the bed smoking while Sylvia stared out the window at the animals.

"I want to know more about Jan Litost," Gideon said. "He was the first victim and the key to this puzzle must lie with him."

"Jan was extremely talented," Bertie Foxe said, taking a long drag on his cigarette. "We'd been friends for years and it seemed a natural thing to accept Archibald's kind invitation to visit the zoo after the London concert."

"Did the three of you travel together frequently?"

"Quite frequently," Sylvia answered from the window.

"You'll forgive me but I must ask this next question. Was there any sort of romantic involvement between yourself and Jan, Mrs. Foxe, which might have made your husband jealous?"

"See here!" Bertie barked, jumping to his feet.

But Sylvia answered calmly, "Certainly not. Bertie and I are happily married and always have been."

"There was nothing between them!" Bertie growled, stepping forward. "Take your dirty little thoughts elsewhere, Parrot!"

Gideon walked to the window and stared out across the tiled roof of the zoo building. He seemed to be looking at the tops of the elephants' heads, barely visible in their enclosure, as he said, "We're all like those animals at times. We meet, and mate, and sometimes kill. It's human nature, or the animal side of human nature, for the males to clash over a female—"

His words were interrupted by a sharp scream from somewhere downstairs.

"Come on!" I shouted, breaking for the door.

We found Archibald Knore at the foot of the stairs, holding onto the maid, Winifred. "What is it?" Gideon demanded as we hurried down to join them.

"I lost my head," Knore muttered, releasing the girl at once. "I was questioning her and she told me a lie. When I grabbed her she screamed."

"A lie about what?"

Winifred was sobbing softly. "He accused me of

wantin' to run off with Mr. Oakes, the butler. I never would do a thing like that, sir."

"They've been carrying on behind my back. I know they have!"

"And the Dish ran away with the Spoon," Gideon quoted. "You thought it referred to your butler and maid."

"What else could it refer to?" Knore said. "They did it and now they're going to run off."

"You think the butler did it?" I asked in amazement.

"You have books on nursery rhymes in the library. Let's check them," Gideon suggested to Knore, "and let this young woman be about her work."

The library, next to Knore's study, was a pleasant room with books reaching from floor to ceiling and the odor of leather bindings in the air. It took Gideon only a few moments' search to find what he sought. "See here—the same theory that links the rhyme to Queen Elizabeth says that the Dish was a courtier honored by being assigned to carry golden dishes into the state dining room."

"A butler, in other words," Knore insisted.

"Or a custodian of something valuable, at least. And the Spoon was a beautiful young woman at court who was taster at the royal meals, insuring that the king or queen had not been poisoned."

"I know all that," Knore grumbled. "It still adds up to butler and maid in this household."

"If you'll pardon me," said Gideon, "the maid, Winifred, could hardly be described as beautiful. And the duties of taster seem more closely to resemble your secretary, Lois. In fact, I saw her taste the breakfast porridge just a few minutes ago."

"That's right!" I agreed.

"Lois?" Knore repeated, frowning with puzzlement.

The Foxes had come back downstairs, and as we left the library I saw Sylvia emerge from the kitchen carrying a rolled-up newspaper in her gloved hand. "I'm going outside for a little reading," she said. "Call me if anything happens, Bertie."

Bertie Fox grunted and said to us, "How do you suppose Taupper's coming along with the boat repairs?"

"Want me to take a look?" I said. But Gideon ignored the question. His mind was still on the problem of the rhyme.

"If the Spoon referred to Lois Lanchester, couldn't the Plate refer not to the butler but to the custodian of your most valuable property, Archibald?"

Knore looked puzzled. "I have no gold."

"The animals, man! Peter Taupper is the custodian of your animals! He is the Plate of the rhyme!"

"Taupper and Lois?" I asked. "You think they're running away together?"

"That's the only way the rhyme can work out," Gideon answered grimly. "Come quickly—there's not a moment to lose."

He led the way, with Knore, Bertie, and me following along. We hurried out of the house and down the path toward the boat dock. I was vaguely aware that the morning's strong winds had let up, but right now we were concerned with more important matters than the weather.

It was the note that stopped us, at the final turn before the boat landing. It had been tacked to a tree like the others, and it read: AND THE DISH RAN AWAY WITH THE SPOON. This time the period was firmly in place at the end of the line. A finish had been reached.

"We're too late," I said.

"Maybe not!" Gideon plunged on and I followed, outdistancing the others.

The first thing we saw was Peter Taupper's body sprawled by the dock, and then Lois struggling with Sylvia Foxe. Sylvia's newspaper lay near Taupper. As Gideon and I hurried to pull them apart I said, "What happened? Did Sylvia come upon them as they were about to get away?"

"That's what it was," Sylvia gasped, struggling in my grip. "Turn me loose!"

But Gideon cautioned, "Hang onto her! She was about to add two more victims to her list! Sylvia Foxe is our nursery-rhyme murderess!"

Peter Taupper had only been stunned by the blow, and he and Lois were able to confirm the attack by Sylvia. She'd used the rolled-up newspaper, which she had soaked in water and put into the kitchen freezer until it froze into a club of ice. The victims never suspected a thing when they saw her walking toward them with a newspaper. All she needed was a reasonable amount of strength behind that ice club to crush their skulls. And the weapon could be dropped anywhere unnoticed.

"I *saw* her coming out of the kitchen with the paper," I confirmed. "But why did she want to kill them all?"

"I expect Bertie can tell us about the first murder," Gideon said.

Bertie Foxe hung his head. "I always suspected Jan was having an affair with my wife. I spoke to him about it back in London, man to man, and I had the impression he was going to break it off."

"I imagine he tried to," Gideon agreed. "That's why she killed him. Then when she saw Milo Lune working nearby she must have feared he'd seen her. So he had to die too. The fact that Litost was a violinist and Lune's name means 'moon' must have suggested the nursery rhyme to her as a means of putting us off the track. But in truth it put us *on* the track. In the original rhyme and in her messages, there were eight words beginning with capital letters besides the first word in each line. There are Cat, Fiddle, Cow, Moon, Dog, Craft, Dish, and Spoon. She gave each one the meaning of a person, animal, or thing. Cat was the tiger, Fiddle was Litost, Cow was the female elephant, Moon was Lune, Craft was the sunken boat, Dish was Taupper, for reasons I've explained, and Spoon was Lois."

"What about Dog?" I asked.

"It was a clue to her own identity. A fox is indeed a member of the dog family, and when no other meaning presented itself I saw what she meant—*The little Dog laughed,* just as Sylvia Foxe herself must have laughed when the boat sank."

"She was going to kill Taupper and Lois just to finish the rhyme?" Knore asked.

"I imagine she would have weighted their bodies and pushed them off the dock. If they had seemed to run away, as in the rhyme, we would have blamed them for the prior killings."

Lois Lanchester still couldn't believe it. "And you knew all this just because a fox is a member of the dog family? Why couldn't the killer have been Bertie Foxe instead of Sylvia?"

"There were other things," Gideon admitted. "It was Sylvia who persuaded you to accompany Taupper to the dock, where she could kill you both. And remember yesterday when Sylvia called down from her window that she saw Lune's body up against the fence in the elephant enclosure? When I stood at that same window this morning I could barely see the tops of the elephants' heads. The zoo building blocked the view. She could only have known about the body if she'd put it there herself a few minutes earlier."

There was a throbbing in the sky and we looked up to see the police helicopter coming in for a landing. Out beyond the big house one of the elephants trumpeted a greeting.

THE CYPRIAN CAT

by Dorothy L. Sayers

It's extraordinarily decent of you to come along and see me like this, Harringay. Believe me, I do appreciate it. It isn't every busy K.C. who'd do as much for such a hopeless sort of client. I only wish I could spin you a more workable kind of story, but honestly I can only tell you exactly what I told Peabody. Of course, I can see he doesn't believe a word of it, and I don't blame him. He thinks I ought to be able to make up a more plausible tale than that, and I suppose I could, but where's the use? One's almost bound to fall down somewhere if one tries to swear to a lie. What I'm going to tell you is the absolute truth. I fired one shot and one shot only, and that was at the cat. It's funny that one should be hanged for shooting a cat.

Merridew and I were always the best of friends, school and college and all that sort of thing. We didn't see very much of each other after the war, because we were living at opposite ends of the country; but we met in town from time to time and wrote occasionally, and each of us knew that the other was there in the background, so to speak. Two years ago he wrote and told me he was getting married. He was just turned forty and the girl was fifteen years younger, and he was tremendously in love. It gave me a bit of a jolt. You know how it is when your friends marry. You feel they will never be quite the same again, and I'd got used to the idea that Merridew and I were cut out to be old bachelors. But of course I congratulated him and sent him a wedding present, and I did sincerely hope he'd be happy. He was obviously over head and ears, almost dangerously so, I thought, considering all things. Though except for the difference of age, it seemed suitable enough. He told me he had met her at—of all places—a rectory garden party down in Norfolk, and that she had actually never been out of her native village. I mean literally—not so much as a trip to the nearest town. I'm not trying to convey that she wasn't pukka, or anything like that. Her father was some queer sort of recluse—a medievalist or something—desperately poor. He died shortly after their marriage.

I didn't see anything of them for the first year or so. Merridew is a civil engineer, you know, and he took his wife away after the honeymoon to Liverpool, where he was doing something in connection with the harbor. It must have been a big change for her from the wilds of Norfolk. I was in Birmingham, with my nose kept pretty close to the grindstone, so we only exchanged occasional letters. His were what I can only call deliriously happy, especially at first. Later on, he seemed a little worried about his wife's health. She was restless; town life didn't suit her; he'd be glad when he could finish up his Liverpool job and get her away into the country. There wasn't any doubt about their happiness, you understand. She'd got him body and soul as they say, and as far as I could make out it was mutual. I want to make that perfectly clear.

Well, to cut a long story short, Merridew wrote to

me at the beginning of last month and said he was just off to a new job, a waterworks extension scheme down in Somerset, and he asked if I could possibly cut loose and join them there for a few weeks. He wanted to have a yarn with me, and Felice was longing to make my acquaintance. They had got rooms at the village inn. It was rather a remote spot, but there was fishing and scenery and so forth, and I should be able to keep Felice company while he was working up at the dam. I was about fed up with Birmingham, what with the heat and one thing and another, and it looked pretty good to me, and I was due for a holiday anyhow, so I fixed up to go. I had a bit of business to do in town, which I calculated would take me about a week, so I said I'd go down to Little Hexham on June 20.

As it happened, my business in London finished itself off unexpectedly soon, and on the sixteenth I found myself absolutely free and stuck in a hotel with road drills working just under the windows and a tar-spraying machine to make things livelier. You remember what a hot month it was—flaming June and no mistake about it. I didn't see any point in waiting, so I sent off a wire to Merridew, packed my bag, and took the train for Somerset the same evening. I couldn't get a compartment to myself, but I found a first-class smoker with only three seats occupied and stowed myself thankfully into the fourth corner. There was a military-looking old boy, an elderly female with a lot of bags and baskets, and a girl. I thought I should have a nice peaceful journey.

So I should have, if it hadn't been for the unfortunate way I'm built. It was quite all right at first. As a matter of fact, I think I was half asleep, and I only woke up properly at seven o'clock, when the waiter came to say that dinner was on. The other people weren't taking it, and when I came back from the restaurant car I found that the old boy had gone, and there were only the two women left. I settled down in my corner again, and gradually, as we went along, I found a horrible feeling creeping over me that there was a cat in the compartment somewhere. I'm one of those wretched people who can't stand cats. I don't mean just that I prefer dogs. I mean that the presence of a cat in the same room with me makes me feel like nothing on earth. I can't describe it, but I believe quite a lot of people are affected that way. Something to do with electricity, or so they tell me. I've read that very often the dislike is mutual, but it isn't so with me. The brutes seem to find me abominably fascinating, make a beeline for my legs every time. It's a funny sort of complaint, and it doesn't make me at all popular with dear old ladies.

Anyway, I began to feel more and more awful, and I realized that the old girl at the other end of the seat must have a cat in one of her innumerable baskets. I thought of asking her to put it out in the corridor or calling the guard and having it removed, but I knew how silly it would sound and made up my mind to try and stick it. I couldn't say the animal was misbehaving itself or anything, and she looked a pleasant old lady; it wasn't her fault that I was a freak. I tried to distract my mind by looking at the girl.

She was worth looking at, too—very slim and dark with one of those dead-white skins that make you think of magnolia blossom. She had the most astonishing eyes, too—I've never seen eyes quite like them—a very pale brown, almost amber, set wide apart and a little slanting, and they seemed to have a kind of luminosity of their own, if you get what I mean. I don't know if this sounds—I don't want you to think I was bowled over or anything. As a matter of fact, she held no sort of attraction for me, though I could imagine a different type of man going potty about her. She was just unusual, that was all. But however much I tried to think of other things I couldn't get rid of the uncomfortable feeling, and eventually I gave it up and went out into the corridor. I just mention this because it will help you to understand the rest of the story. If you can only realize how perfectly awful I feel when there's a cat about—even when it's shut up in a basket—you'll understand better how I came to buy the revolver.

Well, we got to Hexham Junction, which was the nearest station to Little Hexham, and there was old Merridew waiting on the platform. The girl was getting out too—but not the old lady with the cat, thank goodness—and I was just handing her traps out after her when he came galloping up and hailed us.

"Hullo," he said, "why that's splendid! Have you introduced yourselves?" So I tumbled to it then that the girl was Mrs. Merridew, who'd been up to Town on a shopping expedition, and I explained to her about my change of plans, and she said how jolly it was that I could come—the usual things. I noticed what an attractive low voice she had and how graceful her movements were, and I understood—though, mind you, I didn't share—Merridew's infatuation.

We got into his car; Mrs. Merridew sat in the back, and I got up beside Merridew and was very glad to feel the air and to get rid of the oppressive electric feeling I'd had in the train. He told me the place

suited them wonderfully and had given Felice an absolutely new lease on life, so to speak. He said he was
very fit, too, but I thought myself that he looked
rather fagged and nervy.

You'd have liked that inn, Harringay. The real, old-
fashioned stuff, as quaint as you make 'em, and everything genuine—none of your Tottenham Court Road
antiques. We'd all had our grub, and Mrs. Merridew
said she was tired; so she went up to bed early, and
Merridew and I had a drink and went for a stroll
around the village. It's a tiny hamlet quite at the other
end of nowhere; lights out at ten, little thatched
houses with pinched-up attic windows like furry ears.
The place purred in its sleep. Merridew's working
gang didn't sleep there, of course; they'd put up huts
for them at the dams, a mile beyond the village.

The landlord was just locking up the bar when we
came in, a block of a man with an absolutely expressionless face. His wife was a thin, sandy-haired woman
who looked as though she was too downtrodden to
open her mouth. But I found out afterward that was
a mistake, for one evening when he'd taken one or
two over the eight and showed signs of wanting to
make a night of it, his wife sent him off upstairs with
a gesture and a look that took the heart out of him.
That first night she was sitting on the porch and hardly
glanced at us as we passed her. I always thought her
an uncomfortable kind of woman, but she certainly
kept her house most exquisitely neat and clean.

They'd given me a noble bedroom, close under the
eaves with a long, low casement window overlooking
the garden. The sheets smelled of lavender, and I was
between them and asleep almost before you could
count ten. I was tired, you see. But later in the night

I woke up. I was too hot, so took off some of the blankets and then strolled across to the window to get a breath of air. The garden was bathed in moonshine, and on the lawn I could see something twisting and turning oddly. I stared a bit before I made it out to be two cats. They didn't worry me at that distance, and I watched them for a bit before I turned in again. They were rolling over one another and jumping away again and chasing their own shadows on the grass, intent on their own mysterious business, taking themselves seriously, the way cats always do. It looked like a kind of ritual dance. Then something seemed to startle them, and they scampered away.

I went back to bed, but I couldn't get to sleep again. My nerves seemed to be all on edge. I lay watching the window and listening to a kind of soft rustling noise that seemed to be going on in the big wisteria that ran along my side of the house. And then something landed with a soft thud on the sill—a great Cyprian cat.

What did you say? Well, one of those striped gray-and-black cats. Tabby, that's right. In my part of the country they call them Cyprus cats, or Cyprian cats. I'd never seen such a monster. It stood with its head cocked sideways, staring into the room and rubbing its ears very softly against the upright bar of the casement.

Of course, I couldn't do with that. I shooed the brute away, and it made off without a sound. Heat or no heat, I shut and fastened the window. Far out in the shrubbery I thought I heard a faint meowing, then silence. After that, I went straight off to sleep again and lay like a log till the girl came in to call me.

The next day Merridew ran us up in his car to see

the place where they were making the dam, and that was the first time I realized that Felice's nerviness had not been altogether cured. He showed us where they had diverted part of the river into a swift little stream that was to be used for working the dynamo of an electrical plant. There were a couple of planks laid across the stream, and he wanted to take us over to show us the engine. It wasn't extraordinarily wide or dangerous, but Mrs. Merridew peremptorily refused to cross it and got quite hysterical when he tried to insist. Eventually he and I went over and inspected the machinery by ourselves. When we got back, she had recovered her temper and apologized for being so silly. Merridew abased himself, of course, and I began to feel a little *de trop*. She told me afterward that she had once fallen into the river as a child and been nearly drowned, and it had left her with what d'ye call it—a complex about running water. And but for this one trifling episode, I never heard a single sharp word pass between them all the time I was there; nor, for a whole week, did I notice anything else to suggest a flaw in Mrs. Merridew's radiant health. Indeed, as the days wore on to midsummer and the heat grew more intense, her whole body seemed to glow with vitality. It was as though she was lit up from within.

Merridew was out all day and working very hard. I thought he was overdoing it and asked him if he was sleeping badly. He told me that, on the contrary, he fell asleep every night the moment his head touched the pillow and—what was most unusual with him— had no dreams of any kind. I myself felt well enough, but the hot weather made me languid and disinclined for exertion. Mrs. Merridew took me out for long drives in the car. I would sit for hours, lulled into a half slumber by the rush of warm air and the purring of the engine and gazing at my driver, upright at the wheel, her eyes fixed unwaveringly upon the spinning road. We explored the whole of the country to the south and east of Little Hexham, and once or twice went as far north as Bath. Once I suggested that we should turn eastward over the bridge and run down into what looked like rather beautiful wooded country, but Mrs. Merridew didn't care for the idea; she said it was a bad road and that the scenery on that side was disappointing.

Altogether I spent a pleasant week at Little Hexham, and if it had not been for the cats I should have been perfectly comfortable. Every night the garden seemed to be haunted by them—the Cyprian cat that I had seen the first night of my stay, a little ginger one, and a horrible stinking black tom were especially tiresome. And one night there was a terrified white kitten that mewed for an hour on end under my window. I flung boots and books at my visitors till I was heartily weary, but they seemed determined to make the inn garden their rendezvous. The nuisance grew worse from night to night; on one occasion I counted fifteen of them, sitting on their hinder ends in a circle, while the Cyprian cat danced her shadow dance among them, working in and out like a weaver's shuttle. I had to keep my window shut, for the Cyprian cat evidently made a habit of climbing up by the wisteria. The door, too, for once when I had gone down to fetch something from the sitting room, I found her on my bed, kneading the coverlet with her paws— *pr'rp, pr'rp, pr'rp*—with her eyes closed in a sensuous ecstasy. I beat her off, and she spat at me as she fled into the dark passage.

I asked the landlady about her, but she replied rather curtly that they kept no cat at the inn, and it is true that I never saw any of the beasts in the daytime. One evening, however, about dusk I caught the landlord in one of the outhouses. He had the ginger cat on his shoulder and was feeding her with something that looked like strips of liver. I remonstrated with him for encouraging the cats about the place and asked whether I could have a different room, explaining that the nightly caterwauling disturbed me. He half opened his slits of eyes and murmured that he would ask his wife about it, but nothing was done, and in fact I believe there was no other bedroom in the house.

And all this time the weather got hotter and heavier, working up for thunder, with sky like brass and the earth like iron, and the air quivering over it so that it hurt your eyes to look at it.

All right, Harringay, I am trying to keep to the point. And I'm not concealing anything from you. I say that my relations with Mrs. Merridew were perfectly ordinary. Of course, I saw a good deal of her, because as I explained Merridew was out all day. We went up to the dam with him in the morning and brought the car back, and naturally we had to amuse one another as best we could till the evening. She seemed quite pleased to be in my company, and I couldn't dislike her. I can't tell you what we talked about—nothing in particular. She was not a talkative woman. She would sit or lie for hours in the sunshine, hardly speaking, only stretching out her body to the light and heat. Sometimes she would spend a whole afternoon playing with a twig or a pebble, while I sat and smoked. Restful! No. No, I shouldn't call her a restful personality exactly. Not to me, at any rate. In the evening she would liven up and talk a little more, but she generally went up to bed early and left Merridew and me to yarn together in the garden.

Oh, about the revolver! Yes. I bought that in Bath, when I had been at Little Hexham exactly a week. We drove over in the morning, and while Mrs. Merridew got some things for her husband, I prowled around the secondhand shops. I had intended to get an air gun or a peashooter or something of that kind, when I saw this. You've seen it, of course. It's very tiny—what people in books describe as "little more than a toy"—but deadly enough. The old boy who sold it to me didn't seem to know much about firearms. He'd taken it in pawn sometime back, he told me, and there were ten rounds of ammunition with it. He made no bones about a license or anything, glad enough to make a sale, no doubt, without putting difficulties in a customer's way. I told him I knew how to handle it and mentioned by way of a joke that I meant to take a potshot or two at the cats. That seemed to wake him up a bit. He was a dried-up little fellow, with a scrawny gray beard and a stringy neck. He asked me where I was staying. I told him at Little Hexham.

"You better be careful, sir," he said. "They think a heap of their cats down there, and it's reckoned unlucky to kill them." And then he added something I couldn't quite catch, about a silver bullet. He was a doddering old fellow, and he seemed to have some sort of scruple about letting me take the parcel away, but I assured him that I was perfectly capable of looking after it and myself. I left him standing in the door of his shop, pulling at his beard and staring after me.

That night the thunder came. The sky had turned to lead before evening, but the dull heat was more oppressive than the sunshine. Both the Merridews seemed to be in a state of nerves—he sulking and swearing at the weather and the flies, and she wrought up to a queer kind of vivid excitement. Thunder affects some people that way. I wasn't much better, and to make things worse I got the feeling that the house was full of cats. I couldn't see them, but I knew they were there, lurking behind the cupboards and flitting noiselessly about the corridors. I could scarcely sit in the parlor and was thankful to escape to my room.

Cats or no cats I had to open the window, and I sat there with my pajama jacket unbuttoned, trying to get a breath of air. But the place was like the inside of a copper furnace. And pitch-dark. I could scarcely see from my window where the bushes ended and the lawn began. But I could hear and feel the cats. There were little scrapings in the wisteria and scufflings among the leaves, and about eleven o'clock one of them started the concert with a loud and hideous wail. Then another and another joined in—I'll swear there were fifty of them. And presently I got that foul sensation of nausea, and the flesh crawled on my bones, and I knew that one of them was slinking close to me in the darkness.

I looked around quickly, and there she stood, the great Cyprian, right against my shoulder, her eyes glowing like green lamps. I yelled and struck out at her, and she snarled as she leaped out and down. I heard her thump on the gravel, and the yowling burst out all over the garden with renewed vehemence. And then all in a moment there was utter silence, and in the far distance there came a flickering blue flash and then another. In the first of them I saw the far garden wall, topped along all its length with cats, like a nursery frieze. When the second flash came the wall was empty.

At two o'clock the rain came. For three hours before that I had sat there, watching the lightning as it spat across the sky and exulting in the crash of the thunder. The storm seemed to carry off all the electrical disturbance in my body; I could have shouted with excitement and relief. Then the first heavy drops fell, then a steady downpour, then a deluge. It struck the iron-baked garden with a noise like steel rods falling. The smell of the ground came up intoxicatingly, and the wind rose and flung the rain in against my face. At the other end of the passage I heard a window thrown to and fastened, but I leaned out into the tumult and let the water drench my head and shoulders. The thunder still rumbled intermittently, but with less noise and farther off, and in an occasional flash I saw the white grille of falling water drawn between me and the garden.

It was after one of these thunderpeals that I became aware of a knocking at my door. I opened it, and there was Merridew. He had a candle in his hand, and his face was terrified.

"Felice!" he said abruptly. "She's ill. I can't wake her. For God's sake, come and give me a hand."

I hurried down the passage after him. There were two beds in his room—a great four-poster, hung with crimson damask, and a small camp bedstead drawn up near to the window. The small bed was empty, the bedclothes tossed aside; evidently he had just risen from it. In the four-poster lay Mrs. Merridew, naked, with only a sheet upon her. She was stretched flat

upon her back, her long black hair in two plaits over
her shoulders. He face was waxen and shrunk, like
the face of a corpse, and her pulse, when I felt it, was
so faint that at first I could scarcely feel it. Her breathing was very slow and shallow and her flesh cold. I
shook her, but there was no response at all. I lifted
her eyelids and noticed how the eyeballs were turned
up under the upper lid, so that only the whites were
visible. The touch of my fingertip upon the sensitive
ball evoked no reaction. I immediately wondered
whether she took drugs.

Merridew seemed to think it necessary to make
some explanation. He was babbling about the heat—
she couldn't bear so much as a silk nightgown—she
had suggested that he should occupy the other bed—
he had slept heavily—right through the thunder. The
rain blowing in on his face had aroused him. He had
got up and shut the window. Then he had called to
Felice to know if she was all right; he thought the
storm might have frightened her. There was no answer. He had struck a light. Her condition had
alarmed him, and so on.

I told him to pull himself together and to try
whether, by chafing his wife's hands and feet, we
could restore the circulation. I had it firmly in my
mind that she was under the influence of some opiate.
We set to work, rubbing and pinching and slapping
her with wet towels and shouting her name in her ear.
It was like handling a dead woman, except for the
very slight but perfectly regular rise and fall of her
bosom, on which—with a kind of surprise that there
should be any flaw on its magnolia whiteness—I noticed a large brown mole, just over the heart. To my
perturbed fancy it suggested a wound and a menace.

We had been at it for some time, with the sweat pouring off us, when we became aware of something going on outside the window—a stealthy bumping and scraping against the panes. I snatched up the candle and looked out.

On the sill, the Cyprian cat sat and clawed at the casement. Her drenched fur clung limply to her body; her eyes glared into mine; her mouth was opened in protest. She scrabbled furiously at the latch, her hind claws slipping and scratching on the woodwork. I hammered on the pane and bawled at her, and she struck back at the glass as though possessed. As I cursed her and turned away she set up a long, despairing wail.

Merridew called to me to bring back the candle and leave the brute alone. I returned to the bed, but the dismal crying went on and on incessantly. I suggested to Merridew that he should wake the landlord and get hot-water bottles and some brandy from the bar and see if a messenger could not be sent for a doctor. He departed on this errand, while I went on with my massage. It seemed to me that the pulse was growing still fainter. Then I suddenly recollected that I had a small brandy flask in my bag. I ran out to fetch it, and as I did so the cat suddenly stopped its howling.

As I entered my own room the air blowing through the open window struck gratefully upon me. I found my bag in the dark and was rummaging for the flask among my shirts and socks when I heard a loud, triumphant mew and turned around in time to see the Cyprian cat crouched for a moment on the sill, before it sprang in past me and out at the door. I found the flask and hastened back with it, just as Merridew and the landlord came running up the stairs.

We all went into the room together. As we did so,

Mrs. Merridew stirred, sat up, and asked us what in the world was the matter.

I have seldom felt quite such a fool.

Next day the weather was cooler; the storm had cleared the air. What Merridew had said to his wife I do not know. None of us made any public allusion to the night's disturbance, and to all appearance Mrs. Merridew was in the best of health and spirits. Merridew took a day off from the waterworks, and we all went for a long drive and picnic together. We were on the best of terms with one another. Ask Merridew. He will tell you the same thing. He would not—he could not, surely—say otherwise. I can't believe, Harringay, I simply cannot believe that he could imagine or suspect me. I say, there was nothing to suspect. Nothing.

Yes—this is the important date—the twenty-fourth of June. I can't tell you any more details; there is nothing to tell. We went back and had dinner just as usual. All three of us were together all day, till bedtime. On my honor I had no private interview of any kind that day, either with him or with her. I was the first to go to bed, and I heard the others come upstairs about half an hour later. They were talking cheerfully.

It was a moonlight night. For once, no caterwauling came to trouble me. I didn't even bother to shut the window or the door. I put the revolver on the chair beside me before I lay down. Yes, it was loaded. I had no special object in putting it there, except that I meant to have a go at the cats if they started their games again.

I was desperately tired and thought I should drop off to sleep at once, but I didn't. I must have been overtired, I suppose. I lay and looked at the moon-light. And then, about midnight, I heard what I had been half expecting: a stealthy scrabbling in the wisteria and a faint meowing sound.

I sat up in bed and reached for the revolver. I heard the *plop* as the big cat sprang up onto the window ledge; I saw her black-and-silver flanks and the outline of her round head, pricked ears, and upright tail. I aimed and fired, and the beast let out one frightful cry and sprang down into the room.

I jumped out of bed. The crack of the shot had sounded terrific in the silent house, and somewhere I heard a distant voice call out. I pursued the cat into the passage, revolver in hand, with some idea of finishing it off, I suppose. And then, at the door of the Merridews' room, I saw Mrs. Merridew. She stood with one hand on each doorpost, swaying to and fro. Then she fell down at my feet. Her bare breast was all stained with blood. And as I stood staring at her, clutching the revolver, Merridew came out and found us—like that.

Well, Harringay, that's my story, exactly as I told it to Peabody. I'm afraid it won't sound very well in court, but what can I say? The trail of blood led from my room to hers; the cat must have run that way; I *know* it was the cat I shot. I can't offer any explanation. I don't know who shot Mrs. Merridew, or why. I can't help it if the people at the inn say they never saw the Cyprian cat; Merridew saw it that other night, and I know he wouldn't lie about it. Search the house, Harringay. That's the only thing to do. Pull the place to pieces, till you find the body of the Cyprian cat. It will have my bullet in it.

THE TRINITY CAT

by Ellis Peters

He was sitting on top of one of the rear gate-posts of the churchyard when I walked through on Christmas Eve, grooming in his lordly style, with one black leg wrapped round his neck, and his bitten ear at an angle of forty-five degrees, as usual. I reckon one of the toms he'd tangled with in his nomad days had ripped the starched bit out of that one, the other stood up sharply enough. There was snow on the ground, a thin veiling, just beginning to crackle in promise of frost before evening, but he had at least three warm refuges around the place whenever he felt like holing up, besides his two houses, which he used only for visiting and cadging. He'd been a known character around our village for three years then, ever since he walked in from nowhere and made himself agreeable to the vicar and the verger, and finding the billet comfortable and the pickings good, constituted himself resident cat to Holy Trinity church, and took over all the jobs around the place that humans were too slow to tackle, like rat-catching, and chasing off invading dogs.

Nobody knows how old he is, but I think he could only have been about two when he settled here, a scrawny, chewed-up black bandit as lean as wire. After three years of being fed by Joel Woodward at

Trinity Cottage, which was the verger's house by tradition and flanked the lych-gate on one side, and pampered and petted by Miss Patience Thomson at Church Cottage on the other side, he was double his old size, and sleek as velvet, but still had one lop ear and a kink two inches from the end of his tail. He still looked like a brigand, but a highly prosperous brigand. Nobody ever gave him a name, but he wasn't the sort to get called anything fluffy or familiar. Only Miss Patience ever dared coo at him, and he was very gracious about that, she being elderly and innocent and very free with little perks like raw liver, on which he doted. One way and another, he had it made. He lived mostly outdoors, never staying in either house overnight. In winter he had his own little ground-level hatch into the furnace-room of the church, sharing his lodgings matily with a hedgehog that had qualified as assistant vermin-destructor around the churchyard, and preferred sitting out the winter among the coke to hibernating like common hedgehogs. These individualists keep turning up in our valley, for some reason.

All I'd gone to the church for that afternoon was to fix up with the vicar about the Christmas peal, having been roped into the bell-ringing team. Resident police in remote areas like ours get dragged into all sorts of activities, and when the area's changing, and new problems cropping up, if they have any sense they don't need too much dragging, but go willingly. I've put my finger on many an astonished yobbo who thought he'd got clean away with his little breaking-and-entering, just by keeping my ears open during a darts match, or choir practice.

When I came back through the churchyard, around half-past two, Miss Patience was just coming out of

her gate, with a shopping bag on her wrist, and heading toward the street, and we walked along together
a bit of the way. She was getting on for seventy, and
hardly bigger than a bird, but very independent.
Never having married or left the valley, and having
looked after a mother who lived to be nearly ninety,
she'd never had time to catch up with new ideas in
the style of dress suitable for elderly ladies. Everything had always been done mother's way, and fashion, music, and morals had stuck at the period when
mother was a carefully-brought-up girl learning domestic skills, and preparing for a chaste marriage.
There's a lot to be said for it! But it had turned Miss
Patience into a frail little lady in long-skirted black or
gray or navy blue, who still felt undressed without
hat and gloves, at an age when Mrs. Newcombe, for
instance, up at the pub, favored shocking pink trouser
suits and red-gold hair-pieces. A pretty little old lady
Miss Patience was, though, very straight and neat. It
was a pleasure to watch her walk. Which is more than
I could say for Mrs. Newcombe in her trouser suit,
especially from the back!

"A happy Christmas, Sergeant Moon!" she chirped
at me on sight. And I wished her the same, and
slowed up to her pace.

"It's going to be slippery by twilight," I said. "You
be careful how you go."

"Oh, I'm only going to be an hour or so," she said
serenely. "I shall be home long before the frost sets
in. I'm only doing the last bit of Christmas shopping.
There's a cardigan I have to collect for Mrs. Downs."
That was her cleaning-lady, who went in three morn-
ings a week. "I ordered it long ago, but deliveries are
so slow nowadays. They've promised it for today. And

a gramophone record for my little errand-boy."
Tommy Fowler that was, one of the church trebles,
as pink and wholesome looking as they usually con-
trive to be, and just as artful. "And one mustn't forget
our dumb friends, either, must one?" said Miss Patience cheerfully. "They're all important, too."

I took this to mean a couple of packets of some
new product to lure wild birds to her garden. The
Church Cottage thrushes were so fat they could hardly
fly, and when it was frosty she put out fresh water
three and four times a day.

We came to our brief street of shops, and off she
went, with her big jet-and-gold brooch gleaming in
her scarf. She had quite a few pieces of Victorian
and Edwardian jewelry her mother'd left behind, and
almost always wore one piece, being used to the belief
that a lady dresses meticulously every day, not just on
Sundays. And I went for a brisk walk round to see
what was going on, and then went home to Molly and
high tea, and took my boots off thankfully.

That was Christmas Eve. Christmas Day little Miss
Thomson didn't turn up for eight o'clock Communion,
which was unheard of. The vicar said he'd call in after
matins and see that she was all right, and hadn't taken
cold trotting about in the snow. But somebody else
beat us both to it. Tommy Fowler! He was anxious
about that pop record of his. But even he had no
chance until after service, for in our village it's the
custom for the choir to go and sing the vicar an au-
bade in the shape of "Christians, Awake!" before the
main service, ignoring the fact that he's been up for
four hours, and conducted two Communions. And
Tommy Fowler had a solo in the anthem, too. It was

a quarter-past twelve when he got away, and shot up the garden path to the door of Church Cottage.

He shot back even faster a minute later. I was heading for home when he came rocketing out of the gate and ran slam into me, with his eyes sticking out on stalks and his mouth wide open, making a sort of muted keening sound with shock. He clutched hold of me and pointed back toward Miss Thomson's front door, left half-open when he fled, and tried three times before he could croak out:

"Miss Patience. . . . She's there on the floor—she's bad!"

I went in on the run, thinking she'd had a heart attack all alone there, and was lying helpless. The front door led through a diminutive hall, and through another glazed door into the living-room, and that door was open, too, and there was Miss Patience face-down on the carpet, still in her coat and gloves, and with her shopping-bag lying beside her. An occasional table had been knocked over in her fall, spilling a vase and a book. Her hat was askew over one ear, and caved in like a trodden mushroom, and her neat gray bun of hair had come undone and trailed on her shoulder, and it was no longer gray but soiled, brownish black. She was dead and stiff. The room was so cold, you could tell those doors had been ajar all night.

The kid had followed me in, hanging on to my sleeve, his teeth chattering. "I didn't open the door— it was open! I didn't touch her, or anything. I only came to see if she was all right, and get my record."

It was there, lying unbroken, half out of the shopping-bag by her arm. She'd meant it for him, and I told him he should have it, but not yet, because it might be evidence, and we mustn't move anything. And I got him out of there quick, and gave him to the vicar to cope with, and went back to Miss Patience as soon as I'd telephoned for the outfit. Because we had a murder on our hands.

So that was the end of one gentle, harmless old woman, one of very many these days, battered to death because she walked in on an intruder who panicked. Walked in on him, I judged, not much more than an hour after I left her in the street. Everything about her looked the same as then, the shopping-bag, the coat, the hat, the gloves. The only difference, that she was dead. No, one more thing! No handbag, unless it was under the body, and later, when we were able to move her, I wasn't surprised to see that it wasn't there. Handbags are where old ladies carry their money. The sneak-thief who panicked and lashed out at her had still had greed and presence of mind enough to grab the bag as he fled. Nobody'd have to describe that bag to me, I knew it well, soft black leather with an old-fashioned gilt clasp and a short handle, a small thing, not like the hold-alls they carry nowadays.

She was lying facing the opposite door, also open, which led to the stairs. On the writing-desk by that door stood one of a pair of heavy brass candlesticks. Its fellow was on the floor beside Miss Thomson's body, and though the bun of hair and the felt hat had prevented any great spattering of blood, there was blood enough on the square base to label the weapon. Whoever had hit her had been just sneaking down the stairs, ready to leave. She'd come home barely five minutes too soon.

Upstairs, in her bedroom, her bits of jewelry hadn't taken much finding. She'd never thought of herself as having valuables, or of other people as coveting them. Her gold and turquoise and funereal jet and true-lover's-knots in gold and opals, and mother's engagement and wedding rings, and her little Edwardian pendant watch set with seed pearls, had simply lived in the small top drawer of her dressing-table. She belonged to an honest epoch, and it was gone, and now she was gone after it. She didn't even lock her door when she went shopping. There wouldn't have been so much as the warning of a key grating in the lock, just the door opening.

Ten years ago not a soul in this valley behaved differently from Miss Patience. Nobody locked doors, sometimes not even overnight. Some of us went on a fortnight's holiday and left the doors unlocked. Now we can't even put out the milk money until the milkman knocks at the door in person. If this generation likes to pride itself on its progress, let it! As for me, I thought suddenly that maybe the innocent was well out of it.

We did the usual things, photographed the body and the scene of the crime, the doctor examined her and authorized her removal, and confirmed what I'd supposed about the approximate time of her death. And the forensic boys lifted a lot of smudgy latents that weren't going to be of any use to anybody, because they weren't going to be on record, barring a million to one chance. The whole thing stank of the amateur. There wouldn't be any easy matching up of prints, even if they got beauties. One more thing we did for Miss Patience. We tolled the dead-bell for her on Christmas night, six heavy, muffled strokes. She was a virgin. Nobody had to vouch for it, we all knew.

And let me point out, it is a title of honor, to be respected accordingly.

We'd hardly got the poor soul out of the house when the Trinity cat strolled in, taking advantage of the minute or two while the door was open. He got as far as the place on the carpet where she'd lain, and his fur and whiskers stood on end, and even his lop ear jerked up straight. He put his nose down to the pile of the Wilton, about where her shopping bag and handbag must have lain, and started going round in interested circles, snuffing the floor and making little throaty noises that might have been distress, but sounded like pleasure. Excitement, anyhow. The chaps from the C.I.D. were still busy, and didn't want him under their feet, so I picked him up and took him with me when I went across to Trinity Cottage to talk to the verger. The cat never liked being picked up, after a minute he started clawing and cursing, and I put him down. He stalked away again at once, past the corner where people shot their dead flowers, out at the lych-gate, and straight back to sit on Miss Thomson's doorstep. Well, after all, he used to get fed there, he might well be uneasy at all these queer comings and goings. And they don't say "as curious as a cat" for nothing, either.

I didn't need telling that Joel Woodward had had no hand in what had happened, he'd been nearest neighbor and good friend to Miss Patience for years, but he might have seen or heard something out of the ordinary. He was a little, wiry fellow, gnarled like a tree-root, the kind that goes on spry and active into his nineties, and then decides that's enough, and leaves overnight. His wife was dead long ago, and his daughter had come back to keep house for him after her husband deserted her, until she died, too, in a bus accident. There was just old Joel now, and the grandson she'd left with him, young Joel Barnett, nineteen, and a bit of a tearaway by his grandad's standards, but so far pretty innocuous by mine. He was a sulky, graceless sort, but he did work, and he stuck with the old man when many another would have lit out elsewhere.

"A bad business," said old Joel, shaking his head. "I only wish I could help you lay hands on whoever did it. But I only saw her yesterday morning about ten, when she took in the milk. I was round at the church hall all afternoon, getting things ready for the youth social they had last night, it was dark before I got back. I never saw or heard anything out of place. You can't see her living-room light from here, so there was no call to wonder. But the lad was here all afternoon. They only work till one, Christmas Eve. Then they all went boozing together for an hour or so, I expect, so I don't know exactly what time he got in, but he was here and had the tea on when I came home. Drop round in an hour or so and he should be here, he's gone round to collect this girl he's mashing. There's a party somewhere tonight."

I dropped round accordingly, and young Joel was there, sure enough, shoulder-length hair, frilled shirt, outsize lapels and all, got up to kill, all for the benefit of the girl his grandad had mentioned. And it turned out to be Connie Dymond, from the comparatively respectable branch of the family, along the canal-side. There were three sets of Dymond cousins, boys, no great harm in 'em but worth watching, but only this one girl in Connie's family. A good-looker, or at least most of the lads seemed to think so, she had a dozen

or so on her string before she took up with young
Joel. Big girl, too, with a lot of mauve eye-shadow
and a mother-of-pearl mouth, in huge platform shoes
and the fashionable drab granny-coat. But she was
acting very prim and proper with old Joel around.

"Half-past two when I got home," said young Joel.
"Grandad was round at the hall, and I'd have gone
round to help him, only I'd had a pint or two, and
after I'd had me dinner I went to sleep, so it wasn't
worth it by the time I woke up. Around four, that'd
be. From then on I was here watching the telly, and
I never saw nor heard a thing. But there was nobody
else here, so I could be spinning you the yarn, if you
want to look at it that way."

He had a way of going looking for trouble before
anybody else suggested it, there was nothing new
about that. Still, there it was. One young fellow on
the spot, and minus any alibi. There'd be plenty of
others in the same case.

In the evening he'd been at the church social. Miss
Patience wouldn't be expected there, it was mainly for
the young, and anyhow, she very seldom went out in
the evenings.

"*I* was there with Joel," said Connie Dymond. "He
called for me at seven, I was with him all the evening.
We went home to our place after the social finished,
and he didn't leave till nearly midnight."

Very firm about it she was, doing her best for him.
She could hardly know that his movements in the evening didn't interest us, since Miss Patience had then
been dead for some hours.

When I opened the door to leave the Trinity cat
walked in, stalking past me with a purposeful stride.
He had a look round us all, and then made for the

girl, reached up his front paws to her knees, and was on her lap before she could fend him off, though she didn't look as if she welcomed his attentions. Very civil he was, purring and rubbing himself against her coat sleeve, and poking his whiskery face into hers. Unusual for him to be effusive, but when he did decide on it, it was always with someone who couldn't stand cats. You'll have noticed it's a way they have.

"Shove him off," said young Joel, seeing she didn't at all care for being singled out. "He only does it to annoy people."

And she did, but he only jumped on again, I noticed as I closed the door on them and left. It was a Dymond party they were going to, the senior lot, up at the filling station. Not much point in trying to check up on all her cousins and swains when they were gathered for a booze-up. Coming out of a hangover, tomorrow, they might be easy meat. Not that I had any special reason to look their way, they were an extrovert lot, more given to grievous bodily harm in street punch-ups than anything secretive. But it was wide open.

Well, we summed up. None of the lifted prints was on record, all we could do in that line was exclude all those that were Miss Thomson's. This kind of sordid little opportunist break-in had come into local experience only fairly recently, and though it was no novelty now, it had never before led to a death. No motive but the impulse of greed, so no traces leading up to the act, and none leading away. Everyone connected with the church, and most of the village besides, knew about the bits of jewelry she had, but never before had anyone considered them as desirable loot. Victoriana now carry inflated values, and are in demand, but this still didn't look calculated, just wanton. A kid's crime, a teen-ager's crime. Or the crime of a permanent teen-ager. They start at twelve years old now, but there are also the shiftless louts who never get beyond twelve years old, even in their forties.

We checked all the obvious people, her part-time gardener—but he was demonstrably elsewhere at the time—and his drifter of a son, whose alibi was non-existent but voluble, the window-cleaner, a sidelong soul who played up his ailments and did rather well out of her, all the delivery men. Several there who were clear, one or two who could have been around, but had no particular reason to be. Then we went after all the youngsters who, on their records, were possibles. There were three with breaking-and-entering convictions, but if they'd been there they'd been gloved. Several others with petty theft against them were also without alibis. By the end of a pretty exhaustive survey the field was wide, and none of the runners seemed to be ahead of the rest, and we were still looking. None of the stolen property had so far showed up.

Not, that is, until the Saturday. I was coming from Church Cottage through the graveyard again, and as I came near the corner where the dead flowers were shot, I noticed a glaring black patch making an irregular hole in the veil of frozen snow that still covered the ground. You couldn't miss it, it showed up like a black eye. And part of it was the soil and rotting leaves showing through, and part, the blackest part, was the Trinity cat, head down and back arched, digging industriously like a terrier after a rat. The bent end of his tail lashed steadily, while the remaining eight inches stood erect. If he knew I was standing watching him, he didn't care. Nothing was going to deflect him from what he was doing. And in a minute or two he heaved his prize clear, and clawed out to the light a little black leather handbag with a gilt clasp. No mistaking it, all stuck over as it was with dirt and rotting leaves. And he loved it, he was patting it and playing with it and rubbing his head against it, and purring like a steam engine. He cursed, though, when I took it off him, and walked round and round me, pawing and swearing, telling me and the world he'd found it, and it was his.

It hadn't been there long. I'd been along that path often enough to know that the snow hadn't been disturbed the day before. Also, the mess of humus fell off it pretty quick and clean, and left it hardly stained at all. I held it in my handkerchief and snapped the catch, and the inside was clean and empty, the lining slightly frayed from long use. The Trinity cat stood upright on his hind legs and protested loudly, and he had a voice that could outshout a Siamese.

Somebody behind me said curiously: "Whatever've you got there?" And there was young Joel standing open-mouthed, staring, with Connie Dymond hanging on to his arm and gaping at the cat's find in horrified recognition.

"Oh, no! My gawd, that's Miss Thomson's bag, isn't it? I've seen her carrying it hundreds of times."

"Did *he* dig it up?" said Joel, incredulous. "You reckon the chap who—you know, *him*!—he buried it there? It could be anybody, everybody uses this way through."

"My gawd!" said Connie, shrinking in fascinated horror against his side. "Look at that cat! You'd think he *knows*. . . . He gives me the shivers! What's got into him?"

What, indeed? After I'd got rid of them and taken the bag away with me I was still wondering. I walked away with his prize and he followed me as far as the road, howling and swearing, and once I put the bag down, open, to see what he'd do, and he pounced on it and started his fun and games again until I took it from him. For the life of me I couldn't see what there was about it to delight him, but he was in no doubt. I was beginning to feel right superstitious about this avenging detective cat, and to wonder what he was going to unearth next.

I know I ought to have delivered the bag to the forensic lab, but somehow I hung on to it overnight. There was something fermenting at the back of my mind that I couldn't yet grasp.

Next morning we had two more at morning service besides the regulars. Young Joel hardly ever went to church, and I doubt if anybody'd ever seen Connie Dymond there before, but there they both were, large as life and solemn as death, in a middle pew, the boy sulky and scowling as if he'd been press-ganged into it, as he certainly had, Connie very subdued and big-eyed, with almost no make-up and an unusually grave and thoughtful face. Sudden death brings people up against daunting possibilities, and creates penitents. Young Joel felt silly there, but he was daft about her, plainly enough, she could get him to do what she wanted, and she'd wanted to make this gesture. She went through all the movements of devotion, he just sat, stood and kneeled awkwardly as required, and went on scowling.

There was a bitter east wind when we came out.

On the steps of the porch everybody dug out gloves
and turned up collars against it, and so did young Joel,
and as he hauled his gloves out of his coat pocket,
out with them came a little bright thing that rolled
down the steps in front of us all and came to rest in
a crack between the flagstones of the path. A gleam
of pale blue and gold. A dozen people must have
recognized it. Mrs. Downs gave tongue in a shriek
that informed even those who hadn't.

"That's Miss Thomson's! It's one of her turquoise
ear-rings! *How did you get hold of that, Joel Barnett?*"

How, indeed? Everybody stood staring at the tiny
thing, and then at young Joel, and he was gazing at
the flagstones, stuck white and dumb. And all in a
moment Connie Dymond had pulled her arm free of
his and recoiled from him until her back was against
the wall, and was edging away from him like somebody trying to get out of range of flood or fire, and
her face a sight to be seen, blind and stiff with horror.

"You!" she said in a whisper. "It was you! Oh,
my God, *you* did it—*you* killed her! And me keeping
company—how could I? How could *you*!"

She let out a screech and burst into sobs, and before
anybody could stop her she turned and took to her
heels, running for home like a mad thing.

I let her go. She'd keep. And I got young Joel and
that single ear-ring away from the Sunday congrega-
tion and into Trinity Cottage before half the people
there knew what was happening, and shut the world
out, all but old Joel who came panting and shaking
after us a few minutes later.

The boy was a long time getting his voice back, and
when he did he had nothing to say but, hopelessly,
over and over: "I didn't! I never touched her, I

wouldn't. I don't know how that thing got into my pocket. I didn't do it. I never. . . ."

Human beings are not all that inventive. Given a similar set of circumstances they tend to come out with the same formula. And in any case, "deny everything and say nothing else" is a very good rule when cornered.

They thought I'd gone round the bend when I said: "Where's the cat? See if you can get him in."

Old Joel was past wondering. He went out and rattled a saucer on the steps, and pretty soon the Trinity cat strolled in. Not at all excited, not wanting anything, fed and lazy, just curious enough to come and see why he was wanted. I turned him loose on young Joel's overcoat, and he couldn't have cared less. The pocket that had held the ear-ring held very little interest for him. He didn't care about any of the clothes in the wardrobe, or on the pegs in the little hall. As far as he was concerned, this new find was non-event.

I sent for a constable and a car, and took young Joel in with me to the station, and all the village, you may be sure, either saw us pass or heard about it very shortly after. But I didn't stop to take any statement from him, just left him there, and took the car up to Mary Melton's place, where she breeds Siamese, and borrowed a cat-basket from her, the sort she uses to carry her queens to the vet. She asked what on earth I wanted it for, and I said to take the Trinity cat for a ride. She laughed her head off.

"Well, *he's* no queen," she said, "and no king, either. Not even a jack! And you'll never get that wild thing into a basket."

"Oh, yes, I will," I said. "And if he isn't any of

the other picture cards, he's probably going to turn
out to be the joker."

A very neat basket it was, not too obviously meant
for a cat. And it was no trick getting the Trinity cat
into it, all I did was drop in Miss Thomson's handbag,
and he was in after it in a moment. He growled when
he found himself shut in, but it was too late to complain then.

At the house by the canal Connie Dymond's mother
let me in, but was none too happy about letting me
see Connie, until I explained that I needed a statement from her before I could fit together young Joel's
movements all through those Christmas days. Naturally I understood that the girl was terribly upset, but
she'd had a lucky escape, and the sooner everything
was cleared up, the better for her. And it wouldn't
take long.

It didn't take long. Connie came down the stairs
readily enough when her mother called her. She was
all stained and pale and tearful, but had perked up
somewhat with a sort of shivering pride in her own
prominence. I've seen them like that before, getting
the juice out of being the center of attention even
while they wish they were elsewhere. You could even
say she hurried down, and she left the door of her
bedroom open behind her, by the light coming
through at the head of the stairs.

"Oh, Sergeant Moon!" she quavered at me from
three steps up. "Isn't it *awful*? I still can't believe it!
Can there be some mistake? Is there any chance it
wasn't . . . ?"

I said soothingly, yes, there was always a chance.
And I slipped the latch of the cat-basket with one
hand, so that the flap fell open, and the Trinity cat

was out of there and up those stairs like a black flash,
startling her so much she nearly fell down the last
step, and steadied herself against the wall with a small
shriek. And I blurted apologies for accidentally loos-
ing him, and went up the stairs three at a time ahead
of her, before she could recover her balance.

He was up on his hind legs in her dolly little room,
full of pop posters and frills and garish colors, pawing
at the second drawer of her dressing-table, and singing
a loud, joyous, impatient song. When I came plunging
in, he even looked over his shoulder at me and stood
down, as though he knew I'd open the drawer for him.
And I did, and he was up among her fancy undies like
a shot, and digging with his front paws.

He found what he wanted just as she came in at
the door. He yanked it out from among her bras and
slips, and tossed it into the air, and in seconds he was
on the floor with it, rolling and wrestling it, juggling
it on his four paws like a circus turn, and purring fit
to kill, a cat in ecstasy. A comic little thing it was, a
muslin mouse with a plaited green nylon string for a
tail, yellow beads for eyes, and nylon threads for
whiskers, that rustled and sent out wafts of strong
scent as he batted it around and sang to it. A catmint
mouse, old Miss Thomson's last-minute purchase from
the pet shop for her dumb friend. If you could ever
call the Trinity cat dumb! The only thing she bought
that day small enough to be slipped into her handbag
instead of the shopping bag.

Connie let out a screech, and was across that room
so fast I only just beat her to the open drawer. They
were all there, the little pendant watch, the locket,
the brooches, the true-lover's-knot, the purse, even
the other ear-ring. A mistake, she should have ditched

both while she was about it, but she was too greedy. They were for pierced ears, anyhow, no good to Connie.

I held them out in the palm of my hand—such a large haul they made—and let her see what she'd robbed and killed for.

If she'd kept her head she might have made a fight of it even then, claimed he'd made her hide them for him, and she'd been afraid to tell on him directly, and could only think of staging that public act at church, to get him safely in custody before she came clean. But she went wild. She did the one deadly thing, turned and kicked out in a screaming fury at the Trinity cat. He was spinning like a humming-top, and all she touched was the kink in his tail. He whipped round and clawed a red streak down her leg through the nylon. And then she screamed again, and began to babble through hysterical sobs that she never meant to hurt the poor old sod, that it wasn't her fault! Ever since she'd been going with young Joel she'd been seeing that little old bag going in and out, draped with her bits of gold. What in hell did an old witch like her want with jewelry? She had no *right*! At her age!

"But I never meant to hurt her! She came in too soon," lamented Connie, still and for ever the aggrieved. "What was I supposed to do? I had to get away, didn't I? *She was between me and the door!*"

She was half her size, too, and nearly four times her age! Ah, well! What the courts would do with Connie, thank God, was none of my business. I just took her in and charged her, and got her statement. Once we had her dabs it was all over, because she'd left a bunch of them sweaty and clear on that brass candlestick. But if it hadn't been for the Trinity cat and his single-minded pursuit, scaring her into that ill-judged attempt to hand us young Joel as a scapegoat, she might, she just might, have got clean away with it. At least the boy could go home now, and count his blessings.

Not that she was very bright, of course. Who but a stupid harpy, soaked in cheap perfume and gimcrack dreams, would have hung on even to the catmint mouse, mistaking it for a herbal sachet to put among her smalls?

I saw the Trinity cat only this morning, sitting grooming in the church porch. He's getting very self-important, as if he knows he's a celebrity, though throughout he was only looking after the interests of Number One, like all cats. He's lost interest in his mouse already, now most of the scent's gone.

LITTLE MIRACLES

by Kristine Kathryn Rusch

We found the cat just as we were about to seal off the house. Its throat had been slit, and its coat was matted with blood. Some instinct made me crouch down to touch it. Its skin was warm, and its body struggled with shallow breaths. Life among the carnage.

I snapped my fingers for the paramedics. They glanced at each other and didn't move.

"Gentlemen, kindly get your asses over here," I said.

"But, sir, it's a cat."

"And it's still breathing. Get over here."

They crouched over the cat, placed a bandage over its neck, and did something to ease its breathing. I directed them to a veterinarian down the street, then returned my attention to the bloodbath before me. In the kitchen, a woman's body, curled in a fetal hug, clutching a knife in what appeared to have been self-defense. In the bedroom, two children, slaughtered. And in the master bathroom, a man collapsed over the bathtub, also dead. In the living room, the TV stand was empty. The door to the empty stereo cabinet in the dining room stood open, and pictures were missing from the walls.

It looked like a desperate act of a startled burglar.

But the cat was the clue. Sliced on the way out for the sheer pleasure of the act. Cats don't bark. They don't threaten killers. Cats hide from frightening circumstances. The killer flushed the cat and slit its throat just to see the blood.

Wrote up the preliminary report and went home, washed the blood-stink off my skin. It was raining. Felt like it was always raining. Oregon: land of the nonexistent sun.

The house was a mess—dishes in the sink, dirty clothes tumbling out of the closet. No time to clean, not even now, with another crazy on the loose. I opened the fridge, searching for a beer, and heard Delilah's voice: *I don't know how you can come home and assume you lead a normal life, as if nothing happened to you all day*. In the early days, she had liked that, the way I could leave my job behind me. But she never could. She always wanted to know the details, relishing the jargon as if it was a new language. *Was there high velocity blood?* she would have asked about this case.

All over the house, I would have replied. *Especially the bathroom and the kitchen. The man must have gone first, but the woman put up quite a fight.*

I would never have told her about the blood's odd trajectory, indicating that the killer used a sharp weapon, knife perhaps, but not a normal kitchen knife. I would never have trusted her that far.

I closed the refrigerator door without the beer. I never did leave the work at the office. It was always there, one corner of the brain assessing the evidence, searching for the clue that would lead us to the creep of the week. Maybe that was why Delilah left. Maybe her words had always been sarcasm, her questions medicine to draw out the poison.

Grabbed the car keys and let myself out the back door. The car, the only thing she left me, a 1988 Saab, drove itself. We stopped in the slanted parking lot at the vet's, a place I hadn't been since her dog nearly died chewing a steak bone. Pulled open the door, stepped into the scent of disinfectant, matted fur, and frightened animals. The woman behind the reception desk didn't recognize me, which was fine, since I didn't remember seeing her before.

I flashed my badge. "Some of my paramedics brought a cat in earlier."

She shuddered delicately. Just once, but enough for me to notice. "What an awful thing to do to an animal," she said.

You should have seen what happened to the people, I nearly said, but since the paramedics had followed procedure and not said anything, I wouldn't either. "I was wondering if you folks had ever seen the cat before."

"I haven't, but let me check with the doctor." She got up, a tidy woman in a green dress, her age nearly impossible to determine. I glanced around the room. Empty now, but I had seen it filled with worried people hovering over their animals as if the animals were as precious as children. Something in the back set off the dogs, and one of them howled, followed by another. She returned with the vet, the man I remembered, a big-boned redhead with a touch that even the most skittish animal trusted.

"Frank," he said, and held out a well-scrubbed hand. I shook it.

"Doug." We have never socialized, only saw each

other in this small building, but the familiarity put me at ease when I hadn't even realized I was uncomfortable. "Ever see the cat before?"

"No," the vet said. "And he's got distinctive markings. I would have remembered."

"Family named Torgenson, lived just down the block. Ever treat their animals?"

He nodded, looking thoughtful, too polite to ask why Torgenson. "They had a dog, died of old age about a month ago. He always brought the dog in. She was allergic to cats. They both came to put the dog down, and she was a mess by the time they left even though we keep this place as dander-free as modern technology allows."

The news startled me. The cat had been found beside her.

"He's awake. Want to see him?"

It took me a moment to realize that the vet was talking about the cat. "Sure," I said, feeling more than a bit uncomfortable. I'd lived through this scene a number of times in hospitals, seeing the survivor, asking preliminary questions. But I couldn't ask the cat why he'd been there, what he'd seen.

The vet led me through the narrow hallway into a large room filled with steel tables. In the back, rows of cages lined the walls. Cats, in various stages of distress, stared at me. I didn't see any dogs, figured they must be kept elsewhere.

The vet showed me a cage on the far side of the wall. A white cat with an orange mustache stared at us through the mesh. His eyes were still wide with the effect of the drug. A gauze bandage had been taped in place around his neck. He saw me and rolled on his back, paws kneading the empty air.

"Amazing, huh?" the vet said. "I've never seen such a friendly cat. Especially one drugged and wounded."

"He'll live?"

"He probably used up eight of his nine lives, but yeah, he'll make it." The vet opened the door, reached in, and scratched the cat's stomach. "What do you plan to do with him?"

I hadn't realized I had given the cat any thought. "Take him home," I said.

The station was a dingy gray. The walls were made of steel and concrete, built during the Vietnam era when everything had to be bombproof. The ventilation was poor, and the place smelled of old cigarettes, stale coffee, and sweat. My desk was the only spotless one among the detectives, mostly because I shoved everything in drawers. When I arrived the morning after the killings, though, files were piled five inches high on the top.

I sat down and sorted through them. Autopsies, blood analyses, request forms for DNA scans, forensics results, photos of the house's contents . . . amazing how much reading could be generated in one night. I pulled out the autopsy reports and the photographs of the crime scene.

All night I had been thinking about the cat. Hell, I even stopped at the grocery store and bought litter, a little pan, and food dishes. The vet said he would give me food when Rip—that's what they were calling the little guy—was ready to go home.

But that wasn't all I was thinking about. I was thinking about the kind of person who would slit a cat's throat. I was thinking about the woman dead on the kitchen floor. I was thinking about the knife in her hand.

It would have been easy enough for her to surprise her husband in the bathroom. A bit of a struggle and he would be down, then attack the sleeping children. In the kitchen, a quick slash across the throat of a stray cat, and then the final act—a knife to her own gut, enough times to bleed to death.

A domestic tragedy, something I had seen so often that it no longer turned my stomach. The papers would play it up, and the D.A.'s office would look into her life just enough to give her a motive before the case closed completely.

I pulled out the pictures, studied them, realized my theory was wrong. No wounds on Mrs. Torgenson's chest, face, or neck. All in the back. She had been stabbed in the back, surprised in her own kitchen, knife in hand. Not self-defense as I had earlier thought. Surprised chopping an onion for the family dinner.

And Rip, blood matted on his fur, running down his front as it should in a neck wound, but no pool beneath his body. Blood on his back, his tail, his ears. Someone else's blood. I picked up the pictures, turned them. Handprints. He had been moved.

I set the photos down, put my face in my hands. Amazing the details I had missed. I used to approach a crime scene as if it were a complete jigsaw puzzle. All the clues were there; I just had to notice them and arrange them in the correct order. That way each detail went into the brain, from the day-old cigarette stub on the driveway to the pattern of the bloodstains on the wall. In those days, I would have seen the onions on the sideboard, noticed her shredded back, commented on the handprints covering Rip.

Ceramic clanged against the metal surface of my desk, and the aroma of fresh coffee hit me. "Breakfast, Frank?"

Denny, one of the few men who had been in the station as long as I have. Fifteen years sounds like a long time, but I could remember the days when we were enthusiastic about our work, when we concentrated on catching the creeps and then having a few brews after a rough day. We hadn't spent time together in I couldn't remember how long.

I brought my hands down casually, as if I had been resting my eyes instead of berating myself. He had put a cup of coffee on one of my files. I took it, sipped.

"Tough case, huh?" He half-sat, half-leaned on my desk. "I hate seeing kids sliced up like that."

I stared at him, seeing instead the little girl clutching her stuffed bunny, eyes still closed as if she were asleep. Her older sister, eyes wide with terror . . .

Rip had bothered me more than they had. But Rip had been the anomaly at the crime scene.

"Yeah," I said.

Denny looked at me strangely. Once he pulled me off a perp who'd been caught molesting a five-year-old girl. The murder case I'd busted my ass working on because I knew the mother had tried to strangle her daughters and I didn't want her to regain custody of them.

"You okay?" he asked.

"No different than I've been."

He nodded once, as if my comment ended the conversation, and disappeared around the corner to his own desk. When Delilah left, he invited me over for dinner for weeks until it became clear that I would never go. I didn't want to see him and Sheila, perfect examples of conjugal bliss. I didn't want to socialize with anyone.

I sighed, pulled out my legal pad. Options: The killer was (1) someone they knew; (2) some sicko creep just starting; (3) some sicko creep with a pattern; (4) a burglar, caught in the act; (5) a family member.

I pushed the list aside, filled out the DNA forms, sent a notice of the killing across the wire to see if anyone else picked up a pattern. Then I read the files, crossed off the family member—since, with that bloodbath, the entire family died—and assigned one of my men to monitor the fences in town. I was preparing a list of interviews when McRooney stopped.

"Frank, my office."

I set my pen down and followed him through the maze of desks to the only walled-off office in the place. McRooney had a large glass door through which he saw damn near everything. Fake plants hung from the fluorescents, and filing cabinets stood like soldiers behind his desk.

He pulled the blinds on the door.

"Sit," he said.

I did as I was told. McRooney was an okay guy— political, ambitious, people-savvy. I remember when he was a green kid, puking at the scene of his first murder. Long time ago.

"Hear you missed some things at the Torgenson house."

"Too damn much," I said. No use lying to the man. He knew.

"Crime lab boys caught some of it. Forensics more. You're usually ahead of the game, Frank."

"I know," I said.

"You've been slipping these past six months. You didn't take time when the wife left. You need to."

"When the case is wrapped."

"Now," McRooney sat behind his desk, looking like a politician in a thirties movie. "I'm going to reassign. This kind of thing is too important."

"To trust to a guy who's screwing up."

"Your words, Frank." He pulled out a sheet of paper, stamped it, and slid it toward me. "A leave with pay. As much time as you need. Your heart's gone."

I ignored the paper. "I'll just sit at home and get sloshed. Gimme a week. If I haven't got the case wrapped by then, I'll go."

"It'll be cold then."

"If I continue to screw up, you mean?"

"You never used to be so defensive." He leaned back in his chair. It groaned under his weight.

"I never used to notice my own mistakes, either." I sighed, adjusted my trouser legs. "I don't think staying home is the way for me. I got a glimmer in this case, first interest I've felt in a while. Let me try."

He pulled the paper back, looked at it, crumpled it. Missed the hook shot to the garbage can. "Three days. That way we don't lose too much ground."

Three days. As if he expected nothing from my work. I stood. I wouldn't expect much from my work, either. I grabbed the doorknob.

"Frank?"

Stopped, waited, head down, not turning.

"Is she worth all this?"

Friend. The comment of a concerned friend. I let my breath out slowly, feeling truth come with it. "I don't think it's her. I think it's been building for a long time. Her going was just a symptom."

"Studen is a good shrink."

Flush rose on my cheeks—anger canceling truth. "You gave me three days," I said, and let myself out.

Not so much as a half-formed fingerprint by five. Neighbors heard nothing. No, the family was quiet, kept to themselves. Dog was loud, but it died months ago.

Called the vet. Rip was doing better. Could go home in a few days. Quite the survivor, huh?, a comment I took to mean that the vet had seen the papers, understood what happened to the cat.

A little miracle, I replied as I hung up.

Closed the files, went down to the Steelhead for a beer and a burger. The inside was crowded, but not too, just enough so that I had to take a table instead of a booth. Three screens played the news, and the music blared country-western, unusual for a yuppie bar. Glanced at the menu, glanced at the microbrews being sipped at the tables around me. Three days. And day one nearly gone.

When the waitress showed, I ordered a bacon-cheddar burger, fries, and a coffee nudge without the nudge. I'd get more work done with caffeine as the drug of choice.

Woman sat across from me, alone. Blonde, leggy, nail polish, and lip gloss. Not usually my type. She smiled, I smiled back, and it felt good. But the burger arrived before I could pick myself up and sit beside her. Then the boyfriend showed, three-piece suit and silk tie, and I leaned back, outclassed.

Not that I was too disappointed. I'd picked up too

many women in that bar, both before and after Delilah, never for conversation, always for exercise and sometimes not enough of that. Couldn't imagine bringing a woman to my place now, with its ancient dishes and unwashed sheets. Guess it had been a long time. I did the laundry just after Delilah left, months ago.

The burger settled me, the coffee buzzed me. I wandered back to the station, half wishing the cat had died so we could have sent his body to the lab to check for prints. Uncharitable thought—remembering the little guy on his back, trusting paws kneading the air, the cat box at the house, waiting. We'd had cats at home, barn cats who sat on my shoulders while I milked the cows at five in the morning. Two cats, both killed one morning when they got loose in the cow pen. I cried until my momma shamed me.

Men don't cry, she said. They get mad.

Yeah, Momma, I thought. What happens when the anger goes, too, and you're just a big hulking shell?

She would have no answer for that. I squinted, wondered when we last spoke. Wasn't even sure if I'd told her Delilah was gone.

Opened the door to the station, stepped into the familiar noise and stink. Place never changed, day to night, always busy, always crazy. Problems everywhere, even in a small city like this one.

Three new files on my desk: fax-sent cases, one from Washington, one from California, one from Utah. Sat down and read. Perp never caught. One scene left a dog, thought to be a stray, throat slit. Another a cat, belonged to the neighbors, throat slit. Yet another cat, black, purchased from a pet store, throat slit.

California, skipped Nevada, Utah, skipped Idaho,

Washington, and now Oregon. New pattern? Or getting sloppy? Hard to tell with a random crazy.

I put my head on my desk. A random crazy. The worst kind.

Typed up a new report, flagged it for McRooney, and reminded him to notify the FBI. The case was theirs now, not that I couldn't work on it, too.

On the drive home, found myself wondering what the crazy would think if he knew the cat lived. First survivor. The thought gave me a pang, made me half-swerve to head for the vet's, then forced myself to continue the drive home. Silly idea. The cat was safe. As if it mattered.

Opened the door, turned on the lights, blared Tchaikovsky on the CD, and dug into the dishes. Grunge work for relaxation. Had to get the case out of my mind. The best detecting happened in the subconscious—comparing details, fitting pieces. The subconscious still worked, I knew that. The path to the conscious was blocked. I'd seen everything at the murder site but couldn't remember it until something jogged me. Not good. Not good at all.

Left the dishes to soak, went into the living room, and flopped on the couch. Closed my eyes and walked through the Torgenson house again.

First thing: stale-death reek of blood, even before we walked through the door. Into the sunken living room, done in modular white, with chrome lamps, decorative books. An unused room. And nothing, except a little mud leading up the stairs. Half-moon pattern. Man's shoe.

Den. Sloppy with toys, half read books, another stereo still there. Television cabinet empty, VCR gone. No evidence of search, of a mess other than the intentional one.

Into the formal dining. Stereo cabinet door open, equipment gone. Nothing else touched. No prints on the cabinet glass.

Kitchen. Blood-spattered. Woman on her side, fetal position, knife in her hand. Onions chopped on the sideboard, eggs unbeaten in a mixing bowl, meat burned on the stove. The smell of hamburger mixed with fresh blood. Cat left like a calling card beside the back door. Blood pattern on the carpeted steps— dripping blood, spatters on the rug, not the wall.

Follow the stairs twisting to the second story. No handprints, no marks at all on the white walls. Odd for people with children. Fresh paint?

Blood trail leads to the bathroom. Man doubled over the tub, throat slit, blood pouring down the drain. (Drain cleaned? Something else hiding in there? Some missing evidence?) High velocity blood patterned on the mirror around the sink and onto the toilet. Why couldn't he see perp in mirror? Mirror has unusually high placement. Perp too short? Or too quick? With throat slit, man unable to scream. First victim, then. The children might have screamed, at least the second girl. Woman didn't hear—why?

Back to the kitchen, searching, searching, realized the answer in the dining room, now missing. Stereo probably blaring. How, then, could the children sleep? And why was she cooking?

Onions, hamburger, eggs on the sideboard. She was making breakfast.

Back up stairs. Master bedroom, again in white. King-sized bed, made army style—by him, retired colonel, probably his last act. More decorative books in wall cases. Television propped near headboard. Another VCR, more movies. Didn't have to look to guess the kind. Television still there, as is VCR. Half-moon footprints leading to the bathroom, mud plus blood leading out. Confirmed: killer stopped here first. Knew the morning routine well enough to avoid the woman, get the man, the children, and finally her in the kitchen, alone and terrified.

Followed prints to the girls' room. Took the youngest first, nearest the door. Quick slash, throat again, killed her before she could wake. Blood trickles off the bed onto the floor. No prints. Went around to kill her sister. Awake, eyes open, body curled. Sister tried to escape, got caught in the man's arms, watched him kill her. . . .

Opened my eyes, took a deep sigh, body shaking. Relieved to be in my own living room, *Marche Slav* repeating over and over on the CD. Picked up the remote and shut the music off, deciding silence was more amenable than the noise.

He arrived early morning, interrupted the routine, just as he had in the other states. They thought he was a nighttime killer, but he wasn't. He had a set time for attack, and a set plan, and he carried it through. Letting Rip live was no accident. He was trying to get caught. Each set of deaths more dangerous than the last, as if he were searching for the final adrenaline rush, the final opportunity . . .

I leaned over the couch's arm, picked up the phone, and ordered the forensics squad to return to the house, check the drain, the prints. Hung up and remembered the details from the other reports. Each place he had taken something large, something different. Microwave from California, computer from Utah, china and silver in Washington. He wasn't fencing, or even masquerading as a burglar. He was furnishing his home. Souvenirs.

And Rip. Not a calling card, but a clue. A stray dog, a neighbor's cat. Animals didn't belong to the perp, but were associated with him, somehow. A job, maybe, that took him into certain neighborhoods at particular times of the morning? Allowed him to travel, and to watch patterns. Not animal welfare. Those were city jobs, stable because they paid well, not likely to take a drifter. Vet? Perhaps, but again, stability was the key. Needing to build a practice, to get good references.

Vet. Finally the light bulb went off. I picked up the phone, called the station again, asked Vinnie to doublecheck the files. Yes, a vet close to each murdered family.

Thumbed through the phone book, found Doug the vet's home address, grabbed my coat and shield, and left. Ten o'clock might be too late to go visiting in some neighborhoods, but not in mine.

Took five minutes after I knocked for him to come to the door. Out of his smock, he looked younger—aided, I think, by his tousled hair. I half-expected a female voice to query, an admonition not to wake the kids. Instead got a shirtless, sleepy man clutching a beer, TV blaring in the background, cats emerging from all parts of the house, and a quiet dog padding its way to the door.

"Frank?" Doug—he didn't seem like a vet any more to me—ran his hand over his face. "You got a problem? There's an emergency vet on Walker."

"Need to talk to you about the Torgenson case. Got a minute?"

"Sure." Rubbing the sleep from his eyes, pushing back a cat with his foot.

"Come on in."

The place smelled like home. Unwashed dishes piled in the kitchen, blanket on the couch. He tossed a cat off the recliner, bade me sit, used the remote to shut off the TV. "Sorry about the mess. Wife left a few weeks ago, and I can't bring myself to clean."

Vets have lives, too. "It's been six months for me, and I've been thinking about hiring a service."

"Thing is," Doug said, sitting on the couch, feet propped on the coffee table, "I always thought I did a lot of chores."

I nodded. Recognition that my situation was not unique warmed me. "Sorry to bother you so late. Just need a few questions answered. You hire anyone new in the last few months?"

He shook his head. "I haven't hired anyone for two years. Got college kids cleaning the cages—they've been with me since they started school. One's a junior, the other'll graduate in spring. My receptionist has been there for nearly two years, and the lab techs since I started."

The air left me, as a feeling of failure grew. Somehow I'd assumed that his night attendants, cage cleaners, would be the ones. Transient, short-term jobs—

Then felt a flood of relief. If that were true, Rip would have died the first night.

"Who else comes through?"

He closed his eyes. I liked his concentration. Most folks always wanted to know why I needed the information. "Medical supply people like any doctor's office, deliveries—"

"Any in the morning?"

"Cat food, sometimes, about once a month. Arrives seven A.M. sharp, and gets annoyed if no one's at the door to let him in. But he's not new, either. Been servicing us as long as I can remember."

"But only once a month?"

"Sometimes not even that. Got quite a route. Heard him brag to Sally—that's my receptionist. He can cover six states in thirty days if he has to, although he runs Oregon, Nevada, usually, picking up supplies in California as he drives through."

"Don't like him much." No need to make that a question. I could feel the animosity in Doug's every word.

Doug opened his eyes, looked at me, hand on a black cat that decided to stare at me from his lap. "No, I don't. He's odd. Animals don't like him, but they come because he smells like food. Animals always know."

Strays. The neighbor's cat. Food.

"Remember his name?"

Doug gently eased the cat away, got up. "No, but I've got his card around here, somewhere, if I can find my wallet." He walked barefoot over to a desk mounded with open envelopes, pushed them aside, and picked up a leather wallet, thumbed through it, and produced a card. I took it. Black lettering on white.

Jonathan Kivy.

Had him.

I still sweated it. FBI wanted to make the collar—allowed them to take him anywhere they needed to.

They found him in Southern Oregon, TV, VCR, stereo, and paintings in the back of his truck, and radioed, promising to bring him in to me.

All night I'd dreamed about Rip walking up to him, trusting but nervous, hoping that a man who smelled like food would provide him with some. Saw the arm flash down, the quick throat slash, the one-handed bloody carry into the Torgensons' kitchen, dumped by the door like a single sack of cat food.

Woke up, tears on my cheeks, anger in my gut, repeating *it doesn't matter, it doesn't matter.* Remembered nights like that, Delilah's arms around me, soothing, dreams of dead children, bodies in the river, perps with guns, and perps with knives. She'd tell me it was over. I knew it would never be over, so all I could do was drown the tears, let the anger serve. Repeating *it doesn't matter, it doesn't matter,* until it didn't any more.

They showed up about eleven A.M., two men in black suits with regulation haircuts, leading a small man, hands in cuffs. I started shivering, anger running through my body, looking for an escape. One leap across the desk, fingers against his throat, showing him how it felt to be small and helpless and dying . . .

But I didn't move. Clasped my hands under the desktop, waited for them to stop. McRooney left his office, watched me. He said he'd abide by my decision.

They brought him to my desk. Stared at his hands, long slender fingers, strong. Pictured Rip in them, then the little girl, gripped by the hair, head pulled back—

It didn't matter.

But it did.

—throat slashed, one quick movement, her sister screaming. . . .

"He's yours, if you want him, detective," Adams, one of the FBI men, said. They had praised me the night before for saving them so much headache.

I looked at the perp's eyes. Cold, black, reflecting only my face. How close had I gotten to that empty stare?

"Extradite him. Utah. They have a death penalty there, and they're not afraid to use it. Tell them I'll cooperate in any way I can." The words came out angry, so forceful that I almost spit at him.

The perp's face didn't change. I didn't so much care about the death penalty as the trial. Oregon's prisons were overcrowded, good reason, sometimes, to opt for an insanity defense. I didn't want the perp's abusive childhood—if he had one—or an anti-social personality disorder, which he did have, to get in the way of his punishment.

They led him into McRooney's office to prepare the paperwork, perhaps allow him a phone call. I leaned back, wondering why he did it, and then realizing that it didn't matter. He would have some reason, some crazy rationale, but it would just mask the compulsion. I read a lot on serial killers in the early days. Random crazies, triggered by an unknown mechanism. Human, but not human, threatening us all.

I stood up, staggered with the force of released emotion. Denny stopped by my desk, concern on his face. "You okay?"

Reached up, found wet cheeks. Odd that the tears would come now. "Fine," I said.

McRooney had left his office, coming to pat me on the back. I didn't want him to touch me, didn't want anyone to touch me just then. I swallowed, made the lump disappear. "I'm going to take that leave," I said. "Starting now."

McRooney watched, slight frown on his face. To his credit, he didn't comment on my appearance. "You deserve it, Frank. We'll set the details later. Good work on this."

"Thanks," I said. Grabbed my jacket, and half-ran from the station, knowing that on the leave, I would have to think about my future, too. Maybe homicide was no longer for me. Maybe being a cop was no longer for me.

The thought sobered the weird elation building in my gut. Doug said I could get Rip today, and I would. Funny. A cat started my emotional lockup, and a cat undid it. Because he was an anomaly, the only living thing I had not trained my emotions to hide from at a crime scene. I remembered him on his back, paws kneading the air. Like a little child. Delilah used to say pets brought out the parenting instinct. Fine. I needed something to mother, to take the attention from myself.

I got in the car, wondering how Rip would like the drive. Wondering if I could clean the house in an afternoon. Wondering if Doug would drop by after work for a brew. A man without a wife, without conjugal bliss. We could complain about women, get royally sloshed, laugh and cry until we were sure the emotions ran both hot and cold.

Had to clear the icewater from my veins.

Whoa, body, heat wave moving in.

I shivered one last time.

The heat would feel good.